The Sunriver Murders

Ted Haynes

Copyright 2024 by Ted Haynes. All rights reserved.
This is a work of fiction. Names, characters, and events are fictitious or are used fictitiously.

ISBN 978-1-7331544-6-8

Library of Congress Control Number: 2024905346

Book design by Jim Bisakowski www.BookDesign.ca
Back cover art by Ellen Moon https://ellenleichmoon.com/
Map of River Road by Alejandro Zapata

The Robleda Company, Publishers
1259 El Camino Real, Ste 2720
Menlo Park, CA 94025
www.robledabooks.com

For Deon Stonehouse

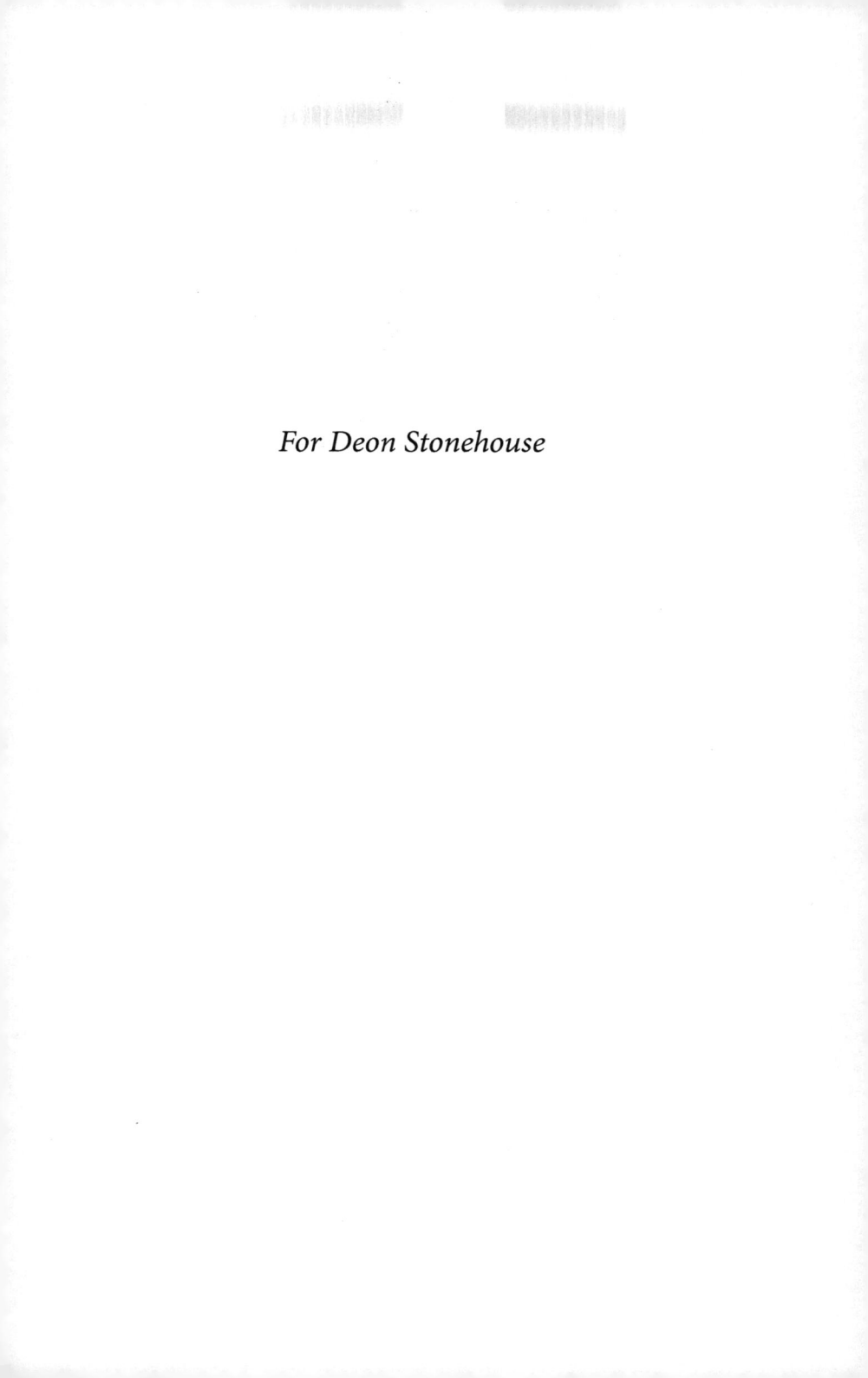

Contents

Chapter 1	Trapped 1
Chapter 2	Bewildered 4
Chapter 3	Plein Air 11
Chapter 4	Escape. 19
Chapter 5	Making Sense 23
Chapter 6	The Bad News 27
	Illustration – Map of River Road in Sunriver. . . . 29
Chapter 7	Gossip. 35
Chapter 8	The Journey I. 41
Chapter 9	A Friend in Need 45
Chapter 10	Wedge Shots 51
Chapter 11	Other Women 57
Chapter 12	Canvassing 65
Chapter 13	The Journey II 76
Chapter 14	Ye Shall Find 80
Chapter 15	Liabilities 89
Chapter 16	The Return of the Prodigal 93
Chapter 17	His Brother's Keeper. 102
Chapter 18	A Bad Impulse 107
Chapter 19	A Family Heirloom 112
Chapter 20	The White Car 117
Chapter 21	A Second Chance 119
Chapter 22	What Tommy Knew. 124
Chapter 23	Race for Glory 127
Chapter 24	Sleeping in Seattle 138
Chapter 25	An Evil Light. 141

Chapter 26	A Fast Retreat	147
Chapter 27	Disaster Preparedness	152
Chapter 28	Flight I	158
Chapter 29	The Devil's Due	160
Chapter 30	Reversal of Fortune	168
Chapter 31	Flight II	171
Chapter 32	Menace	173
Chapter 33	Follow the Money	176
Chapter 34	Race for Redemption	185
Chapter 35	The Tipping Point	191
Chapter 36	Who Knew What	196
Chapter 37	Confessions and Repentance	202
Chapter 38	Revelation	206
Chapter 39	Cries and Whispers	212
Chapter 40	Can I Get A Witness?	216
Chapter 41	Lifesaving	222
Chapter 42	A New Perspective	228
Chapter 43	Arrested Development	236
Chapter 44	The War Between the States	243
Chapter 45	Ashland	249
Chapter 46	Resolutions and Reconciliations	251
	Acknowledgements	256
	Fact and Fiction	257
	About the Author	258
	Books by Ted Haynes	258

Principal Characters

Carl Breuninger – Deschutes County Sheriff's Detective

Dylan Crabtree – Ex-con

Ben Crabtree – Dylan's brother, lives in Sunriver

Leon Martinez – Artist, retired art teacher

Elizabeth Martinez – Leon's wife

Geoff Pennstead – Investor

Dara Pennstead – Geoff's wife

Ward Beacham – Pennstead neighbor

Lester Westlake – Leon's former pupil

Tommy Westlake – Lester's son

Gabriel and Maria Isabel Torres – Leon's childhood friends

Chapter 1

Trapped

Dylan Crabtree was not supposed to be here. Not supposed to be in Sunriver. Not supposed to be in Deschutes County. Not supposed to be in Oregon. And now, if he didn't get a move on, the police were going to find him alone in the house and he'd be back where he started. They'd be knocking on doors looking for anyone who saw what happened. They hadn't even arrived yet. There were no sirens. But they'd be here soon, Dylan was certain. A pool of blood spread across East Cascade Road.

Dylan was sure no one had seen him enter his family's vacation house the night before. One story, two small bedrooms, a one-car garage, not very different from other houses in Sunriver. He'd walked three miles along the bike paths from where the bus dropped him off at the gas station. He'd worn big sunglasses on the bus to hide his very memorable black eye. The glasses even looked fashionable. He didn't look like a bum. He looked like a thirty-year-old fit blond man on a leisurely walk through the resort. A vacationer. Clean-shaven, short hair, golf shirt, and a daypack on his back. He didn't look like a criminal and, by nature, he was not a criminal. At least he didn't think of himself that way.

Dylan's brother Ben lived in the house now, and expected him. Gave him beer and dinner. They told stories, had a laugh or two. Dylan hadn't laughed in a long time. They managed to forget that

Dylan was breaking the law. Vague about whether Ben was breaking the law by hosting him. Taking their chances. But succeeding. They were pulling it off. The law was a pain in the neck. They weren't doing anybody any harm.

The brothers had come to this house all their lives. Skied with their parents in the winter, swum and played tennis in the summer. Out all day on their bikes.

When he knew the police were coming, Dylan's first instinct was to run out the front door and disappear in the woods. But that wouldn't work today. First of all, the family in the rental house across the street was taking forever to pack up their car, as though they had scattered their belongings at random throughout the house and were searching every nook and cranny to find them again. The father, the mother, and the two young teenagers, a boy and a girl, came out independently, at completely unpredictable intervals, to put clothes, golf clubs, knapsacks, shopping bags, coolers, and skateboards in the car. From time to time one parent would rearrange what was already stowed only to have it rearranged by the other parent ten minutes later. If Dylan walked out of the house by the front door one family member or another was bound to see him.

The house had no back door and only one back window. Dylan's parents hadn't wanted to spoil the rustic feel of their location by watching cars go past on East Cascade, even if the road was partially screened by lodgepole pines between the house and the road. And they didn't want to be on display for people driving by. They'd built a walled patio on the back of the house so they could still be outside, enjoying the warm weather and the beautiful blue sky.

It wouldn't work to not answer the door, to stay in the house all day, not making a sound. As soon as Ben got home from fishing, the police would be back. Ben would not know what the police knew or didn't know already. He wouldn't know what had happened out on East Cascade. He wouldn't know whether Dylan was involved in it or whether Dylan was still in the house or long gone. Or perhaps arrested already or hauled in by the police for questioning. Ben might give Dylan up or get himself in trouble by lying. The police might enter the house and find Dylan after all. No. Dylan had to be gone before Ben got home.

Dylan did know another way to get out of that house. He hadn't used it since he was a boy and he was a lot bigger now. He might get stuck. Even it if worked, it wouldn't be enough for Dylan to simply disappear. He'd have to erase every trace that he'd been there.

He wished he could have prevented what happened on East Cascade. Then he could have stayed with Ben a few more days in Sunriver. He could have gone on long walks. He and Ben could have rented a canoe at the marina and floated down the river, maybe even had lunch up at Paulina Lake. None of that was going to happen. He had to leave.

Ben would be sorry to find Dylan was gone. He'd worry how much Dylan was involved with the trouble on East Cascade. But Dylan couldn't leave Ben a note. A note would prove Dylan had been there. Ben would have to figure it out for himself when the police showed up. He would be smart enough and loyal enough not to mention Dylan at all. Dylan's duty was to make sure he'd left no hint of himself to trip up his brother's story. He looked around carefully, remembering his movements through the house.

Chapter 2

Bewildered

"For God's sake, put a tarp over that body," yelled Carl Breuninger, Deschutes County Sheriff's Department detective, stepping out of his car. Carl believed that keeping to proper procedures helped keep the world in order as much as the law did. He accepted that people couldn't be perfect, that the world bumbled on in spite of mistakes and inefficiencies. But if you made too many allowances, life went downhill for everyone. Carl was in his late fifties, had a little extra weight on his five-foot-eight frame, and he looked, with his square-shaped head and straight-across lips, not necessarily angry but strict.

A Sunriver policewoman, the only other person in sight, was stringing yellow crime scene tape from tree to tree around a section of East Cascade Road to fence in a silver Mercedes sedan and, thirty feet behind it, a headless body.

"Haven't got a tarp," the patrolwoman shouted back, business-like, professional, with a tiny trace of "back off" in her voice. Carl had met this patrolwoman before but didn't remember her name. The County Sheriff's Department and the Sunriver Police generally worked well together and Carl shrugged off the woman's testiness. It was a taut situation for both of them. He got an orange tarp from the back of his own SUV, walked over to the body, and flung the tarp out in the air to settle over the corpse like a bedsheet. There was no reason to call an ambulance. The man, and Carl was pretty sure it was a man, lay in a pool of blood and the ragged stump of his neck pointed to a messy pile of white, red, and gray. The body smelled of Old Spice aftershave.

Shotgun, thought Carl from five feet away or less. It would take the Medical Examiner and the Crime Lab a week to make it official but Carl knew what the conclusion would be. Death by shotgun—unless the man had been killed by something else before he lost his head.

"Sorry for my tone, officer," said Carl. "I got the call while I was driving from Bend to La Pine. What have we got here?" He remembered her name now. It was Katy Maples, officer Maples. She was about thirty-five and looked too slim to be an imposing police officer until you saw how wiry and strong she was.

"No sign of the shooter," she said. "Doesn't look like suicide to me. The gun would still be here. The guy who called it in is waiting in his car over there. I haven't interviewed him but he told me he didn't see what happened. He saw the body in the road and he stopped. The chief went up towards Beaver Drive to get public works in place to close the road."

Carl had come in on the other end of East Cascade, from Cottonwood, and another Sunriver officer had let him through. The police department had only a few people on duty at 7:30 in the morning. They'd emptied the stationhouse to secure the scene.

The man who had called 911 saw Carl coming. He stopped talking to his rearview mirror, opened his door, stepped out, and stood beside the vehicle, a green Ford Escape. He was a red-haired man in his thirties wearing a lightweight long-sleeved shirt with button-down breast pockets and loose-fitting jeans. Carl introduced himself.

"First let me ask you who you've told about what you've seen," said Carl.

"Just the 911 call and the friends I'm meeting to hike up past Tumalo Falls. I had to tell them I'd be late."

"So not the media? Not the *Bulletin* or KTVZ?"

"No."

"Okay. What time did you arrive here?"

"I did post a photo on Instagram," said the man. "From right here. I didn't go near the dead guy."

"Did you give the location?"

The man thought about this for a second. "I said Sunriver but I didn't say what road."

"Okay," said Carl. "Don't send out any more photos or information." He tried not to show how ticked he was. The more people who knew about this, the more spectators they'd have at the scene, the more media attention they'd get, the more questions they'd have to answer, the more garbage information they'd have to sort through, and the more panic and rumors they'd have to handle. If the Sheriff or the police wanted the public's help on this they could put it on the media once they had a better idea what happened.

"So what time did you get here?"

"About 7:15, I'd guess," the man said. "But I called 911 right away, within thirty seconds. I'm sure they'd know when I called in."

"Did you see anyone else around, any cars?"

"Not a thing," he said. "I looked at both sides of the road and behind me too. I thought whoever shot the guy might come after me. So I looked carefully."

"Did you hear anything?"

"No. When I drove up, I had the windows closed and I was playing music. I didn't hear a shot or anything else."

Carl took the man's name and address from his driver's license. The man, Simon Carr, told Carl his phone number.

"What happened to your front bumper?" asked Carl. The middle of the low bar on the front of the Escape was scratched and dented but had no blood or dirt on it that Carl could see.

"I was off road and I hit a rock," said Carr.

He's probably telling the truth, thought Carl, and he doubted very much that the man would strike the victim with his car, shoot him, and then call 911. But the dent and the explanation were worth remembering. Simon Carr might know something, or remember something, that he hadn't told Carl.

"Okay. Thanks for your help," Carl said. "If you think of something more, give me a call."

"Will do. Can I go now?" the man asked. He had done his duty but it had taken his time and he was anxious to get going.

"Yeah, sure," said Carl.

"Can you take down the tape for a second?" asked the man. "I'll stay away from the body and the car. I was going to head out Cottonwood and I'm already late."

"Negative," said Carl. "You need to turn around."

While the man took two back-and-forths to turn around, Carl called his boss, Sheriff Gordon Knapp. Gordon would want to know whether to alert the public.

"One man dead," said Carl. "Shotgun. Might have been robbery but it looks personal. No description of the shooter and he took the gun with him. There's a Mercedes parked here which is probably the victim's. Looks like the victim got out of his car voluntarily." Carl was guessing at that but it might help Gordon decide what to tell the rest of the Sheriff's Department and the media. "I'd also bet the shooter is not planning to kill more people. If a guy's going to do a mass shooting, he wouldn't start with a lone guy on an empty road." Carl knew Gordon could follow his logic. And they both knew a mass shooter wouldn't want a shotgun. He'd want an automatic rifle.

"I'll need deputies to canvass the area," Carl told Gordon. "The houses here are in the trees back from the road but somebody may have seen something."

"You'll need Kristen and Susan out there too," said Gordon. Kristen Valle was the county Medical Examiner. Susan McCarthy was a crime scene investigator contracted by the county. "I'll get them on their way. Meantime get someone to take photos while the scene is fresh."

"We have a Sunriver policewoman who put up tape and she's already taking pictures," Carl replied. Susan McCarthy would take the more technical photos from the right angles. But the photos Katy Maples took before Susan got here might pick up something that would change before Susan arrived.

"And I'm sending a deputy with a dog to find the gun," added Gordon.

"We'll need them all."

Carl looked up at a beautiful summer morning, sunlight slanting through the lodgepole pines. Temperature still in the sixties but rising rapidly. It was one of the few places in Sunriver, Carl realized, where the houses were far enough from the road that it was hard to see them and difficult for people in the houses to see the road. All of the driveways emptied onto side roads, none of them onto East Cascade. Had the killer chosen this place for that reason? That would suggest premeditation and intent. There would be no "Sorry, the gun went off by accident."

Sunriver was a resort community, a family place, a happy place. Clear skies most of the year, a welcome relief from rainy Portland and Seattle. "The heart and soul of the great northwest," said the advertising. Two murders in its fifty-year history. Four thousand homes in a lodgepole forest surrounding a central lodge, two golf courses, tennis courts, swimming pools, a spa, a rural shopping mall, and a bunch of restaurants. The Deschutes River ran along the resort's western edge with the national forest and the Cascade Mountains stretching beyond. Bend, a fast-growing city of a hundred thousand people, was seventeen miles north over Lava Butte Pass.

Three spectators were standing outside the yellow tape now—a man in his seventies, another in his thirties, and a dark-haired girl of about eight. They hadn't been there when Carl first arrived. Carl wanted to know what they saw or heard that brought them to the scene. And he wanted their names. Everyone was a suspect. Well, maybe not the little girl. At least everyone had things they wanted to tell and things they didn't. He walked over to the trio with his mouth set and his eyebrows furrowed. He'd address them as concerned citizens, supporting the law and wanting answers every bit as much as Carl did. That might change.

The girl, who'd been outside with her dog, had heard two shots right together, less than a second apart. They sounded different, she said, but she couldn't describe the sounds. She'd never fired a gun herself. Never been to a range, never hunted, and her family didn't own guns. None of the three had seen the shooting or anyone coming or going. The girl had been on the far side of her house and she didn't know where the shots had come from, or really that they were shots at all, until she told her father, the man in his thirties, about the funny sounds, like firecrackers in tin cans. He had walked around his house, investigating to indulge his daughter, and saw the flashing lights of Katy Maples' police car.

The older man said he hadn't heard the shots. He was taking a walk on a side road, parallel to East Cascade, when he heard sirens in the distance and saw the flashing lights through the trees. No one remembered seeing the Mercedes before or any other car parked where it was now.

Carl got their names and phone numbers. Then he told them the first thing that Kristen, the medical examiner, would do when she got there was put a tent up over the victim before she took the tarp off. And if the crime scene investigator found anything, she would do her best to keep it hidden from onlookers. In other words, there would be nothing to see.

"Can we take pictures?" asked the older man.

"The law says you can," said Carl, "but I'd rather you didn't. And be careful. Crossing the tape to take a picture would be a crime. Putting a photo online or giving it to the press could be interfering with an investigation. And recording video with any audio in it could violate wiretapping laws. The law draws funny lines sometimes. You don't want the district attorney to haul you into court. Best bet, I'd say, is go home and get back to your life."

The girl and her father left. The older man apparently had nothing better to do.

Carl went to the body and lifted the tarp away from the old man. To estimate the victim's height, Carl imagined himself lying side by side with him. About five-ten, two inches taller than Carl. Not as stocky. People said Carl looked like a concrete bunker.

The corpse was wearing brown leather shoes, not dressy but not built for hiking either. Khaki slacks. A long-sleeved cotton shirt with a dark blue windowpane pattern on it. A black fleece-lined leather bomber jacket, overly warm for summer. He wore a thick gold wedding ring. The wrinkles on his hands indicated an older man, maybe in his seventies. Nice-looking leather belt that cost at least two hundred dollars. Not super expensive clothes but they fit with a guy who drove a Mercedes.

Blood and dirt had soiled the khakis by the man's upper legs and Carl bent down to look more closely. The thighs looked oddly depressed, possibly broken. Stretching a yard or more toward Cottonwood was a faint red tire track. A car or truck had run over the man's legs. It was after the man was already dead, Carl reasoned, or there would have been a pool of blood underneath the legs, pushed out by a beating heart. And who would drive over a man's body but his killer? The crime lab would be able to tell him about the car that made those tracks. Had Simon Carr run over the victim in his Ford Escape and then backed around the corpse before calling 911? Highly unlikely given Carr's composure and the fact that he called 911 rather than leaving the scene as fast as he could.

It's too early for theories, Carl thought, *but not too early for questions.* Did the Mercedes belong to the victim and, if it did, why was his body thirty feet from the car? If the car belonged to the victim, why did he park it where he did? Ultimately, of course, who was the victim and why did someone kill him? *Gather what evidence you can,* Carl told himself, *and hope the picture gets clearer.* It might get frustrating, even embarrassing, but at least this case would be an interesting puzzle. Most murders were people getting drunk—often the victim as well as the killer. An argument starts and one person shoots the other person. It could as easily have been the other way around. Carl was fairly sure nothing like that happened here. An older, decently dressed man, probably driving a Mercedes, was not likely to get into a drunken argument at this early hour, if at all.

Chapter 3

Plein Air

Leon Martinez hadn't expected to be painting a crime scene. He had come out early to paint the portrait of a low-lying black lava rock in a park in Sunriver. His idea was to catch the morning sun raking over the rubble-strewn surface. A geologist told him the rock had been there at least seventy-five thousand years. It was older than Lava Butte, the prominent cinder cone by the road to Bend, and even older than Mt. Bachelor, the nine-thousand-foot volcano that dominated the skyline to the west.

Leon packed his painting kit and collapsible easel into a backpack to put in the back of his ten-year-old Acura SUV. He slid his six-foot tall frame into the driver's seat. In his seventies, he still had the ramrod straight back and easy gait of much younger man. He was retired from teaching art at Bend High School and painted because he still enjoyed the challenge. From time to time he taught watercolor to adults, a way to exercise his teaching skills and make life a little brighter for others. He saved plenty of time and energy for his own painting, golf, and spending time with Elizabeth, his wife of almost fifty years.

Driving around one of Sunriver's tree-filled traffic circles, he passed a row of orange cones and a public works truck blocking off East Cascade Road. Lights flashed white and yellow on the roof. The most likely explanation, Leon calculated, was that someone had hit a mule deer and the utilities man was blocking the road while they cleared it. Deer wandered all through Sunriver, sauntering through back yards and crossing roads with no regard for oncoming cars. Leon's son, Dan, had once hit a fawn. It jumped right in front of him. The deer ran off into the woods, impossible to know whether it was unhurt or looking for a place to die.

Maybe it wasn't a deer. Leon drove back to ask the man standing by the truck a question.

"My wife came this way a little earlier. Has there been an accident?"

"What kind of car was your wife driving?" The man's question had brought Leon's blood pressure up a notch.

"A Toyota Camry. Blue."

"Not involved, as far as I know. And the only one hurt was a man." Blood pressure down. "Would your wife have had a passenger?"

"I don't think so," Leon said. "She was on her way to a golf game with other women. If she had a passenger, it might have been a woman but it wouldn't have been a man."

The public works man was ready for Leon to move on.

"Is it okay if I walk down there?" Leon asked.

"It's a free country. Stay outside the yellow tape. And you can't park here."

Leon drove around the circle and parked in the dirt on a side road. He called Elizabeth's cell and the call went to voicemail. That was almost reassuring. She would have turned off her phone as soon as she got to the golf course. Leon called the golf shop at the Woodlands to ask whether she'd checked in for the tournament.

"Yup," said the young man on the phone. "Went off about five minutes ago. Should be on the first fairway."

Okay, Leon thought when he hung up. *Not to worry.* He put on his favorite outdoor painting hat, yellow straw with a circular brim that curved down around his head. He walked through the trees and bunch grass to see what a crime scene might look like. He was a straight-backed man, carrying his folding easel and painting supplies in a gray backpack.

Leon had never painted a crime scene. He'd painted all his adult life, mostly abstracts in acrylic. Sometimes he revised the painting again and again over a period of years. After he retired from teaching, he'd switched to watercolor, a different kind of discipline. You couldn't go back and change a watercolor. You couldn't scrape away your errors. When a watercolor was done, it was pretty much done, for better or worse.

He'd imposed a further discipline on himself by choosing plein air painting. It meant starting and finishing an outdoor scene within a limited period of time. It was a kind of game, like soccer or blitz chess. Once he started, all his training and experience went into rapid decisions, almost instinctive. He had no time for analysis or a slow weighing of pros and cons. The light, shadows, and colors of the scene changed while he was painting and he had to allow for that.

A side benefit of plein air painting was it got him out of the little studio he had at home, much as he loved it. What could be better than finding an interesting scene and doing what he loved in the light of the morning sun?

The scene of the crime, when Leon got to it, was beautiful—light filtering through the lodgepole pines, police lights flashing, law enforcement doing whatever it was doing. Very much in the spirit of plein air painting, the scene was transitory. This stretch of East Cascade Road would never look the same again.

Leon unpacked the easel and extended its legs. He placed his drawing board on it and clipped a sheet of paper to it. The board leaned toward the horizontal so the watercolors wouldn't run. A shelf attached below the drawing board. It supported a folding box of watercolors, a hook to hold a collapsible bucket of clean water, and, extending to the left, a small shelf with holes in it to hold five brushes. Leon's palette, for mixing colors, would be the lid of the paint box. Leon's backpack, now resting on the ground, held tubes of paint, a water bottle, more watercolor paper, rags to clean the brushes, and a muffin for a mid-morning snack.

He studied the landscape in front of him. A perfect setup. The desert blue sky, the brown vertical lines of trees, the horizontal lines of the road, the sparse tree branches of green needles, scrubby bushes, bunch grass about a foot high, light brown dirt, and the reddish cinders on the shoulder of the road. A stump in the foreground offered shadows that would challenge him. The bright tarp toward the right would be balanced by the silver gray of the Mercedes on the left. Leon wouldn't put the yellow police tape in his painting. It would be too dominant.

Outside the tape to the left stood a Sunriver police SUV, another SUV from the Deschutes County Sheriff's department, and a Sunriver Fire Department truck with its engine rumbling. Lights flashed from all of them. Four men and one woman, in different uniforms, were standing between the vehicles and the tape. They wouldn't be in the painting. Keep it focused—one person standing by the car in a brown Sheriff's Department uniform and a black tactical vest looking at the tarp.

A woman in the dark blue uniform of the Sunriver police was inside the tape now, taking photo after photo, careful not to touch the car or the tarp. Choosing subjects, pointing and clicking away. Leon lifted his cell phone and took a single picture for his own purpose. While he was painting, the sunlight would shift. The shadows of the trees would move. Leon would check the photo later so he could paint the light and shadow where they were when he started. *Don't chase the light,* he reminded himself.

Composition first. Leon picked up a pencil to sketch in the proportions of the road, the car, the tarp, and a few of the trees. Leon had lightly penciled in the major features when one of the men in uniform started toward him. Not fast, but strong and purposeful. It was Carl something or other. Started with a B. Sheriff's detective. To Leon's surprise, the man remembered his name.

"Hello, Leon."

"Hello, Carl. Looks like you're going to have a busy day."

"Good to see you, Leon, but let me ask—how do you happen to be here?"

"I was on my way to paint something else and I thought this would be more interesting."

"You didn't hear about it on the news or online?"

"Nope. I saw the road blocked off and the fellow from public works told me the police were investigating something. I thought it might be a good subject. Turned out I was right."

"Ever seen that Mercedes before?"

"Don't remember it." Leon had nothing to tell Breuninger and, though he wanted to be courteous, he wanted to get to his painting.

"I need to see the painting when you're done with it," said Carl.

"Great. I'll make sure you see it." A vague but sincere commitment. Leon would be happy to show Carl the painting. But he might finish it in his studio at home and he didn't want to think through the logistics of where he and Carl would be when the painting was finished. Maybe the detective would be happy if Leon emailed him a photograph of it. Carl turned and left.

A new sheriff's car arrived and a man in a deputy's uniform let a German shepherd out of the rear door and put a leash on him. The dog jumped and pranced as much as he could on the leash, looking back at the deputy, dying to get to work. The deputy talked a bit with Detective Breuninger and then said something to the dog. He led the dog around the outside of the tape, the dog smelling the ground as he went. Leon bent to his painting as the man and the dog walked in ever-widening circles around the car and the tarp. They came right up to Leon on the third circle. The dog sniffed Leon and the easel before lifting its head at the painting and quickly dismissing it.

"Not a connoisseur," said Leon.

The deputy did not catch Leon's joke. He was focused on the dog. "Excuse us," said the deputy.

"No problem," said Leon.

Leon didn't notice at first that Breuninger was coming through the trees again.

"Sorry about the dog," he said. "He would never have hurt you."

"I have confidence in the Sheriff's Department," Leon said, taking off his hat. "But I appreciate your reassurance. What's the dog looking for?"

"A gun."

"Did he find one?"

"Not yet."

"Do you know who the dead man is? I assume it's a man."

"Don't know for sure yet. We'll look for his wallet once the medical examiner gets a look at the body."

Leon was surprised Breuninger would tell him even that much.

Carl walked back to the gaggle of police and Leon began to apply watercolors to the paper, starting with the black road and the car. He erased his earlier pencil lines as he went. He'd save the trees, grass, and underbrush for last. At least a dozen lodgepoles with prolific branches and subtle shading would take time.

Off to the left, beyond the police and sheriff cars, a large white van with KTVZ on the side rolled in and parked off the side of the road. The police must have let it through. A satellite dish hinged up from the roof. Two men stepped out of the van and walked toward the yellow tape. The one in the suit veered off to talk to Carl. After a minute of dialogue he walked up to the edge of the tape. The other man, carrying a video camera on his shoulder and standing outside the tape, pointed his camera toward the tarp, stood steady for a moment, then slowly panned left and right about thirty degrees in each direction, wide enough to catch the silvery Mercedes slightly off to the cameraman's left. Then the man in the suit stood beside the yellow tape and the cameraman backed up to get him, the tape, the car, and the tarp in the same picture. The man in the suit took a microphone from the cameraman and started talking. He paused after twenty seconds, lowered the mic, and had a brief conversation with the cameraman. He turned slightly to his right, brought the microphone to his mouth again and gave another talk. Leon guessed they were the exact same words the man had spoken earlier. Two takes for someone back in a studio to choose from.

That was it. The men climbed back in the truck. The cameraman never pointed the camera back at the police and sheriff's cars or at any of the officers or deputies. Apparently Carl had declined to be interviewed. The truck turned around with two short back and forth runs to keep the wheels on the road. Then it left, passing a new car with a yellow, blue, and green Deschutes County seal coming to the scene.

A short red-haired woman in a long white lab coat got out with a blue bag in her hand, like a carry-on bag to take on an airplane. She talked with Carl and they walked over to the tarp, picked up two corners, and folded it back over to the far side of the body. She hadn't put up a tent as Carl had told the spectators she would. Only the one old man was watching now.

The policewoman came over and took pictures while Carl and the woman in the white coat held the tarp up. Leon tried to hold the picture in his mind of the moment the tarp was lifted. He penciled in outlines of Carl, the woman, the corpse, and the drape of the tarp. Then he erased the lines. The three forms, two alive and one dead, were too complicated and too depressing. But he kept looking.

He could see the body but he couldn't make sense of it. He thought it was a man from the way it was dressed. But it had no head. Or what had been his head was exploded like a pumpkin dropped from the sky. Blood splayed out toward Leon's side of the road. Leon wasn't going to paint that. Thank God for the tarp. The police photographer took another dozen photos from multiple angles.

The small red-haired woman in the white coat knelt beside the body, poking and prodding it with black-gloved hands and with thermometers. Carl and the woman rolled the body over. More police photographs by Katy Maples. The examiner poked and prodded a bit more and then pulled the man's pants down around his knees. More photos. Then she pushed a thermometer into him. After she read it and wrote down something, she sat back on her haunches and said something to Carl. She got up, pulled her blue bag away from the body, and gripped the nearest corner of the tarp. She and Carl laid the tarp back over the body and walked away.

Another woman arrived in an unmarked car and in plain clothes. She placed yellow cones all around the body and into the woods on Leon's side of the road, beyond where the blood was visible. She took many, many pictures. She measured distances and wrote them down in a notebook. She picked up bits of material, presumably shotgun pellets. She scraped and wiped samples off the road in multiple places.

A hearse had arrived in the meantime and a deputy cut the police tape to let the driver back up to the body. Four of the deputies and officers spread out another tarp, narrower, black, with loop handles around the edges. They wrapped the orange tarp around the body and rolled it onto the black tarp, picked up the black tarp by the handles, and gently, but not ceremoniously, slid it into the back of the hearse. The driver closed the wide back door. So much for whoever it was. It struck a note of finality in Leon's mind, as though a hope of resurrection, of putting the body back together, lasted as long as it lay where it fell and people were fussing over it. Not anymore.

Leon had left the trees for last and painting them would take a while. He studied the photo he'd taken earlier on his phone in order to place the shadows and help remind him where the light was when he first arrived.

A large tow truck arrived to haul the Mercedes up onto its bed and carry it away. A patrolman took down the crime scene tape. A Sunriver fire department truck washed down the road and drove off. The two women, Carl, the sheriff's deputies, and the Sunriver Police all left. Traffic began to move again along East Cascade.

Leon remained alone in the forest, rocking back and forth on his feet to keep the blood flowing while he finished the painting. It was a good morning's work. He packed his equipment into his backpack and walked away. For the first time he stopped thinking about what the scene looked like and began to think what it meant. Somebody, rightly or wrongly, had lost his life. There would be repercussions. Leon hoped they didn't extend to him or anyone he knew.

Chapter 4

Escape

The time Dylan had taken to destroy any evidence of his being in the house had cost him the chance to sneak out a window. If he went out that way now, the police would stop him and ask questions. The woman who was aiming her camera away from him right now would inevitably snap a photo of him. They would check his ID and he would be in trouble right away. He wasn't supposed to leave the State of Washington. Back to jail if he did.

Dylan had thought this trip would be a safe bet. He had called his brother from a pay phone to say he was coming. He'd worn big sunglasses and a floppy hat on the buses from Seattle to Bend. He'd stayed away from people. But back amidst memories of happier times, sitting on the enclosed patio talking with Ben, drinking beer and eating pizza as evening came on, he thought it had been worth the risk.

Any minute the law would come knocking on doors asking if anyone had seen or heard anything suspicious. They would politely ask for his ID. But once they ran him through their database they'd tell his probation officer he left Washington and he'd be back in prison. He wouldn't answer the door, of course, but if he walked out later, even at night, someone might see him or a dog might bark at him and call attention. The neighbors would be on heightened alert after today and would notice the man they hadn't seen before.

If he didn't leave soon, the police would come back later when Ben was home. They might want to search the house. Ben would have to lie for him in any case and he had to make that as risk-free for Ben as he could. He'd thrown out every trace of himself he could think of. Put his towels, sheets, and pillowcase in the laundry hamper. Washed all the dishes and put them away. He had no place to hide the beer bottles but it was credible that one man could have drunk that much beer over a day or two. It would be strange, though, to find that the beer bottles had been washed. Who washes beer bottles? But Dylan's fingerprints were on half of them. He washed them all. He kept the dishwashing gloves on his hands so he wouldn't leave any new fingerprints.

Dylan hadn't opened the trap door in his bedroom for years. It led to the crawlspace under the house and the crawlspace led to small door, more of a hatch, that led to the cave where he and Ben had played and hid things. The cave was part of a lava tube, much smaller than the mile-long tourist attraction on the other side of Highway 97. But it had formed the same way. When the lava flow cooled, thousands of years ago, the top of a lava cooled to solid rock while the hotter lava underneath was still liquid. Then the liquid lava ran out and left an empty tube behind. There were hundreds of lava tubes all over Central Oregon, mostly unknown unless the roof fell in.

The lava tube under the Crabtrees' house ran about two hundred feet and came out in the crawlspace of the house across the street, the house where the family finally looked like they were leaving. They had shut and locked the front door.

When Dylan was eight, he and Ben and the children in the other house crawled back and forth between the houses. The tube had seemed big at the time. It would be a laugh for years, he thought, if in trying to dodge the police he starved to death wedged in the rock where no one would find him.

Dylan took a quick peek over the patio wall to see what was happening on East Cascade. Four police and sheriff's vehicles were out there now, three with their lights flashing, and a gaggle of law enforcement milling about inside and outside of a yellow tape strung from tree to tree. A man in a brown sheriff's uniform and a woman in a blue Sunriver Police uniform left the group and headed through the woods directly toward Dylan. It was time for Dylan to make a break.

A flashlight. He would need a flashlight. He got the one from the kitchen drawer where it had always been and checked that it worked. Dylan rolled back the rug over the trap door and lifted up the ring handle. He slid two feet into the crawlspace. God, it was cramped already. He tugged the rug back over the trapdoor and slowly lowered the door into place again.

As a boy Dylan could walk through most of the tube, bent over in the low places. Now he had to crawl, dragging his backpack behind him. For a three-foot section, he had to shimmy on his stomach like a soldier under machine gun fire. He'd taken the few clothes he'd brought with him along with bread, peanut butter, two apples from the kitchen, and two bottles of water. He would have taken cash if he could find any but he didn't. His brother, Ben, would understand. Dylan had a hundred twenty of his own, enough for bus fare from Bend to Seattle. He didn't leave Ben a note.

The trapdoor into the house across the street wasn't nailed shut or wedged under heavy furniture. Dylan listened closely from the tunnel and opened the trapdoor slowly. He paused to listen again, making sure no one had come back for something they'd forgotten. He put on the latex dishwashing gloves he'd brought from Ben's house so he wouldn't leave fingerprints in this house either. The trapdoor came up in a bedroom in the front of the house. Dylan could hear adult voices out in the driveway. The police were here talking with the family about to drive away. He'd heard enough police voices to recognize the serious tone, the deliberate rhythm in their speech.

The back door in this house, he knew, led toward the forest and escape. But Dylan couldn't go yet. His face and hands were dirty from the tunnel. His clothes were filthy. He stepped into a bathroom but didn't want to run water that the police out front might hear. He carefully lifted the top off the toilet tank and dipped in a washcloth and soap, using them to scrub his face, neck, and hands. He swapped his clothes for the shirt and pants in the backpack and wiped down the backpack. He took the washcloth with him. If the owners missed it, they would assume the renters took it.

Dylan walked carefully and slowly to the sliding glass door then to the back deck. He did not hear the voices of the family or the high but authoritative voice of the policewoman anymore. He would not be able to lock the sliding door from the outside and whoever came to the house next might wonder if there had been a burglary. For that matter a burglar might actually find his way in that door if it stayed unlocked long enough. He could hope.

Chapter 5

Making Sense

When Carl decided he couldn't learn anything more at the scene, he asked Bob Bobletz, the Sunriver Police Chief, to meet him at the police station. Susan McCarthy, the crime scene investigator who had measured the scene and taken photographs, would join them. The pair that had canvassed the local houses—sheriff's deputy Adam Wallhagen, and Sunriver police officer Katy Maples—would be party of the meeting too. Adam was ex-army. Not afraid of anything. Katy was almost bashful when she wore civvies, but in her uniform, with the force of the law behind her, she could be as assertive as any officer in the department. She was subtle when she needed to be and she was good at talking with people. Carl had counted on her to do most of the interviewing when she and Adam went house to house.

The group gathered in the windowless conference room in the center of the small police building and Carl finally got his second coffee of the day.

"We're going to assume," Carl began, "that the wallet that Kristen pulled from the victim's pocket belonged to him. It still had his ID, credit cards, and six dollars in it. If that's true our victim is a man named Geoffrey Pennstead, seventy-seven years old, who lives at the end of River Road on the far side of the airport. Oregon DMV says the Mercedes is registered to a Dara Pennstead at the same address.

A fifty-year-old female, presumably the man's wife or his daughter. I'm going to her house as soon as we're done here. So I want to quickly put together a timeline based on what we know. The 911 call came in at 7:23 a.m. and I arrived at 7:35. What time, Bob, did you set up the roadblocks?"

"It was a scramble but we blocked off the north end about 7:27 and the south end about 7:30. The only vehicles that came into the area between 7:30 and 11:15 when we opened up the road again were law enforcement, the fire department, one camera truck from KTVZ, the medical examiner, the crime scene investigator, and the hearse. Nobody drove out except those same people and the guy you interviewed who called 911." Carl wrote the times down on the conference room whiteboard with brief notations of what occurred.

"Kristen, the medical examiner, arrived at 8:10," said Carl, "and examined the body as soon as she got there. She puts the time of death between 7:15 and 7:25. She says she can be that precise because it hadn't been long since the man died. So the 911 caller came upon the victim within eight minutes max after he was killed. The caller didn't see anyone else in the area. Kristen also says she didn't find any injury or other sign of violence aside from the shotgun blast and being run over, which she says happened after he was already dead.

"Between 7:50 and 8:00, I interviewed three bystanders. They hadn't seen the shooting and had no useful information. I'll interview them again if we learn more and I think they might know something they thought was irrelevant at the time.

"At 8:00 o'clock, a man I know, Leon Martinez, arrived and started painting the scene. Stopped at the roadblock and walked in. I interviewed him. Hadn't seen anything. Doesn't know anything. Solid citizen.

"At 8:15, we have enough people to start canvassing the nearby houses and I'll ask Adam and Katy to tell us what they learned.

"At 8:30, the K-9 unit arrives and we send the dog out to look for guns. The dog doesn't find any," said Carl. "Kristen, the medical examiner, says she'll know more from the autopsy and tox screen next week. Aside from that, she says, she can only state the obvious.

The victim had his head blown off by a shotgun at short range. Susan, what can you tell us from your investigation?"

Susan began. "The shotgun pellets indicate he was shot twice, once with birdshot and once with buckshot. Kristen should be able to tell us which came first but I think they were fired in very quick succession. The other thing I can add is the tire treads that went over the body were bigger and knobbier than a sedan, most likely an SUV or a pickup truck built for heavy loads. The lab may be able to pin them down further."

"So it wasn't the Mercedes sedan," said Carl. "Let's move onto the reports from the canvassing."

Adam said Katy should give the report since she did most of the talking and Adam backed her up.

"No houses at all are close to East Cascade along that stretch," said Katy. "We called on twenty houses on the dead-end roads that parallel East Cascade on either side. No answer at ten of them. We got the license numbers of all the cars parked outside the houses, including three of the no answers. No likely suspects. No criminal histories. No serious traffic violations. Four respondents said they owned the houses and six were short term rentals. Got their contact information. Nobody saw anything—not the area where the shooting took place, no unusual activity on their street. One man said he might have heard a shot but he wasn't sure and he didn't remember the time. One girl heard the shots but didn't note the time. Renters at one house were outside packing up to leave. They had been in and out of the house at the time but even they hadn't heard a shot. Hadn't seen anybody else out of doors at that hour.

"I asked all the respondents whether they had a gun in the house or if they knew of anyone on the road who had a gun. Two houses with a pistol each and another with a hunting rifle locked in a rack. No one admitted to having a shotgun or knew of anyone who did. Nobody's been brandishing a weapon. They don't all know each other. With all the renters, it's not much of a neighborhood. But no one knew of any feuds going on or anyone who's angry or acting strange. That's about it. Names and contact information will be in our report."

"Thanks," said Carl. "We'll go back to the empty houses later to see who's come home. And we'll find out who owns the vacant houses and who might be renting them."

"Sorry we didn't find anything useful," said Katy, "but the house where a family was leaving is across the street from the two houses closest to the crime scene. The rental has a doorbell camera that uploads to the cloud. We called the owner and he gave us the web address, his username, and his password. Adam and I are going to look at the video from 7:00 a.m. to 10:00 a.m. It only records motion so we won't have to watch a solid three hours."

"Even if you don't see anyone, the information will be useful," said Carl. "We have to eliminate a lot of possibilities before we get to the answer. We'll know more when we get lab results. I'm going to visit the woman the Mercedes is registered to. Katy, can you visit the lodge and see who checked in or checked out this morning between 6:00 and 10:00? Maybe they saw someone coming or going. Ask which employees came or left work between 7:00 and 8:00 and talk to all the ones you can find.

"Keep in touch. And don't say any more about the killing than you absolutely have to. We want to let Sheriff Knapp and Chief Bobletz decide what to tell the press. KTVZ already has video of the crime scene and we can't help that. But don't add to what the public already knows. We want to solve this quickly but we want to minimize the worries. No rumors. No guesses."

"Any theories we should be checking out?" asked Adam. Deputy Wallhagen planned to be a detective himself one day. He was trying to get a head start.

"Too early. We're sucking up information while it's fresh," said Carl. "We should know a lot more by tomorrow. And we'll have all the lab reports in a week."

Chapter 6

The Bad News

Carl Breuninger didn't like uncertainty. He was at war with it. He was driving, he knew, into a carnival of uncertainty. He snaked around the curving roads and traffic circles in Sunriver where he could never find a direct route to anywhere he wanted to go. Carl didn't know Dara Pennstead from a hot rock and Officer Carrie Finch, in the car behind him, didn't know her either. Would she simply be a woman whose car had been stolen? Or a woman who was about to learn that her husband or father was dead? Perhaps a woman who was somehow responsible for the man's death? Maybe a woman already a victim herself, lying dead on her kitchen floor, blood spattered all over the kitchen cabinets by another shotgun blast? Worse yet, a hostage with the killer inside the house, threatening to kill Dara and aiming a gun out the window at Carl and Carrie as they approached?

Carl would ask the Sunriver police to stop traffic on East Cascade for the next few mornings to find people who came that way every day. That would be the few homeowners who weren't retired and went to work in Bend every morning. The Sunriver Police Department was short-staffed and Bobletz might say he couldn't spare the manpower. But any officer stopping traffic could still respond to emergency calls if there were any. The emergency that took a lot of the department's time was finding lost children. That didn't happen as much in the early morning.

And, of course, Carl realized, golfers on their way to tee off at the Woodlands Golf Course could have seen something. The course was on the north end of the resort and maybe half of the people going there would come on East Cascade. Carl called dispatch to get the number of the Woodland pro shop and reached it as he was driving. He told the youngster who answered that he needed the names and phone numbers of everyone who played this morning.

"This about the shooting at East Cascade?"

"Most likely," Carl said.

"Sure," he said. "For residents with golf passes, we have all their names and numbers. Emails too. But for visitors, we only have contact information for the person who made the reservation. I can email you everything we've got. But do you want to talk to them as they come off the course? That should start around noon. You could wait for them as they finish the eighteenth green." Carl definitely didn't want to stand around in the sun for hours waylaying people who would be more eager to get to their cars, or the bathroom, or a cold drink, than remember what they had seen on their way to play golf.

"Good idea but we may not be able to do that," Carl said. "Could you get your guys who take the carts to ask for names and numbers of all the players who come in? Tell them the sheriff is looking for witnesses before and after a crime."

"We'll do what we can but the employees can't force them if the players blow them off." He paused. "You know what might help? The Sunriver Ladies have a member guest tournament this morning. Teed off between 7:30 and 9:00 a.m. We have names for all of the ladies who played and phone numbers for all the members. The members can probably give you the phone numbers for their guests. And the ladies are going to have lunch in McDivot's Café next to the pro shop. If you come back about one o'clock, you can talk to them all."

Carl, with Carrie Finch following him, took River Road past the Nature Center, the marina, and the airport. It was the longest stretch of road in Sunriver that had no houses along it except at the very end.

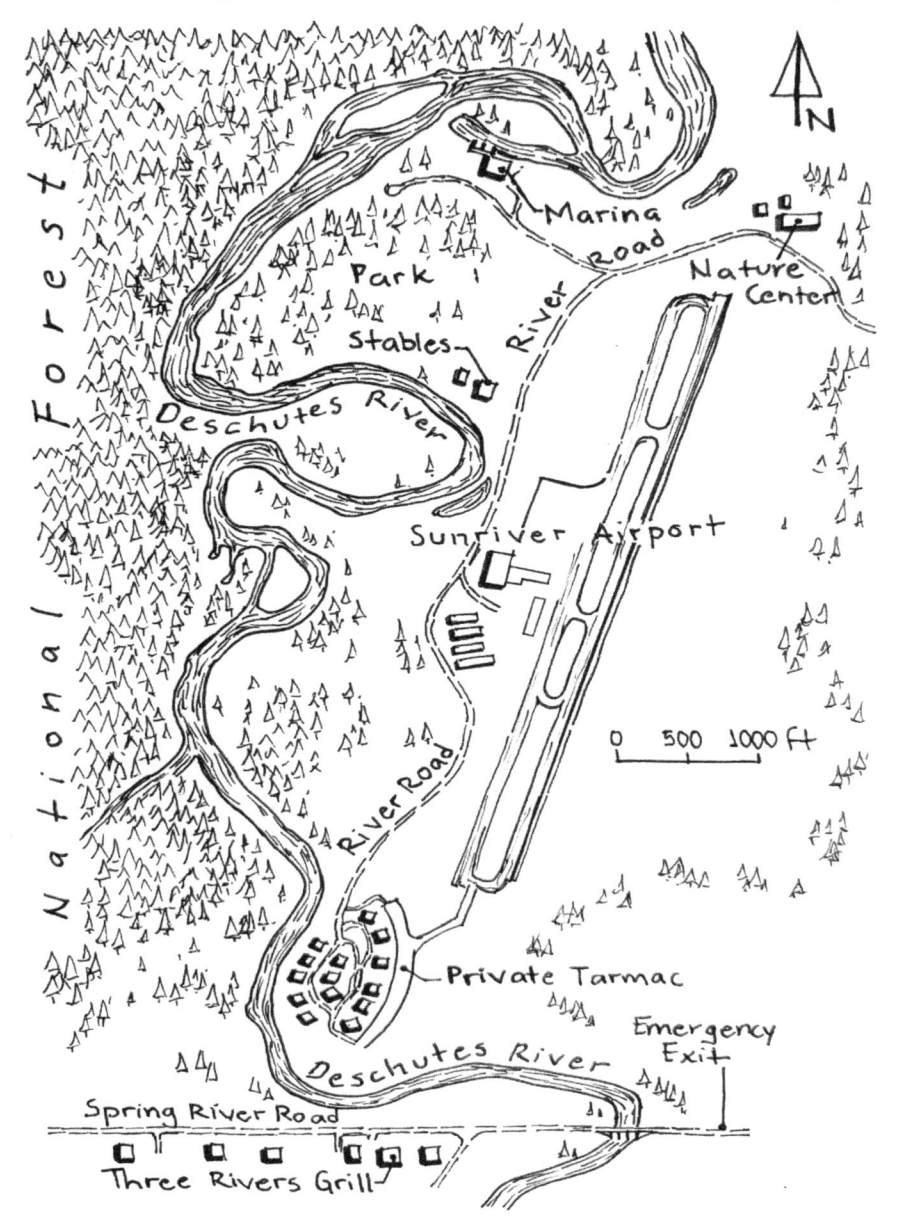

RIVER ROAD IN SUNRIVER

Off in their own neighborhood, the houses were among the most expensive in the whole development. The houses that backed up to a private taxiway that extended from the airport were certainly the biggest—they had airplane hangars built into them. The Pennsteads' house was one of them. Carl parked in the driveway in front of the single car garage and Carrie parked on the street. The Pennstead house was well-built, with light gray board and batten above stone wainscotting. It would have good views of Mt. Bachelor out the west windows on the second floor. But maintenance was overdue. The paint had faded and was peeling in the direct sun. The shrubs by the house were dead or sickly and the lawn had bare spots in it.

Carl checked his holster and gun. Carrie had her hand on her pistol and the two walked up to the door together.

If the Pennsteads' windows had any shades or drapes, they were open. Carl saw no one inside and no movement. But soon after he rang the doorbell, he heard a quick light step, a woman's step, coming to the door.

"Oh, hello," the woman said, looking surprised but not alarmed. Then in a friendly, confident tone, "Is there something wrong?" She was about five-foot-six, short dark hair, trim figure. Flushed and perspiring with no make-up. Sneakers, shorts, and a t-shirt over a sports bra. "Forgive my appearance," she said. "I was on the Peleton." She kept her poise, an attractive woman accustomed to having the world treat her well. She would be polite to him, even friendly, as though she were welcoming a handyman who had come to fix a leaky faucet. People in Sunriver, in all of Central Oregon, were generally friendly. It was the custom of the place.

Gordon, Carl's boss, had once said to him, "It's a funny thing. But I think the more guns a town has, the friendlier it is. People want to assure each other they are not a threat and they wish the other guy well."

Dara Pennstead might be friendly, thought Carl, but he didn't know who might be with her.

"Are you Dara Pennstead?" Carl's tone was optimistic.

"Yes, I am," said Dara.

"I'm Lieutenant Detective Carl Breuninger with the County Sheriff's Department and this is Officer Finch with the Sunriver Police Department. Are you alone in the house?"

"Yes." Dara smiled a winning smile.

Carl squeezed up the corners of his mouth into his long-practiced imitation of a smile. "We're gathering information on a recent crime and I think you might be able to help us. May we come in?" If Mrs. Pennstead got emotional, and she might wind up that way, she wouldn't want to be standing in the doorway.

"Would you like some coffee?" she said. "I made it about an hour ago but it's still hot."

"No thank you," said Carl. What he had to say was important, life changing. He could not delay it for social niceties. But he didn't want Dara to collapse on the floor.

"Could we sit down?" he asked. "This might take a few minutes."

"Sure," she said. "Let's go in the living room." They walked back into the house and Dara gestured toward a grass-colored sofa. She sat in one of two leather armchairs five feet away and a few inches higher than the couch. She smiled at Carl and Carrie, a citizen ready to help.

"We found a Mercedes S430 by the side of the road in Sunriver this morning, registered to you. Do you know who last had the car?"

A trace of concern flickered across Mrs. Pennstead's face. "My husband took it this morning. Did it break down? He cares about his plane but he puts off fixing his cars. That car is ready for hospice."

"We're having it towed. We don't know yet whether it broke down. But, and this is why we are here, we also found the body of a man we could not identify next to the car. We don't know for sure it is your husband but your husband's wallet was in the man's pocket. Can you tell me when you last saw your husband?"

Dara Pennstead's mouth dropped open and she sank back into her chair.

"Geoff flew back this morning from a business trip," she said. "He was in a hurry to get to Bend. Didn't even have breakfast. I handed him an apple."

"What does he look like and what he was wearing?"

"Handsome man," said Dara, shakily now. "Older. Seventy-seven. Five-foot-ten. Gray hair. Brown eyes. Medium build. Brown oval birthmark on his left shoulder. He was wearing a Tattersall shirt and a black bomber jacket. He might have taken the jacket off. Oh, and he left here about seven o'clock this morning."

"Did he bring anything from the plane or take anything with him in the car?" asked Carl.

Dara thought about the question a minute. "I didn't see him get out of the plane but he was carrying a gym bag with him when he went to the car."

"What did that look like?"

"Black with handles and a shoulder strap. Kind of big for a gym bag. He used it sometimes as an overnight bag. Did you find it?"

"No," said Carl. "But now we know to look for it."

"I'd like to have it," said Dara. Her eyes, dry the moment before, burst forth in a flood of tears. "Oh God, what happened?" Dara leaned on her forearms, pressed on the arms of the chair, as if she were at the top of a roller coaster about to take a steep plunge. Her gaze was locked on the floor until she slowly turned toward Carl. "Are you sure it's Geoff?"

"Ninety-nine percent," said Carl. "If he's ever been fingerprinted, we'll compare the prints."

"He was fingerprinted when he got his pilot's license. What happened?"

"He was shot. We don't know yet by whom or what the circumstances were. Sorry to come to you with a shadow of a doubt whether the victim is your husband or not. But the quicker we start our investigation, the more likely we'll get to the true facts. It's a serious crime and Deschutes County is committed to finding the perpetrator."

"Oh God," she said, looking at her open hands in her lap. "What next? How did it come to this?" She shook her head side to side.

"How did what come to this?" Carl asked.

"All this business. All these investments. All this financing. All this wheeling and dealing. We had a nice life. We should have been happy."

"And what happened?" Carl asked, immediately concerned about the bluntness of his question.

Dara sucked her breath in and looked at Carl with narrowed eyes, as if she hadn't really taken him in before. "I think I probably need a lawyer," she said.

Dammit, thought Carl. If Dara hired a lawyer, it would take weeks to learn what she could easily tell him in the next five minutes. Search warrants, subpoenas, court hearings, God knew what else. If she wouldn't paint the whole picture of Pennstead's finances, maybe she would answer a simpler question.

"Where did Mr. Pennstead go on his business trip?"

"I don't know. He didn't tell me."

"How long was he gone?"

"He flew out two days ago and came back this morning."

"Do you think you are in danger yourself?" Carl asked in a voice of concern.

Dara swept her eyes around the comfortable, orderly living room. She was shocked, Carl thought, that she could no longer feel safe in her own house. A killer could come to her door as easily as Carl had.

"Wait a minute," said Dara. "Was this a random shooting or some kind of argument Geoff got into on the spot? Road rage or something? Or did somebody shoot Geoff on purpose?"

"We don't know." Carl didn't tell her his first thought was the shooting was spontaneous, not planned. A calculating killer would use a quieter weapon in a private place, not a shotgun on a public road.

"I can't think why anyone would want to kill Geoff."

"Nobody was angry with him? Nobody thought he'd cheated them or embarrassed them, or taken advantage of them?"

"Not that I know of. He's an honest man."

"Does he owe anyone money?"

"Nobody. Well, I mean, not a person. He borrowed money to make investments. But he borrowed from legitimate business people. From banks. He's a private investor. Geoff has all kinds of investments—private companies, real estate, the stock market. I don't know what else."

"Any specific banks?"

"Oh, I don't know. He always said 'the bank.'"

"Do you have a mortgage on the house?"

"That's with Wells Fargo. I know that."

"Do you know where he keeps his financial statements? Can I have a look at them?"

Dara caught herself and paused a minute. "I think I better have a lawyer before you do that."

"Anybody have any disputes with your husband about anything?"

"Not that I know of. Certainly not bad enough to kill him."

"You two getting along okay?"

"Yes. And I'm not going to answer any more questions until I have a lawyer." Dara's face had gotten a pinched look that made her less appealing than before. She was angry but on the edge of tears.

"I understand," said Carl. "We're going to leave for now. Will you call me when you get a lawyer so we can continue our discussion? We both want to know what happened to Geoff and why."

"If it is Geoff after all this," said Dara. "You'll tell me when you're sure and you'll let me see him?"

"Yes, I'll let you know. You may not want to see him but you can if you want. In the meantime, I'll make sure that deputies and the Sunriver police keep a watch on your house to protect you. It's not to keep an eye on you. You are not a suspect." Carl was lying about that. Of course Dara was a suspect. But she'd be more relaxed if she thought Carl didn't have his eye on her. She might be careless in hiding the truth. And, suspect or not, she might truly be in danger.

"And if anyone threatens you or even worries you," said Carl, "be sure and let me know right away. Do you have someone you can call to come talk with you?"

"I don't know," said Dara. "Maybe."

Carl wasn't worried about Dara fleeing Sunriver. Fifty-year-old women with a house, a Mercedes, and even a goddam plane, whether in debt or not, don't disappear to start a new life. They hire lawyers.

Chapter 7

Gossip

Leon knew from experience that it would take time for him to know whether his painting of the crime scene was a good one or not. Whether he was proud of it or not. But he'd enjoyed the morning working on it, getting ideas, solving problems. It was still a lovely day, great to be outside. Elizabeth should have enjoyed her golf game too, and he was happy to think she had.

He packed up his easel and walked back to his car. His next stop would be a lunch he had every week with other men from Sunriver and Upriver Ranch, the smaller community to the south of Sunriver where Leon lived. Five to ten men usually showed up, not always the same ones. This was the fourth week in a row they met at Three Rivers Grill, a place a mile outside of Sunriver on the road up to Mt. Bachelor. It wasn't gourmet but it was nicer than a diner and Leon could get a good Cobb salad. The men liked it because tourists didn't come there. The customers were mostly local. Nobody was wearing golf clothes and about half the men wore their ball caps indoors. The food was good, the service was good, and there was a full bar. The men talked about sports, their golf games, real estate, fishing, and their families. They stayed away from politics because they had very different opinions and they wanted to keep the lunches going.

Leon was early and sat at the counter while he waited for the others. The four TV screens around the grill were usually tuned to sports and Leon asked the tall young barman, who looked strong enough to be working construction, why the screen behind the bar was set to the local channel.

"Some guy died in Sunriver. All you can see is a tarp in the middle of a road. The clip will come around again."

At the moment the TV was showing a newscaster in the KTVZ studio. The sound was off but the caption beneath him said the Sheriff's Department had not yet released the name of the victim.

"Not going to be good for rentals," said a short overweight man pulling out a stool next to Leon and looking up at the TV screen. It was Ward Beecham, another man from the lunch group who had gotten there early. Ward was tolerated more than welcomed. His contributions tended toward the cynical. But he was part of the group anyway. Leon thought that happened more in rural areas. You were going to see the same people time after time and you had to learn how to get along.

The men did feel sorry for Ward. He had lost his son in a bad way. In the middle of the night four years earlier, Ward had shot and killed his son by accident. He thought the son was an intruder. It was in the paper for days. Now Ward's two older children wouldn't speak to him. One of them told *The Bulletin* that he didn't think Ward had killed the boy on purpose but that he'd been careless. Ward had never been in the military but he was serious about guns and home defense. He was never charged with the killing but some people, including his friends in the group, quietly wondered whether that was what happened. Maybe he got carried away in some late-night argument, pointed a pistol at him, and it went off—intentionally, by accident, or some murky calculation halfway in between.

"Violent death does take some shine off vacationing in Sunriver," Leon answered. He immediately regretted what he'd said given Ward's history but Ward didn't act like he'd caught the connection.

"No suspects identified," said the caption on the screen. The television rolled the clip of the orange tarp again. Leon had been at that same location for hours and the TV showed him nothing new.

"I know that car," said Ward, for once sounding positive about something. "It's the right color, kind of a silver metallic with a little brown in it. My neighbor drives a 2001 S430 exactly like that. I'll bet it's his. Geoff Pennstead is his name."

Leon thought Ward was getting over his skis with guesswork. "Now you're going to tell me who shot him."

"No idea. Maybe some chappie who was after his wife. She's much younger than he is. Or was." That sounded like the Ward that Leon expected. The most sordid explanation possible. Ward had stepped over into fantasyland.

Rather than counter him, Leon volunteered a more realistic idea. "Maybe some kind of argument that got out of hand," he speculated.

"I can see that," said Ward. "The guy is driving along at twenty-five miles an hour, like he's supposed to, and somebody else is in a rush. The guy in a hurry gets furious enough to bump the Mercedes or pass Geoff and cut him off. One or both of them get out of their cars. They get into an argument and somebody points a gun and pulls the trigger. Or maybe Pennstead decides it's lovely weather for shooting himself. I saw him leave his house this morning in that car. He landed his plane at the crack of dawn. That's what got my attention in the first place. Then he went out again in his car." Ward lived by the Sunriver Airport and had a new kind of plane that he was very proud of. It was an Epic GX1000 Turboprop, made in Bend. The fastest single-engine prop plane in the world. The Epics were made out of lightweight carbon-fiber composites instead of aluminum. The lighter weight of the composite allowed the planes to fly faster and be more fuel efficient.

"The car could have used a wash," Leon said.

Ward didn't ask Leon how he knew that that. The dirt on the car was hard to see on the TV.

"That's his for sure then," said Ward. "This morning it looked like a month since water touched it."

"Sorry if he turns out to be the guy."

"Me too," said Ward. "But he's not a close friend. We talk planes once in a while."

Five of their lunch partners were heading for their favorite table.

Leon and Ward joined them. There were enough of them now to talk about the guy dead in the road without having to repeat it for every new arrival. Those who were late would have to catch up. Leon waited for someone else to start the topic. Three of the men had read about it on the internet.

"God, you leave your house in the morning and next thing you know, you're dead in the road." This was one of the older men, still an avid golfer. Years ago, he'd been club champion at the golf course in Upriver Ranch. That was before Elizabeth and Leon moved there from Bend.

"Could make you want to stay home and watch old movies," Leon said.

"Or make sure you carry a gun when you go out," said another man. At least half the men in the group had guns at home. One man carried a pistol in his golf bag. The men joked that he got more gimmie putts than he really deserved. The man admitted he probably would not be attacked on the golf course. He said he felt more comfortable having it, like having a full set of clubs and his favorite putter. The gun made him feel complete.

A waitress brought menus. Two more of the group came in. When the waitress came back with water, she asked who was ready to order. The kitchen wouldn't be able to deliver seven or ten lunches all at the same time in any case and she wanted to get the kitchen started on the orders they could. All the men knew the menu and many of them ordered the same thing every time. Two other men sat down before she was around the table and she took their orders too.

"I think the guy was my neighbor," said Ward. "Name is Geoff Pennstead. He left his house early this morning in a car identical to the one they're showing on TV."

"He buys and sells real estate, right?" asked the man to Carl's left.

"And other stuff. He was into a gold mine in Mexico but they couldn't raise enough money to start digging," said another. "I never heard what happened to that. But I know he had eighty acres of scrubland down in La Pine that would have paid off bigtime when Highway 97 was moved. But they never moved the highway.

Pennstead must have lost his shirt on that one."

The conversation turned to golf, first an upcoming PGA tournament and then the men's recent games, new golf clubs, disasters on the course, and pin placements that were hard or even unfair. This week the men talked about whether inflation would slow down, whether the country would drop into a recession, what Congress and the Fed should do or would do. Leon listened but contributed nothing. He had no background in economics and limited knowledge of business. In his heart, he had decided he was a socialist. After all, his parents had named him Leon after Leon Trotsky, one of the founders of the Soviet Union whom Stalin had assassinated. But Leon didn't know enough or care enough to argue for socialism. And this was not the place to test out his ideas. The group was mostly retired businessmen, capitalists to the core. One doctor and one engineer.

And if Leon was a socialist, he knew he was a hypocritical one. He lived in Upriver Ranch, an expensive place for Central Oregon. His wife, Elizabeth, was a capitalist through and through. She worked her way up to area manager for a bank and she made some excellent investments for herself and Leon. Capitalism had paid for their cars, their son's college and his law school, and some very nice vacations. They could never have built the house in Upriver on Leon's teacher's retirement.

Leon's cell phone rang and he stepped away from the table to answer it. The call was from a student who had been in two of Leon's adult watercolor classes. He remembered she worked harder at her painting than his other adult students. She had once been a professional singer and she knew how much patience and hard work it took to develop whatever talent a person was born with. He hadn't seen her for months. Her name was Dara Pennstead. Leon took his phone outside to talk with her.

"Leon, the Sheriff was just here. They think Geoff is dead but they aren't sure it's even him. He doesn't answer his cell phone. The detective asked me all kinds of questions. I can't even think straight. You're the best person I know to talk to. I hope you don't mind."

People told Leon he sometimes cared too much about his students, starting with his high school students. If they were depressed or in trouble, he went out of his way to help them. Girls and boys got picked on. Parents ignored them or even hit them. Kids fell behind academically, athletically, socially, or financially. They despaired of ever making successes of their lives. Leon would buck them up as well as he could and search for ways to make their burdens lighter.

Leon had never heard about Dara's family. He wanted to console her for the death of her husband, if it really was Geoff, or at least he wanted to show that someone cared. But he would be cautious. With an adult, it might be harder to maintain the teacher-student relationship without creating some other kind of dependency. He didn't want to get entangled.

"The detective is sending somebody," said Dara. "'Victim's assistance,' he called it. I don't know about that. I don't need someone to tell me Geoff has gone to a better place and who wants to pray with me. I need someone to tell me what to do."

"You've got some time to sort things out," said Leon. "Take a deep breath and make some lists, as though you were making lists of what you needed to do to paint a picture." It sounded simple and Leon wanted it to sound simple. Familiar, too, like lists they'd made in class—materials needed, steps in preparation, steps in thinking, steps in painting.

"Could you come over?" asked Dara. "I trust you."

Dara hadn't made friends in Leon's adult art class and he sensed she was short on friends overall. Just talking with her got him deeper into her life and her problems than he wanted to be. But he said he would come.

When Leon went back inside, the men's discussion had moved on to whether the eastern counties of Oregon would ever become part of Idaho, as many of their residents wanted. They would be interested to know about the call from Dara Pennstead. He chose to keep it to himself.

Chapter 8

The Journey I

Dylan Crabtree was relieved. More relieved than he should have been because his dangers were not over. He was walking north on a dirt path beside the railroad tracks. The track bed was high enough to hide him from the houses in Sunriver. The ponderosa forest to his right stretched for a mile before it got to Highway 97. Soon the forest would be on both sides and, after that, the track led through a lava field too bleak for anyone to like visiting. Volcanoes might be pretty at a distance but lava fields were ugly jumbles of rough black rock, hot and bone dry in the middle of the day, slow and difficult to get through on foot. The railroad tracks cut straight through the lava. Dylan could walk all the way to Bend without being seen.

Up the tracks ahead, Dylan saw the one road the railroad crossed before it got to Bend. The road led from the highway down to the canoe landing on the Deschutes River. Light traffic. Not a through road. Still, the road ran straight and a driver could see Dylan from a long way off. He stood next to a tree to check no cars were coming and then hustled across like a hiker on a mission.

The tracks went another seven hundred yards through the forest before abruptly cutting into a tall mound of black lava. The lava flow, seven thousand years old, had blocked the river and formed a lake that backed up through what was now Sunriver. The lake would have covered the airport, the stables, and at least one of the golf courses. Centuries later, the river broke through the rock and the lake disappeared. Dylan remembered this history lesson from visits to the Nature Center that his parents had marched Ben and Dylan to when they were boys. He'd dreamed for years that Lava Butte would erupt again.

The tracks ran for two miles through the uneven rock, straight through cuts for two hundred yards at a time and then along man-made embankments that kept the grade as steady as possible. No walking trail paralleled the tracks but the wooden ties between the rails were easy to walk on, less than two feet center to center and each tie six inches wide. Every step brought him closer to Bend and to Seattle and further from the police who would love to know what Dylan knew about the death in Sunriver.

The tracks left the lava field for an airy ponderosa forest. Though the shade was meager, the air felt cooler than out in the lava. Dylan stopped under a tree to drain half a water bottle. Now a dirt trail ran beside the tracks and he scrambled down the embankment to take advantage. He could hear Highway 97 off to his right, the whish of cars, the whining of tires, and the occasional honk of a horn.

After two miles through the forest, houses and streets appeared on Dylan's left, the southernmost reach of the city of Bend. Dylan stuck to the dirt trail on the right side of the tracks. The fewer people who saw him the better. But he didn't look scruffy. He didn't look homeless. He didn't look like a bum or a criminal. The haircut he'd gotten two weeks ago for the benefit of his parole officer hadn't grown out. His shirt and pants were clean and his soft green backpack from North Face made him look like a man hiking for sport, not a man without a car who was trying to distance himself from the police.

One misjudgment, four years ago, had cost Dylan dearly. His supposed friend, Jeffey, talked him into stealing checks out of mailboxes, washing them with chemicals to change who they were made out to, then cashing them. It was foolproof. They would never get caught. But they were caught. A four-year sentence bargained down to two. Then parole. His high school friends didn't want to see him. Women didn't want to date him except for those who had problems of their own—physical health, mental health, drugs, debt, children with no child support, a troublesome ex, criminal records, personality problems, or simply too plain boring to tolerate. All Dylan's problems traced to Jeffey's overly optimistic scheme.

Jeffey had served time too. No time off for good behavior though. Committed a burglary as soon as he got out. OD'd on fentanyl while awaiting trial. Stupid Jeffey. How had Dylan ever gotten mixed up with him?

Dylan's brother Ben was the one rock Dylan could cling to. Steady job. Cute girlfriend in Salem with a good head on her shoulders. Ben had visited Dylan in prison, driven miles to do it. They both thought it was safe for Dylan to come to Sunriver for a few days. Keep a low profile. Enjoy the sunny weather. Get back to the vacation house they'd known since they were children. Be a normal person.

Bad luck messes people up when they're vulnerable. If that car simply hadn't stopped on East Cascade behind Ben's house, Dylan wouldn't be on the run now, trying to be inconspicuous, trying not to be memorable to anyone who might see him.

He was walking on the street now, past house after house. Cars came by every few minutes. People came out of their houses and drove away. Dylan crossed the street when he saw anyone. Or slowed down. Or took a side street. Anything to keep his distance.

A bus route had to run down here somewhere. A city bus would take him to the terminal on Hawthorne Avenue where he could get an intercity bus to Portland. His feet were beginning to hurt. His sneakers were not built for a hike this long. He found Brookswood Boulevard going north, a name he recognized. Sooner or later, a bus stop would appear.

He counted himself lucky he didn't have to walk any further. Where Brookswood crossed Poplar Street there was a bus stop. He climbed aboard a bus that came twenty minutes later. The bus rode the high ridge above the shopping center in the Old Mill District and followed Bond Street right through downtown. Little had changed from his childhood in spite of Bend's rapid growth. He got to Hawthorne Station at half past noon. The next bus to Portland wouldn't leave until the next morning. He stood stock still in the lobby of the bus station, his shoulders sagging. He couldn't wait that long.

Chapter 9

A Friend in Need

Driving to Dara's house would take Leon fifteen minutes. First to the main entrance to Sunriver, then through meandering roads and two traffic circles to reach River Road at the north end of the airport. The Pennsteads lived at the far south end. But, as the crow flies, the house was only four hundred yards away from the Three Rivers Grill. Leon would get there quicker if he walked. He drove a short distance to the parking area where kayakers unloaded their boats from the Deschutes River. He parked and walked into Sunriver through a narrow pedestrian gate and strode down a bike path toward Dara's house. The swiftly flowing river on his left and the meadow on the right looked to be the way God created them. But the land had been through farms and ranches in the early 1900s, an army training camp in World War II, and the resort with its two golf courses built in the '60s. The meadow Leon was walking past, looking fresh as a clearing in Eden, had seen a lot of history.

A couple in a canoe drifted downstream with the current. They worried a raft of ducks that paddled furiously until wheeling up into the air to find water they liked better.

Dara's call to Leon confirmed Leon's impression that she hadn't made friends in Sunriver. His other students, all women, were polite to her while quietly keeping their distance. She was younger than the rest of them and was pegged, apparently, as a scarlet woman who had seduced her older husband Geoff Pennstead away from his first wife. An unhappy man, missing his youth and regretting lost opportunities, could easily seize on Dara as a last hope of love and romance. She'd sung with rock bands when she was younger but the one time Elizabeth and Leon saw her perform in Bend, she was singing torch songs and tunes from the thirties and forties—"I Get Along Without You Very Well," "You Don't Know What Love Is," and "Cry Me a River." She sang more upbeat songs too—"I've Never Been in Love Before," "Give Me the Simple Life," "It Might As Well Be Spring," and "Teach Me Tonight."

Dara could "sell a song" as the expression went. Her voice carried deep emotion, real or simulated. Her listeners hung on her words, the passions of their youth sleepily awakened from their slumber. Bend was saturated with music. It had an eight-thousand-person amphitheater, a converted movie theater, and dozens of pubs and bars where local and visiting bands performed. Dara had once had her place in that fertile community.

Leon had never met Geoff Pennstead but it was easy to guess why he married Dara. She told Leon in art class that Geoff was seventy-something to her fifty. He had children from his first wife but they never visited and hardly had any contact with their father, much less with Dara.

Dara had lost her first husband to drugs, she told Leon. Her singing did not pay the rent and she didn't have the experience to get a good, sit-down, well-paying job with benefits. Geoff meant security, an easy life, and whatever luxuries he chose to share with her. She did wear old clothes in painting class like everyone else. Paint spills and drips. But she wore expensive-looking jewelry.

Leon expected more of Dara than his other students because he could see how very much she wanted to learn. She dwelled on every word he said. But she hadn't tried to build a relationship outside of painting. Leon was a happily married man with a full life. And the last thing Dara needed was another older man.

He crossed a hundred yards of dusty ground between the bike trail and the road that ran past the houses. A Sunriver Police patrol car sat in the Pennstead driveway with a female officer in the driver's seat, windows open. She could see Leon coming, a seventy-two-year-old man in a golf shirt, looking calm and empty-handed. Not a threat. Nonetheless she got out of her car and stopped him with her gaze. The name tag on her shirt said "Maples."

"Are you going to this house?" she asked.

"Yes," he said. "Mrs. Pennstead asked me to come see her. My name is Leon Martinez. I live in Upriver Ranch."

"May I see your identification?" Leon reached for his hip pocket, noting a flicker of wariness in the deputy's eyes. Her hand had been resting on her gun since she first got out of her car. He slowed his movements as he pulled out his wallet. He knew he didn't look suspicious but the deputy wouldn't want to take chances.

Officer Maples eyed Leon's driver's license and glanced up at him. She handed back the license and picked a cell phone out of her shirt pocket.

"I'm going to call Mrs. Pennstead. Hold on a minute."

Before she could punch in the number, Dara opened the front door and called out. "Hello, Leon, please come in."

The officer held Leon with a question. "Did you see anyone on your way here?"

"Two canoers on the river," Leon said respectfully, though he thought his answer was absurdly non-threatening. "A couple. Didn't look suspicious to me."

Dara held her door open for Leon and shut it as soon as he stepped into her front hall. Leon was afraid she would embrace him but she didn't.

"Would you like something?" she asked. "Coffee, tea, a drink?"

"A glass of tap water would be good," Leon said, largely to reassure her the niceties were still being observed, that the world was still on an even keel. She led Leon to the kitchen, took a tumbler out of a cupboard, and pushed it gently into a recessed spigot in the refrigerator. She held it while she got a green paper napkin out of a drawer with one hand. They sat in the living room on straight-back chairs with wooden arms and cushioned seats, facing each other across a glass-topped coffee table.

"I really need to talk with somebody rational," Dara started. "I don't know what to think, what I should be asking, what I'm supposed to do. Everything. The Sheriff was here. Very nice man but he kept asking me questions. When had I last seen Geoff? Where had he been? Who were his friends and who had seen him recently? How had we been getting along? I'm sure he thinks I might have helped get Geoff killed. Which I didn't."

"I'm sure you didn't," said Leon. He wasn't sure at all but he would say comforting things and try to calm her down. "You should get a lawyer to protect you, in any case." The law was unknown territory for Leon but his son Dan was a lawyer and had told terrifying stories about the trouble people could have easily escaped if they had asked an attorney.

"I don't know much about Geoff's business," said Dara. "Sometimes we'd jet off to Italy and stay in a villa. Other times we had to eat tuna fish for weeks and couldn't go out to dinner. We were in tuna fish times right now. I don't know where I'm going to get the money to pay bills. Geoff gave me money every month but I can't sign on his account."

"Did he have a will?"

"We both do. He says he left half his estate to me but I'm not sure. I couldn't read all the fine print."

"You need a lawyer for that, too," Leon said.

"I don't know how I'm going to pay for all these lawyers."

"Geoff's estate will pay for a lot of it, even before the will is settled. That's the way I understand it. You're not the first person whose spouse died suddenly. A lawyer can find ways to handle these things. Try to relax. It will all get worked out."

"I know I should be grieving for Geoff instead of worrying about myself. Don't tell anybody."

"I won't." Leon did wonder why Dara wasn't sadder but he was grateful that she wasn't. Rationality might be her hidden strength. And she was self-centered. Not vicious but inclined, he thought, to see events in terms of how they affected her. She didn't seem to feel sorry for Geoff or even angry at whoever killed him. Still, she needed someone to talk to. She needed a friend. She needed Leon.

"And I have to arrange a funeral," Dara went on. "I mean, I always knew Geoff would die before I did. But not like this. Not so sudden and not so violent. And the detective is worried somebody may try to kill me too. As if. Why would anyone want to do that? I never hurt anyone."

"The detective is being cautious. If some nut comes after you, he doesn't want people to say the Sheriff didn't do enough."

"At least he agreed to call Geoff's children," said Dara. "They'd hang up on me as soon as they knew I was calling. I'm sure they'll tell Detective Breuninger everything negative about me they can think of. Then he'll be back here asking questions."

"He's not after you, Dara. He's after the truth. In the long run, he's on your side." Leon didn't think Dara could fake the distress he saw in her face.

"I asked the detective, whatever his name is," she started.

"Carl Breuninger?"

"Yes, Breuninger. I asked him not to tell the media about Geoff. But Breuninger says he has to do that as soon as he tells Geoff's son and daughter. Then everybody will want to talk to me. I can see it coming. A TV truck will be parked outside the house and reporters knocking on the door."

"Can you stay at a friend's house or at a hotel?"

Dara perched on the edge of her chair, weighing Leon's suggestion. Leon sipped his glass of water but she hadn't touched her own.

"I don't have any friends I can ask. And I don't want to be cooped up in a hotel room. This is my house. I have food enough to last a week or so. I'm going to hunker down and draw the blinds. At least not too many people know my cell phone number. Would it be okay if I called you? I trust you."

Leon didn't look forward to being on call but he said yes. At least Dara didn't ask to stay at his house. Harboring an unhappy woman twenty-four hours a day would have sapped whatever generosity Leon had left. Elizabeth would throw up her hands at the very idea.

"Call me whenever," said Leon. "And I'll get my son Dan to recommend the lawyers you need. Dan does commercial law in Bend and he knows attorneys that do criminal law and estate law and anything else."

Leon had learned, as a teacher, that he could only give so much to any one student at any one time. He had to set limits. Leon had just about reached that point with Dara.

"Have you got someone you can call to talk? A family member?" he asked.

"My family is a trainwreck. I haven't talked with any of them in years. My sister would want to tell me her own troubles and then she'd ask me for money. Maybe one of the musicians I used to sing with. But it's been a while. I pretty much left them behind when I married Geoff."

Dara embraced Leon in the front hall. She needed human contact and Leon held her a moment before he backed off. Leon was not her brother or even a close friend. And he certainly wasn't a replacement for her husband.

He passed two swans in the river as he walked the trail back to his car. Leon thought the swans must have wandered from the pond where they lived on the other end of Sunriver. He hoped they hadn't abandoned their pond for good. People liked seeing them there.

Chapter 10

Wedge Shots

Carl's next stop was McDivot's Café at the Woodlands golf course. The ladies who played in the tournament that day would be having lunch. He wanted them sitting down, paying attention to him, and sparking off each other in recalling what they had seen on the way to the golf course. Deputy Shane O'Connell was waiting for him in the shade of a porch outside the café. Carl had assigned O'Connell to interview employees of the combination gas station and market on Cottonwood. Also the golf course employees, and the golfers who teed off before the ladies' tournament.

"I got a list of ten gas sales from when they opened at seven up until eight o'clock. The list shows what type of gas, how many gallons, the cost, and the last four digits of the credit card if they used one. The station attendant remembered four of the people and their vehicles. I'll include them in my report. The store had seventeen transactions. The clerks could name the locals who came in every day but they were vague about the others. We'll get copies of the surveillance videos when the owner comes in later."

"Good. How about the golf course workers?"

"The greenskeepers, the guys who mow the course and rake the sand traps, started work at 5:30 a.m. when the sun rose. They were out on the course when I got there and I didn't talk to each of them face-to-face. I asked their boss to ask them if they saw anything and he said he would. But he said it was still dark when they were driving in and they would not have seen much.

"The two people in the golf shop got there at 6:30 and didn't see anything. The starters and marshals are volunteers and they were here before 7:00. None of them saw anything unusual but I wrote down names and numbers if we want to interview them again."

"And the golfers?"

"I talked to them as they came off the eighteenth green—all the golfers who started between 7:00 and 8:00, before the ladies tournament started at 8:00. Names and numbers and I took photos of them as they approached the green. A few smart alecks gave me a wide berth and I caught up to them where they had to turn in the carts. We can find these people if we want to. Some of them didn't take much time to try and remember anything but I asked them all to call the sheriff's office if something came to mind. One man said he came along East Cascade around 7:10 and saw a bicyclist in a yellow and green racing outfit. The witness remembered the guy because bikes are supposed to stay on the bike paths and this man was racing down the middle of the road."

"We'll ask the Sunriver Police to keep an eye out for him."

"That's about it," said O'Connell. "The ladies just got here. They're inside having lunch. The lady running the tournament is Elizabeth Martinez. In her sixties, blonde, and wearing a light lavender blouse. Doesn't look like her name would be Martinez."

"I know her," said Carl. Here was a coincidence. Carl was wary of coincidences. Coincidences could lead to answers. But too often they were only that, coincidences, and they could lead into rabbit warrens going nowhere.

Carl had seen Leon Martinez painting the crime scene earlier and here was Leon's wife, Elizabeth, who had been in the area at about the time of the shooting. What kind of coincidence was that? The Martinezes lived in Upriver Ranch, south of Sunriver, and Elizabeth would have naturally come to the Woodlands on East Cascade. The couple were law-abiding citizens. But trouble had followed them in the past. Carl had come to their house a few years ago, tracking down a nutcase with a gun who was after Leon and Elizabeth's daughter-in-law. The man was about to shoot Leon at the front door when Elizabeth crept up behind Leon and shot the man dead with a pistol. She hadn't gripped the pistol with any strength and the kickback knocked the gun out of her hand. She had to ice her wrist for a week and wrap a bandage around it. She'd always hated guns and didn't want anything to do with them. Using a gun to save her husband's life had not changed her mind. She didn't think anybody but the police should have guns.

Out of the twenty or so women crammed into the little café there was another woman Carl knew, Shanti Sergeant. Shanti had led a yoga retreat to Hosmer Lake in the Cascade Mountains where a woman had been shot dead in her tent. Shanti had a yoga studio in Bend.

Elizabeth came over to Carl, a wrapped sandwich in her hand, as soon as she saw him inside the door. They said hello, calling each other by their first names.

"We heard sirens this morning but nobody knew what was going on. Then we heard a man had been killed. Are you here about that?"

"Yes. I want to ask if anyone saw anything on their way to the course. Could you get the group's attention? It would be better if you did it."

"Right away," said Elizabeth. She clapped her hands and raised her voice. "Ladies. We'll get to the awards in a minute but Detective Breuninger is here from the sheriff's department and he wants to talk to us about the sirens we heard."

Carl stepped forward. "Sorry to interrupt your lunch," said Carl, "but we need to gather information as quickly as possible. We had an incident on East Cascade Road this morning shortly after seven o'clock. A man was shot and killed. His wife has been notified. We have not identified the shooter but we don't believe he is a threat to anyone else. We're hoping some of you may have seen something that could help us. First of all, how many of you came by way of East Cascade before the police blocked the road off?"

Three hands went up. Elizabeth's did not.

"Can any of you remember anything you saw along the way—another car, a person by the road, a bicyclist, anything out of the ordinary?"

"I was half asleep," one woman joked. "I'm sorry I don't remember anything."

"Any cars coming the other way?"

"Not that I can remember," said the woman.

"I saw a squashed squirrel on East Cascade near Cottonwood," said the second woman. "I don't suppose it's important but that's all I can remember."

"What time did you see it?" asked Carl. It probably wasn't relevant but he wanted to encourage the women to tell him everything they could think of.

"Must have been about 7:15 but I don't know."

Carl scribbled a line in his notebook. He looked at the third woman.

The woman spoke in a surprisingly low voice. "I saw a silver Mercedes sedan ahead of me slow down and pull off to the side of the road. I thought he was lost and trying to figure out where he was. I thought he could figure it out without my help so I drove right past him. I was in a hurry to get here."

The woman, Carl noticed, had unusually big hands and shoulders. It dawned on him that she might not have always been a woman. That didn't make any difference, he decided, if she could give him some useful information.

"What did the driver look like?" asked Carl.

"I don't know for sure," came the reply in a voice that would be hard to say was a man's or a woman's. "I think it might have been an older man with white hair. But I can't be sure."

"Anyone else in the car or in the area?"

"Not that I saw. Or not that I remember. I was on the phone, you know. On the speakerphone." The woman, who had begun speaking in a confident tone, was getting uncomfortable being the center of attention.

"Can you be sure I get your name and phone number?" said Carl.

"I may have more questions later." The woman nodded.

"Anything else?"

"A car driving very slow on Beaver Drive," said another woman. "I took Beaver Drive because of the roadblock on East Cascade. I was afraid of being late and this car was holding me up. It was a small SUV, black. I don't know what make it was."

Carl scribbled another line. "License number?"

"I didn't even look."

"Anything else?"

The woman who mentioned the dead squirrel piped up. "Who was it? I mean the man who was killed."

"We're not ready to release that information. We're still notifying family members. Thank you, all of you. This has been very helpful. I'll leave some of my cards here. If you remember anything more from this morning, please call the Sheriff's Department and ask for me, Carl Breuninger. Leave me a voicemail with your name and number if I'm not there."

Carl looked around the room. The women were turning to their lunches and their conversations. The woman with the deep voice took a business card out of a little golf purse and handed it to a woman at the next table who passed it on to two other women before it got to Carl. The woman's name was Bobbie Searle and she was a real estate agent in Sunriver.

He walked out the door and stood in the shade of the overhanging roof, looking at his notes and glancing up at two people on the practice green.

The door behind him opened and Shanti Sergeant, the yoga instructor, caught his eye.

"One thing," she said. "I live in Bend so I came in on Cottonwood, not East Cascade. A car coming the other way had a man in it who was scowling at me."

"Description?"

"White guy with brown hair, maybe in his thirties, hefty, even overweight. He had a brownish red beard, medium length, a little raggedy."

"And the car?"

"A white SUV. I don't pay much attention to cars so I can't give you a better description. I didn't get the license plate. I guess it was standard Oregon—three letters and three numbers with a green tree in the middle. If it had been out-of-state, I might have noticed."

"You say he was scowling. Did he look angry?"

"Yes, and staring right at me."

"This will help," Carl said. "And, for what it's worth, I don't think his anger was directed at you. He couldn't even see you. If he was driving east on Cottonwood, the sun would have been in his eyes and you would have been in shadow. He probably had something else on his mind. Anything else you can remember?"

Shanti shook her head. "Afraid not. I was a little upset myself after I saw him. I had to put him out of my mind so I could play golf. I'll let you know if I think of anything more."

Carl thanked her and encouraged her to call. But he would be cautious if she did call. Witnesses who stretched to remember details had a bent toward making things up without even knowing it.

Chapter 11

Other Women

Elizabeth wasn't home when Leon got there. He called his son Dan as he had told Dara he would.

"Before I get lawyers to call Mrs. Pennstead, Dad, what do you know about her ability to pay them?"

"She lives in a nice big house and her husband owned a plane. He had investments and she says sometimes they have money to burn but right now they're pinching pennies. I don't know how much ready cash she has to pay lawyers."

"Well," said Dan, "if she has assets, lawyers can usually get paid before creditors. I can line up some attorneys I know to start down the road on this. Probably not our firm and maybe not top drawer. But capable. And it sounds like Mrs. Pennstead's problems are not going to require the fine points of the law. I'll tell the attorneys what you've told me and then I'll call Mrs. Pennstead."

Leon retreated to his studio and put the watercolor he'd started that morning on his easel. He filled in the sky and the ground between the trees using the colors he'd mixed earlier. The ground had to look different where it was in shadow and where it was in sunshine. Leon transferred the photo he'd taken when he first arrived at the scene from his cell phone to his tablet. He used the photo to place the shadows on the trees and bushes.

Leon decided the painting was finished and he left it on his easel to dry. He was washing his brushes in the studio sink when he heard the garage door go up. He went through the house to find Elizabeth bringing a grocery bag in from her car.

"You want me to help?" he asked.

"No need. There's only this one bag of groceries. I left my golf clubs in the car. They cleaned them at the course and I'm playing again tomorrow."

When Elizabeth put the paper bag on the counter, Leon pulled groceries out of it and spread them out along the countertop. It was better if Elizabeth put them away. Otherwise she'd ask him where he put some jar or can or vegetable and he wouldn't remember.

"Did you hear about the man who was shot and killed today?" he asked.

"Oh, yes. Carl Breuninger came to the lunch after the tournament and asked us if they'd seen anything on their way to the course. Nobody really had. It sounded like he didn't have much to go on. Wouldn't even tell us who was shot."

"It was a man named Geoff Pennstead. His wife was in some of the classes I taught at the resort. You remember we went to hear her sing one time in Bend? Dara Pennstead?"

Elizabeth held a carton of milk in one hand and the refrigerator door handle in the other. Her arm froze for a second before she put the carton on the shelf.

"How did you learn her name?"

"She called me. Carl Breuninger had been to see her."

"And what did this woman want from you?"

"Just to talk. She doesn't have many friends in Sunriver and she isn't close with her family."

"How long did you talk?" Elizabeth was staring at the fresh corn still on the counter, not looking at Leon.

"I went to her house. We talked for about half an hour. I told her she needed legal advice and I put her in touch with Dan."

Elizabeth turned around sharply and raised a reprimanding finger. "You better stay away from that woman!" Elizabeth took a breath. "She's probably desperate and she likes to manipulate men.

She's a snake."

"I don't think she's a snake," said Leon, very surprised his wife had any idea about Dara Pennstead at all. "She's a woman who lost her husband. She needs help."

"Then let her get it from someplace else. Did you promise her anything? You're not going to see her again, are you?"

"I said Dan would find her the lawyers she needed and he's already said he would do that. She may call me again but I didn't promise her anything."

"If she calls you hang up."

"I can't simply hang up. But if you feel that strongly about it, I'll keep the conversation short and I don't need to go to her house again."

"You damn well better not." Elizabeth rarely swore, rarely got this emotional. Did Elizabeth imagine Dara would draw more comfort out of Leon than any single woman had a right to expect of a married man? Elizabeth was not the jealous type. But she protected her marriage. A few times over the years when a woman showed a heightened interest in Leon, or his art, she never seemed to get invited to dinner, cocktails, or golf.

Elizabeth had been unfaithful to Leon only once. Special circumstances. Long ago. More painful for Elizabeth than for Leon and best forgotten. Pretty much forgotten in fact and no risk of recurring.

Leon had been five days with another woman. Also special circumstances. Elizabeth knew about it and had reluctantly agreed to it, with conditions. It was long, long ago when they were much younger. Leon's tryst was very much on his mind right now because the woman and her husband were coming to visit Leon and Elizabeth this summer for the first time. The husband and wife, Gabriel and Maria Isabel Torres, had grown up with Leon in the Claremont suburb of Los Angeles. Elizabeth had met them when she and Leon had visited San Francisco. The couples were friends of a sort, exchanging Christmas cards and occasional emails.

Maria's father had been the manager of an orange grove. Gabriel's family and Leon's had been friends back in Valencia and had fled

Spain together when Franco came to power at the end of the Spanish Civil War. Right out of high school, Gabriel and Maria had married and moved to San Francisco. Gabriel once played guitar with Carlos Santana but his first love was flamenco music.

When Leon and Elizabeth were newly married, Gabriel called Leon with an unusual request.

"Maria and I have thought about this long and hard," said Gabriel, "and you will need to think about it too, though I hope your answer will be yes."

Leon wanted to help his friend and he promised he would consider what his friend asked, whatever it was.

"I was wounded in Vietnam," said Gabriel, "I think you know how. I can walk, talk, and play the guitar. I can still play soccer and basketball. But I'm missing some essential male equipment. Or it is so mangled up, it is of no use. I have to sit down to go to the bathroom. Maria Isabel admits she misses that piece of equipment but, God bless her, she says we are man and wife forever. It's a tragedy but that's life, you know. I could be dead, or blind, or crazy. That's fate. *El destino*. We live with it.

"But the thing is, we want to have a child. And we don't want some random guy to be the father, whether he's a Nobel Laureate or not. We've talked about it and we'd like you to be the father. No obligations on your part beyond insemination. No doctor bills. No child support. No paying for education. Nothing. And we want the child to be ours so it means you may never meet him or her. At least not until the child is older and wants to meet you.

"And we want to do this the old-fashioned way. No artificial insemination. You come. You screw the ever-loving hell out of Maria for a week, and you go back to your wife. You like Maria, don't you? You find her attractive?"

"Yes, of course," said Leon in spite of warnings from all parts of his brain that this was a bad idea. "Maria wants to do this?"

"Yes. She's desperate to have a child and we've both known you most of our lives. She wants the child's father to be you. I have a friend who is going out of town. You can stay at his place and Maria can visit you there. Maria would prefer it that way and I think you would too. I certainly would."

"So you've been thinking of this for some time?"

"Yes. We're sure this is what we want to do, if you agree."

Leon thought about it for three days. Maria was a good friend. She liked to laugh over tapas and wine. And when she danced flamenco, she expressed a full range of emotions, from scornful to plaintive, from delicate to fiery. One moment she might want you as a drowning woman wants air. The next second she might be disgusted with you, or simply bored. It was intimidating and appealing to think of being in bed with her. Dark eyes, dark hair. She was beautiful.

Leon's calmer thoughts turned on the balance between his love and commitment to Elizabeth, the good he could do for Gabriel and Maria Isabel, and the excitement he felt for himself. He knew Elizabeth must give her consent.

"I'm not so concerned you're going to fall in love with Maria," Elizabeth said. "I am concerned you are going to get attached to this child."

"My life is here in Oregon with you and with our own family when we have children of our own. Gabriel and Maria don't plan to tell the child that Gabriel is not its father. And I promise to support them in that. And they promise I will not have any financial responsibility at all. I have no other loyalties."

"We need to get all that in writing," said Elizabeth. Practical Elizabeth. "And you need to promise me, from the bottom of your heart, that our marriage will be intact and you will be loyal to me and as considerate of me as you ever were when you get back."

"I promise."

Leon had summers off from teaching and he had the time to visit San Francisco. Elizabeth herself was advancing her career at the bank. She had only two weeks of vacation a year.

Leon visited art galleries in San Francisco, the De Young Museum, and the museum at the Palace of the Legion of Honor. Not with Maria. Maria came to visit the friend's house the first morning Leon was there, an hour later than the time she said she'd be there.

Leon worried that she'd changed her mind, worried that he ought to change his. They met as friends, as though they had nothing out of the ordinary in mind. They admired the friend's house together. It was a small house on the south edge of the city and had a view that spread from the Golden Gate Bridge on the left to the Bay Bridge on the right, with a sharply pointed pyramid building rising out of the business district.

Leon and Maria had never dated, never kissed. It might be impossible, Leon worried, to shift from being friends, even temporarily, to becoming lovers. Wouldn't it be better to go out for coffee after all, rather than alter their relationship?

"We should take our clothes off," said Maria. "That will put things on a different footing." They moved separately, without touching, without looking toward each other, and hung their clothes on hangers in the closet. Taking clothes off was not difficult, not alarming. They each did it every day.

"Embrace me," said Maria. She'd thought this through. They stood holding each other in front of the window, something they wouldn't do again for fear of being seen. But it was a powerful moment, standing naked with the city spread below them. They stood that way for a full minute, unmoving as desire built within them. Finally Maria let out a sigh and leaned her head against Leon's shoulder as if she were about to cry. He knew she could feel his "equipment," as Gabriel called it, pressing against her. He ran his hand from her shoulder to the small of her back. She raised her head.

"God, yes," she said. She slid her knee up alongside his leg. He bent down to kiss her lips, then her neck, then her shoulder. Fire shot through them both. This was really going to happen. So much excitement now, so much pleasure to come.

Was he betraying Elizabeth after all? It would not be so much the physical act of making love with Maria, of lying with her, of penetrating her. His desire was his betrayal. How could he let himself desire any woman as much as he desired Elizabeth? Had Elizabeth realized this would happen when she granted permission? Was he doing something wrong—wrong in a way he had not anticipated?

But the idea that it might be wrong, that he shouldn't be doing this, only excited him further.

Backwards logic, he thought later. *If I shouldn't be doing this, and I'm still doing it, it must really be worth doing.*

He licked Maria's breasts as her breaths grew stronger and more rapid. She gripped his member and pulled him toward the bed. She didn't let go when she lay back on the bed and separated her legs.

"Ouch," said Leon.

Maria released her grip on him but kept her eye on his genitals as though they might disappear if she didn't watch carefully. He kneeled between her thighs and lowered himself.

That night they went out to dinner with Gabriel. They had thought it would go well—three old friends together. No secrets. Everything planned and agreed to. But they had miscalculated. It was a sad and awkward meal. Maria loved Gabriel. She wasn't going to leave him. Would not even imagine it. But Gabriel could see she and Leon were besotted with desire. Yearned for each other. Could hardly wait to get back into bed.

Leon felt he had injured his friend, shown him up, and stolen a portion of the affection that Gabriel depended on. Gabriel and Leon didn't see each other for the rest of the visit.

Forty weeks later, Leon and Elizabeth received a birth announcement. Dolores Segovia Torres, seven pounds, six ounces. They received Christmas cards with photos of the Torres family until Elizabeth asked them to stop sending them. When Dolores turned fifteen, her parents told her who her biological father was. She said Gabriel and Maria were her parents and she had no need to meet Leon.

"She's just not interested," Gabriel told Leon over the phone. "Sorry. And we're not trying to talk her into it. She is firm in her convictions."

"Like her mother," said Leon. "I understand."

It was years before Leon visited Gabriel and Maria again in San Francisco. Delores was married and living in Madrid by then. Dan was in college. No one mentioned Leon spending time alone with

Maria on this trip. Had she taken other lovers? Had Gabriel known and approved? Leon did not know and did not ask.

This year, for the first time, Gabriel and Maria were coming to see Oregon, staying with Leon and Elizabeth. Gabriel wanted to see a concert at the amphitheater in Bend. A wildly creative young Spanish woman, Rosalia, had added rap and hip hop to traditional flamenco music. She was immensely popular in Spain and had won two Grammys. Leon loved flamenco and would enjoy the concert too. They all hoped Elizabeth would as well. She might not love the music but she always loved the amphitheater, sitting under a blue sky turning to sunset, a crowd of happy people, young and old, and views of the snow-capped mountains in the distance. Beyond the stage stood three giant silver chimneys preserved from a long-gone lumber mill, flags at the top flapping in the breeze. The mill closed when Elizabeth was five years old but the chimneys had been there all her life.

Leon had been scrupulously loyal to Elizabeth ever since his week with Maria. He avoided even the appearance of disloyalty. So he would not visit Dara again if Elizabeth cared that much about it. Most of what he could do for Dara he had already done. He'd been a steadying presence immediately after her husband's death. He'd pointed her toward the lawyers she needed. She would have to find someone else for emotional support. He was done with Dara Pennstead.

Chapter 12

Canvassing

Falling Star Road was a dead-end road that ran parallel to East Cascade. The road ended in a loop with an acre of open lodgepole forest in the middle and six houses around the outside of the loop. Deputy Wallhagen and Officer Maples had canvassed the neighborhood in the morning and Carl's last stop in the afternoon was to knock on the doors of the houses where no one had answered earlier.

The morning canvass had turned up nothing of particular interest. Only one girl had heard a shot. No one had been looking toward East Cascade and no one had noticed anything until the flashing lights from the police cars flickered through their windows. Occupants of three even-numbered houses on the east side of the loop, the side away from East Cascade, didn't know anything had happened at all until the deputies knocked on their door. The family at number 74 had been loading up their car at the time of the shooting, about 7:20 a.m., so they were outside much of that time, going back and forth between the house and the car. They hadn't heard or seen anything. Officer Maples noted that they could not see East Cascade from either the house or the driveway.

If a house was rented out, the owner had to report to the police the name of the rental agent and the rental agent could give the police the name of the current renter if there was one. The five houses on the west side of the loop were numbered with odd numbers 67 thru 75. Wallhagen and Maples had found 67 and 71 occupied.

At number 67, a rental, a teenage boy answered the door, the deputies' report said, after a long delay. The boy said his father was out playing golf. The boy didn't know where. The kid guessed his father left about 7:00 am. The boy himself had been playing *Tomb Raider* with speakers on loud. He hadn't seen or heard anything, including Deputy Wallhagen ringing the doorbell. Wallhagen's notes said he heard the video game going and pounded on the door until the boy showed up. The boy was Tommy Westlake and his father's name was Lester Westlake. They were renting the house and there was no one else staying with them.

The family at number 71 was having breakfast when the deputies arrived. They were the owners and it was their vacation house. They rented the house out for part of the summer but they were in it themselves for a week right now. They'd woken up at 7:00 am but they hadn't heard or seen anything. Deputy Wallhagen interviewed each of the parents separately while Officer Maples interviewed the three children one at a time. The mother was the only one who remembered anything unusual. The day before, a white SUV had made a slow circle of the loop and driven out again without stopping at any of the houses. She hadn't seen the driver, couldn't identify the make or model of the car, and didn't even look at the license plate. It didn't raise her suspicions enough to call the police but now she remembered it.

The three houses where there was no one home were not on rental programs. The deputies had called the owner of each house and reached the owner of number 75. He said no one was staying at the house now. Or at least no one should be staying there. Adam and Katy found all the doors and windows locked and no sign of occupancy. The owners of numbers 69 and 73 had not answered their phones or responded to text messages.

Carl parked where he could watch all five houses on the west side of the loop. At number 67 where the boy Tommy Westlake had been alone playing video games, there was now a silvery gray sedan parked in the driveway. At 71, the family car reported in the morning was still there. Nothing had changed at the three houses where no one answered this morning—no cars in the driveways, no sign of activity at the houses.

Kristen, the medical examiner, called Carl as he sat there.

"I can tell you a little more about your victim and the shooting," she said. "We'll know more once we get the drug screen and the autopsy report in a week or two. I found no needle marks or other signs of drug use. No observable signs of illness or injury prior to the shooting. Not over or under weight. Reasonable muscle tone for a man of his age. Tan lines are consistent with golf. No signs of smoking or drinking to excess. He could still have cancer or heart problems but from what I can tell right now, he was in good health.

"As for the shooting, he was shot twice in very quick succession. Shots probably less than a second apart, both from a shotgun. My report will say it could have been two different shotguns but common sense tells me it was one. I leave it up to you. Anyhow the first shot was birdshot and the second was buckshot. Probably twelve gauge judging from the density of pellets. Fired five to seven feet from the victim at a slightly upward angle. If the victim was standing up, and the blood pattern on the road indicates he was, then the shooter probably fired from the hip. At that range, he didn't have to sight along the barrel to aim. It would be hard to miss."

"You said earlier the victim might have been holding something in his hand."

"His right hand. He had pellets along the backs of his fingers and no pellets in the palm. It's just an idea. If you're instinctively trying to fend off getting shot, you'd tend to hold out both palms. If you think you're going to punch your attacker or if you have a gun yourself, your fist is closed and the backs of your fingers are facing the shooter."

"He could have been holding a gun?"

"Could have been. Could have been a tennis racquet or a hundred other things. Something hard, though, that didn't get squashed or leave a residue. Not a banana."

"Not a snack before dying?"

"No."

"If it was a gun, had he fired it?"

"No, no powder residue."

"Anything else?"

"His corpse was run over after he died. I think you already knew that. That's all I can help you with right now. I'll get you the autopsy and tox screen reports as soon as I get them."

"His wife is going to want the body back. What can I tell her?"

"I'd say two weeks but she should get the funeral home to call Clackamas and keep on top of them. It's better they call than she does. Clackamas is a government office. Sympathy is not their strong suit."

Carl hung up with Kristin and called the crime lab about Geoff Pennstead's car.

"You'll like this, Carl," said Bob Fielding, the tech who'd gone over the car. "Somebody installed a radio activated valve on the fuel line. It's a remote controlled little motor that closes a valve and shuts off the gas going to the carburetor. Kills the engine in a couple of seconds. It's home built but it does the job. Looks like somebody wanted to stop the victim and wanted to control where he did it."

"That certainly knocks out the road rage theory," said Carl. This wasn't spontaneous. But when this case finally got to trial, premeditation would be easy to prove. No bargaining of murder down to manslaughter. "Any fingerprints on it?"

"No. Wiped clean. But the guy who installed it might have touched something else. We're going to fingerprint the whole car."

"Ugh," said Carl. "Finding all the people who touched that car and eliminating them as suspects is a monumental task. Let's hope we find the killer some other way and then check the fingerprints. Any sign of blood or gunpowder or shotgun pellets near the car?"

"None. He couldn't have been near his car when he got blasted."

"Anything else?"

"The brakes are worn. The tires are worn. And the oil needs to be changed. The right rear window won't go down. The guy has not been keeping his car up."

"Thanks, Bob."

"Not so fast," said Bob. "I still haven't gotten to the biggest thing. I found traces of cocaine on the floor in the back seat."

"Jesus," said Carl. "The guy was seventy-seven. Cocaine could give him a heart attack."

"Maybe it wasn't Pennstead using it."

"Maybe not," said Carl. "Kristen said he showed no obvious signs of drug use. Maybe it was his wife using it. Or maybe he was dealing it. He's in financial trouble. Selling drugs might be his quick route to cash."

"Glad I could help," said Bob. "I'll write this up but you've basically got all I have."

Carl didn't know what to make of the cocaine angle but it did give him an opening. The possibility of Pennstead dealing cocaine should be enough to get a search warrant for his house. Carl wouldn't have to wait for Dara Pennstead to give him permission. He used the terminal in his car to fill out a search warrant and send it off to the Deschutes County judge's panel with a copy to Jocelyn Nelson, the assistant district attorney he hoped would be assigned to the case.

A pickup truck with a trailer passed by Carl and the driver skillfully backed the trailer, with an open aluminum boat on it, into the garage of number 73. Carl drove up to the house and parked in front of it. He didn't block the driveway or turn on his flashers. That would look hostile. The man who had been driving the truck was unhooking the trailer. He was alone. He stood up, empty-handed, and forced a smile.

"Hello," the man said.

"Hello," said Carl. "Carl Breuninger, Deschutes County Sheriff's Department. Have you heard about an incident on East Cascade this morning?"

"Not a thing," the man said. "I've been gone all day. Been up to Crane Prairie fishing. What happened?"

"Man was shot. What time did you leave here this morning?"

"Oh, 6:30, quarter to 7:00. You know the best fishing spots in the channels can only take one boat at a time. I got there early." The man, medium height and about forty, did look a little worn out, exactly like a man who had spent all day sitting in a boat in the sun.

"Any luck?"

"Yeah. I caught two twenty-three inchers that I had to put back. They were natives. But I got a nineteen-inch hatchery fish in the cooler. Gonna make a nice dinner."

"You the owner of the house?"

"Yeah. Ben Crabtree. How do you do?"

"How do you do? Anybody staying with you?"

"No, nobody," said the man.

"Have you seen anything unusual in the area in the last few days?"

Ben looked around as if he might notice something unusual now or it might help some memory come to him.

"Can't say as I have," said Ben. "Who was shot?"

"We're not releasing the name yet," said Carl.

"Resident or visitor?" asked Ben.

Carl thought any resident, like Ben, would be interested in knowing the answer. Also anyone who had a stake in who the actual victim might be.

"Resident," said Carl. Did Carl detect a slight relaxation of Ben's shoulders when he heard this?

"That's awful," said Ben. "From this neighborhood?"

"No," said Carl. He didn't like answering questions. He wanted to ask them.

"How about the owners of the other houses?" asked Carl. "Anything suspicious or even unusual in the last few months?"

"I try to mind my own business," said Crabtree. "We say hello and I know some of their names but we're not what you'd call friends. On the other hand, renters come and go. I mostly try to ignore them. If they're still partying hard after ten o'clock, I call the police. The response time is good and the renters shut down pretty quick once the police get here. Haven't had any trouble lately. Do you have any more questions? I kinda need to go inside and take a leak."

"Can I see your driver's license quickly? It's standard procedure so nobody asks me later whether I'm sure who I talked with." The man pulled his wallet out of his back pocket and fished out his Oregon driver's license for Carl. It said Benjamin Crabtree and Carl wrote down his name, birthdate, and license number. Carl asked for a phone number and Crabtree gave it to him.

"Thanks," said Carl, handing back the license. "Call the Sheriff's Department if you're missing anything from your house or you think of anything that might help us."

"Will do," said Ben. "Bye for now." He walked through the garage back into the house and Carl walked back to his car.

Carl's next stop was at number 67 to interview the father of the video game boy. The man, Lester Westlake, answered the door and invited Carl in. They sat at the heavy wood dining room table. Video game sounds came from somewhere else in the house.

"You want a beer?" asked Westlake.

"No thanks. On duty."

"How about iced tea? It's in a bottle."

"Sure. Thanks."

Westlake went to the kitchen and returned with two bottles, lemon-flavored iced tea for Carl and a Mirror Pond Ale for himself. He put them on the table without coasters. The bottles would leave rings on the table but they wouldn't be the first. Carl mentioned "the incident" and asked if Lester knew anything about it.

"I was gone by then. I played Pronghorn today with some buddies, the Nicklaus course in the morning and the Fazio course in the afternoon. It was a hell of a day." He was clearly pleased with himself.

"Was your wife or someone else here in the morning?"

"Just Tommy. My wife and I are divorced. It's my turn to get Tommy and we came here for some time together. Unfortunately," and here Lester rolled his eyes, "all he wants to do is play video games."

And all you want to do is play golf, thought Carl. But he didn't say it.

"Have you seen anything out of the ordinary around here?

"Got here day before yesterday. Never rented this house before. I don't know what's usual and what isn't."

"Anybody acting strangely?"

"The family two doors down left their golf clubs out in the driveway all night. I guess they forgot them. I wouldn't do that. Anyhow, the clubs were still there in the morning."

"Okay," said Carl, scribbling in his notebook. "I'd like to talk to Tommy before I go."

"Tommy!" Westlake shouted toward a hallway door. The video game sounds did not stop. Westlake got up and went down the hall. The sounds stopped and Westlake reappeared with Tommy in front of him.

"I need to talk to Tommy alone," said Carl.

"I've got to go take a shower anyhow," said Westlake. "Do you mind showing yourself out?"

"That'll be fine," said Carl. He turned his attention to the boy. Tommy slumped in his stance and looked at Carl, resigned. The kid was not happy.

"Why don't you have a seat?" said Carl.

"That's okay," said Tommy, not moving.

"This may take a while," said Carl, "and I want to look at you eye-to-eye."

Tommy clearly didn't want to be questioned, didn't even want to be in the room. But he was not defiant. He plunked himself down sloppily in the chair opposite Carl and leaned against the back rest.

"How's the game going?" Carl asked in a serious tone, as though this were important information, not a grown-up's attempt to establish a relationship with a difficult boy. "What role are you in now?" Carl had very little idea what he was talking about but he'd heard his sister's boys discussing roles.

"Hunter," mumbled Tommy. A reluctant answer but at least an answer. Carl had lucked out with his question.

"I know you talked with Officer Maples this morning," said Carl, "but I want to see if you can tell me anything more."

"I don't think so," said Tommy.

"So a little after seven this morning were you sleeping, or getting breakfast, or playing games or something else?" asked Carl.

"I don't know," said Tommy. "I don't remember." Carl sensed Tommy tensing, trying to sit sloppily in his chair and appear bored. The boy didn't want to tell him something. "You know a man was shot and killed on the road behind your house?"

"Yeah, I know." The obvious next question for Carl was "How do you know?" but he didn't ask it. He wanted Tommy to relax, even to feel he could tell Carl anything and not get in trouble.

"Well, we all take that very seriously. People don't get shot very often and everybody—the police, the television stations, the newspapers, all the people who live in Sunriver, the people who run businesses here—everybody wants to know how it happened. We've collected everything we could find from the area. We've had a dog out looking for clues. Did you see the dog?"

"Yeah," said Tommy, "I saw the dog."

Carl hid his satisfaction in hearing this. So the kid had looked out the window at some point. He'd opened up a crack in his "I saw nothing" story that Carl, if he played it right, might expand into something.

"And what was the dog doing?"

"Sniffing around."

"Did he stop or slow down anywhere?"

"He smelled around a man who was painting a picture on the other side of the road."

"Did he sniff on this side of the road?"

"Yeah, I guess so."

"What kind of dog was it?" asked Carl.

"I don't know."

"What did it look like? What color was it?"

"I don't remember. I didn't look close."

"Did you see any guns when you were watching the dog?"

Tommy considered his answer carefully. He had gotten wary. "The police had guns in their holsters."

Carl decided he wouldn't press Tommy right now. The boy would retreat into his "I don't know" story and the story would solidify. If

Tommy got nervous, his father might cut off Carl's access to the boy or get a lawyer. But Carl thought Tommy knew something he wasn't saying. Carl would let him think he was off the hook, let him stew about it for a while, and come back at him in a day or two.

"Well, thanks for your help, Tommy," said Carl. Tommy eyed Carl's gun as Carl got up from the table. "Here's my card. If you think of anything more, you let me know." Carl walked to the front door. Lester Westlake had not returned from the back of the house. "See ya."

"See ya," said Tommy reflexively. Almost friendly. Adults had rarely taken such an interest in what Tommy knew or what he had to say.

"Good luck with your game."

Late in the afternoon, when Carl got back to headquarters, he looked up Lester Westlake and Ben Crabtree in multiple criminal databases. Westlake was not in any of them. Ben Crabtree, the man with the boat who said he'd been fishing at Crane Prairie, had never been arrested. But he was listed as a contact for his brother, Dylan Crabtree, who had been convicted of passing bad checks. Dylan had gone to prison and was now out on parole. Carl picked up his desk phone and called Dylan's parole officer, Alma Oshiro, in Seattle.

"He better not have been in Oregon," said Alma. "Off parole and back to prison if he leaves the State of Washington. Let's see. He showed up for his appointment last Tuesday and he's due for another a week from this coming Tuesday. We took off the ankle bracelet when he got the job at Les Schwab. They're supposed to tell me if he doesn't show up for work. Let me look at my emails."

Carl waited on the line for a full two minutes.

"He's been off work for an injury. A tire slipped off the rim when he was inflating it. The air pressure flipped the whole wheel up and it hit him in the eye socket. Broke some bones. His vision was okay but they gave him a few days off for it anyway. Nobody checked on him. He could have made a quick trip to Oregon if he felt up to it. It's too bad if he did," Alma went on. "No record of drug use. No DUI's. No domestic violence. He always showed up for his appointments. He was at home whenever I checked."

"So far," said Carl, "I have no proof he was in Oregon. I've got no leverage with the guy so there's no point in talking to him unless he was here and he's stupid enough to admit it."

"He's not stupid. He got away with the check writing for at least a year."

"Let's keep in touch," said Carl. "And call me right away if he misses his next appointment."

Carl would keep his eye out for a connection between Crabtree and Pennstead but it was hard to imagine what it would be. And how could Dylan be sure Pennstead would take a route so close to Ben Crabtree's house? Did Dylan injure his eye on purpose to get the time off to commit a murder? A murder planned by a guy whose previous crime was writing bad checks? It didn't look likely.

Chapter 13

The Journey II

All this work, only to get this far. Dylan dreaded spending the night in Bend. Even if the money he had was enough for a hotel, he couldn't afford the risk of making a record of his being here. He could try sleeping in a park or on the street until it was time for the 7:00 a.m. bus. But if he got rousted for vagrancy, the police would look up his priors and see he was violating his parole. Dylan sat on a plastic chair in the bus terminal trying to come up with a plan.

He would hang out in the downtown library until it closed. He'd read the papers and then find a book. Then he'd find a late movie and see if he could sleep through it. Then he'd go to a bar that stayed open late, maybe Corey's or the M&J. He'd have to nurse something along to make sure they didn't ask him to leave early. No calling any attention to himself. No conversations and absolutely no arguments. He could do that part. He and Ben were brought up to be decent, well-behaved kids. He could act that way. But he'd been in prison too. He knew how to spot someone looking for trouble, someone who took offense too easily, someone who wanted to get into a fight. He'd steer clear of anyone with that look in his eye. Maybe he'd meet someone who'd let him sleep on their couch. If not, maybe sit up all night on the second street sidewalk among homeless tents.

But first Dylan had to look as presentable as possible. He took his backpack into the bus station restroom to wash his face and neaten up. Dirt from the lava tube fell out of his hair as he ran his comb through it. But he didn't look too bad in the mirror. Too much sun from his walk. He'd look tired later. But still a credible man. A man who could work all day if need be. Or hike or ski. A man who could put on a tie and jacket and look like he wore them all the time.

Someone had taped a note to the wall next to the mirror.

"Drive me and my car to Corvallis today. Will pay."

Below the message was a phone number. This looked a lot better to Dylan than sitting on the sidewalk all night. Buses ran from Corvallis to Portland all the time with connections to Seattle from there. Dylan could be home by tomorrow, safe and sound.

He found a payphone in the lobby, dropped in fifty cents and dialed the number. A man answered.

"Yes?"

"I'm ready to drive you to Corvallis."

"Leaving now?"

"Yes. I'm at the bus station ready to go."

"You have a valid driver's license?'

"Yes. And I'm a good driver."

"A hundred dollars good enough?" That was a lot less than Dylan thought an Uber driver would charge but he wasn't supplying the car or the gas and he wanted to get closer to Portland anyway. Dylan said that was fine with him.

"I'll pick you up in ten minutes. Wait on the sidewalk by Hawthorne."

"Will do."

The man, when he showed up, was about fifty, with thinning brown hair. Medium height and thirty pounds overweight. His name was Hal Shalen.

"Let me see your eyes," said Hal. Dylan didn't want to reveal the black eye he'd gotten at work but he whipped off his sunglasses and looked Hal in the face, trying to look calmer than he felt. Hal seemed to be satisfied.

"You know the route?" Hal asked as they passed each other around the back of Hal's deep blue Lexus sedan.

"You'll need to tell me," said Dylan. In fact, he'd been over the mountains to the Willamette Valley at least a hundred times. If the man asked him, Dylan would say he had come to Bend with friends to go hiking. Didn't know his way around.

"Route 20 all the way," said Hal. "If you don't know where to make a turn, you need to wake me up. Otherwise, don't worry if I fall asleep. I'm narcoleptic. Can't trust myself to drive that far or that fast."

"Fine," said Dylan. Maybe Hal would sleep the whole way. "We go out through Sisters, right?"

"Right."

Dylan hoped he wouldn't have to spend the next two-and-a-half hours talking, making up lies about himself and keeping them consistent. He was tired after his long walk and he wanted to concentrate on his driving. If he got in an accident, even a minor one, or got pulled over for speeding, the police would know he wasn't in Seattle where he should be. They might guess he'd been visiting his brother and ask him what he knew about the shooting in Sunriver. He definitely didn't want to get connected to that.

Hal wasn't a talker and that was good. Dylan glanced at him periodically but didn't see him nodding off. Dylan idly considered that he could stop worrying about Hal identifying him to the State of Washington if Dylan bumped him off along the way. He could pull over into a forest road, maybe the road to Iron Mountain Trailhead. Get Hal out of the car and hit him with a tire iron or a rock. Dump him down a steep hillside. Drive the car to Portland and leave it on the street. Clearly Hal hadn't passed along Dylan's name to anyone else. He hadn't pulled out a phone to make a call or send a text since he drove up to the bus station.

But killing Hal was a passing thought. It worried Dylan that he'd even thought of it. The idea was not worthy of the person Dylan aspired to be. In addition, of course, it was a terrible idea, not worth the risk even if Dylan were a psychopath. Someone could remember the two men getting in the car. And surely someone would remember Dylan hanging around the bus station. Dylan's fingerprints and

DNA were in the car and no amount of wiping could remove all traces. Hal might put up a fight. Though Dylan was confident he'd be the winner, it might cost him. Some scar, some injury, some blood on his clothes.

Dylan reminded himself his goal was to become a good citizen, to lead a normal life. Get a steady job. Have friends. Find a wife. Have children. Own a house. He wasn't going to be a criminal even if he could get away with it. The disastrous trip to Sunriver had reminded him how careful he had to be.

Chapter 14

Ye Shall Find

The morning after Geoff Pennstead's murder, Detective Breuninger arrived at Dara Pennstead's house a second time—this time with two sheriff's deputies, a Sunriver police officer, and a warrant to search the house, the grounds, whatever cars were on the property, Geoff's airplane, and the airplane hangar. The judge had signed the warrant to include everything Carl asked for. But he had cautioned Carl about Geoff and Dara's financial records. Carl could seize anything that appeared related to drug dealing but Carl didn't get a blank check to take whatever checkbooks, bank statements, credit card statements, or any other records he came across. It would be hard to know where to draw the line but Carl would do the best he could.

For that matter, how much financial trouble was Geoff in and who else might he owe money to? Carl couldn't paw through Geoff and Dara's records without a change in the warrant. And if he happened to find something that didn't closely relate to drug dealing, he couldn't take it and he couldn't act on it. If the information led to Geoff's killer but Carl didn't have a warrant for it, the "fruit of the poisoned tree" would undermine the district attorney if and when the case came to trial.

Dara Pennstead was still in her nightgown and a white robe when Carl knocked on the door.

"I'm sorry to bother you, Mrs. Pennstead, but we found evidence of drugs in Geoff's car. We need to search the house for drugs and anything connected to them. We'll try to leave everything neat and tidy where we found it."

"Oh, God," said Dara, her face sinking. "Couldn't you come back another day?"

"I'm afraid not. We'll try not to take too long."

"Can I get dressed at least?"

"Of course. Deputy Newton will go with you if you don't mind."

"I do mind, dammit. Jesus. Can you just leave me alone?"

"Sorry. The law's the law. And this may help us find Geoff's killer."

"What difference would that make? I need to figure out my life."

"I think you need to care," said Carl. "If your husband was involved with drugs and somebody he did business with comes to search your house, they'll be a lot rougher than the Sheriff's Department. You'll be safer if we've already searched it. Now, before you go change, we're going to send a dog through the house to search for drugs. She'll be a lot faster than we are. First I'm going to have a deputy make sure all the inside doors are open. Are any of them locked?"

"No," said Dara, her eyes pinched in a frown and her teeth unclenched only enough to speak the one word.

"All open, including the door into the garage," said the deputy when he returned, "except I left the door into the airplane hangar closed."

"We'll do that separately," said Carl.

The deputy handling the dog unhooked the leash and held its collar. "Bowser, *Such Rauschgift,*" commanded the deputy. He let go of the collar and Bowser shot forward, sniffing all the corners of the front hall and all the people in the room. He raced into the kitchen and began a thorough search. Carl, Dara, the two deputies and the one Sunriver police officer stood silent, listening to the dog scrambling through the house, its paws thumping on the carpets, its nails clicking on the wood. They stood silently waiting for Bowser to come back.

Carl could see Dara's jaw had relaxed a shade and he theorized she didn't think the canine would find any drugs in the house. Good for her. Bowser came back to the front hall and sat facing his handler. He'd found nothing.

"The search warrant also covers drug paraphernalia," said Carl. "It won't take us long and we'll do your bedroom first if you like so you can change."

Dara waited outside the upstairs bedroom with a woman deputy, Deputy Newton, while Carl and another deputy looked through the room quickly, touching nothing but the closet door handle. Carl did not expect to find bongs or pipes or any other drug paraphernalia. Geoff was a businessman in his seventies, not a likely user. Dara showed no signs of habitual cocaine use—red nose, dilated pupils, sweating, or excess energy or anxiety. Her mood hadn't changed much since Carl arrived. She was irritated and she stayed irritated. But that was understandable.

What Carl did hope to find in the search was a note, a receipt, a map, or some other evidence of how cocaine got into Pennstead's car. And what, if anything, did cocaine have to do with his murder?

Carl located an upstairs bedroom with a large wooden desk and a four-drawer steel filing cabinet. He'd have to get a new search warrant to go pouring through the file cabinet but there was a single file folder open on the desk with bank statements in it from Deschutes River Bank. The top statement, dated over a month ago, was in plain sight. The law clearly allowed Carl to look at it. The statement was for a loan to "New 97 Partners". The loan was for five million dollars, paid down to a little over three million dollars. The status of the loan was "In Arrears." The most recent statement, which should have arrived by now according to the dates, was missing. Carl took a picture of the statement in the folder without touching it. Was Geoff part of the partnership and did he owe the bank money? If Geoff was financially stretched, then who else did he owe money to? The Deschutes River Bank was unlikely to kill people who took out loans. But other creditors might practice more brutal business methods. Whoever or whatever New 97 Partners was, Carl needed to find out.

When the deputies and officers had searched the house and

found nothing of interest, they opened the door into the hangar and entered. The space was almost as large as a high school gymnasium. The wide hangar door, white with aluminum frames, had a hinged joint across it so it could fold up to open. The hangar walls, ceiling, and concrete floor were painted white. Cupboards and metal drawers, also white, were spaced along the walls. A large workbench with a vise stood against one wall and a jack to lift the plane for changing tires sat on the floor next to the workbench. A long extension cord with a work light on the end of it rested on a wall hook. A three-step stepladder leaned against the wall by the work light.

In the middle of the hangar, facing the hangar door, sat a Beechcraft King Air 200, a two-engine prop plane. The plane was white with parallel lines of green and yellow from the nose to the tail. Carl could see the plane hadn't been washed recently and the tires looked scratched.

The handler walked Bowser around the walls of the hangar and got no reaction. He got no reaction when the dog sniffed the tires of the plane. But when the dog sniffed the bottom of the fuselage, he sat down below the cabin door on the left side of the plane and looked longingly upward. The handler reached up, pushed a button to release the door latch, turned the handle on the door, and pulled out the stairway, hinged at the bottom, down to where it almost touched the ground. The dog leapt up into the cabin. The handler climbed up and peeked in.

"The plane smells like Old Spice," said the handler.

"The victim's body smelled the same," said Carl.

"People use stuff like that to hide the smell of drugs. It'll fool a human but it won't fool a dog." Carl could hear the dog's feet thumping on the floor of the cabin.

"He's found something," said the handler. "Good dog!" He backed down the stairs and called the dog who came carefully down the first two steps before jumping to the floor. The handler ruffled the fur on the dog's neck and repeated, "Good dog." He turned to Carl. "It's behind the back passenger seat on the left."

Carl pulled a pair of nitrile gloves and a plastic evidence bag out of his vest and climbed the stairs. In the pocket behind the back seat he found a package the size of a dictionary, tightly wrapped in cellophane, with the black contents showing through the wrapping.

Carl took photos of the package where he found it, then placed it in an evidence bag. He climbed out of the plane with the bag in his hand.

"Looks like two kilos of cocaine," he said to the others, "worth at least a hundred thousand. Maybe two hundred thousand on the street."

"How could anybody leave that behind?" asked the dog handler.

"More important is how did it get there in the first place?"

Carl wrote notes on a label and stuck it on the evidence bag. "Take this directly to the evidence room and get a receipt for it," he told the dog handler. The deputy took the bag and his dog out through the house.

Dara and Deputy Newton were waiting in the living room when Carl came in from the hangar. Dara still looked angry. She'd look a lot more worried, Carl decided, if she knew her husband was ferrying illegal drugs around the country. Carl would be frank with her.

"We found two kilos of what we think is cocaine in your husband's plane. Do you know anything about that?"

Dara's jaw dropped and her eyes bulged out at Carl. "No," she said. "Not anything. What's going on here?"

"Has he ever had drugs in his possession before?"

"No. At least I don't think so. He wasn't into drugs. Didn't even want to take prescriptions."

"Did he ever have contact with anyone who might have dealt in anything illegal?"

"Not that I ever knew about. He was a legitimate businessman. His friends were businesspeople. Or men he played golf with. Nobody like that."

Dara didn't look like a user but, with her time in the music business, Carl suspected she'd at least known people who used drugs, "recreational" or more serious. "Did you or he ever use drugs?"

"No," said Dara, a little too fast and emphatically. "You've searched the house. You didn't find anything in the house, did you?"

"That's right," said Carl, "no drugs in the house. But now my concern about your safety is only greater. If Geoff didn't know about that package, it must belong to someone else. And that someone else will very likely come looking for it. You'll have protection around the clock but if you see something or get a strange phone call, call 911."

"I don't know anything. I don't have anything. I'll tell them to get lost."

Carl didn't think Dara's plan would work if it came to that. But he wasn't about to tear down her confidence.

"I'm going to give you a receipt for the suspected cocaine. Hang onto it and keep it where you can find it. Make a copy. You'll need it if someone comes looking for that package. If they think you still have the drugs, they will not be nice about asking you where they are."

Deputy Newton left for headquarters to write a report that Carl would look at later. Officer Maples stayed to relieve the deputy who had been watching the house.

The house next door to Dara's had first and second floor windows that overlooked the Pennstead driveway. Carl thought the owner might confirm the time Geoff left his house on the morning of his murder. And might having something interesting to say about the Pennsteads. Carl walked up to the door and knocked.

"I've been expecting you," said the man who answered, a short heavy man in his sixties. "My name's Ward Beacham." He offered his hand to shake and Carl took it. "I bet you're here about Geoff Pennstead. I know you have questions but I can tell you straight off, I saw him fly in the day he was murdered and saw him leave in his car right after. You want to come in?"

"I will, if you don't mind," said Carl. "Is there anyone else here?"

"My wife is upstairs. Marilyn. No dogs, by the way, in case you are about to ask. Why don't we sit at the kitchen table so you can have the same view I had that morning? Of course I was upstairs when Geoff flew in. I know his plane. Taxied up to his hangar and drove right in."

They were seated at the table now, Carl facing toward the street where he could plainly see the neighboring driveway out the window.

"What time did he land and what time did he drive out?"

"Put his plane in the hangar at 6:47. I know because I looked at my alarm clock. Idled the engine outside for a minute and backed it into the hangar with a tug. I'd never seen him come in that early in the morning. And he drove out of his garage about seven. Give or take five minutes, I'd guess."

"Anybody with him?"

"I don't know. I hadn't thought of that. I guess I didn't even see Geoff for sure. I knew it was his plane and his car. He got out of his plane in the hangar and got into his car in the garage. I assumed it was Geoff. And I didn't see anyone else."

"Not Dara? Did you see her at all?" Carl was sorry to be asking the question. Sorry to suggest to Ward, and maybe through him to the wider community, that Dara might be a suspect. But he had to ask the question.

"Didn't see her coming or going," said Ward.

"Do you know when Geoff flew out or where he was going?"

"No idea."

"I understand he had to file a flight plan," said Carl

"I'm sure he filed one but it'll take you weeks to get it from the FAA. It's really for the air traffic controllers along the route to help keep you separate from other aircraft. But you probably don't want the flight plan."

"I don't?"

"If the pilot's flying on instruments, a company called Flight Aware tracks the flight. And even if he's flying VFR—sorry, that's visual flight rules—his plane has a transponder that sends out his GPS location and altitude. And the tracking data is available online, free to anyone who wants it. If you know the tail number of a plane, you can look up where it's been and the route it took."

"The tail number is the number painted on the side of the plane, right?"

"Or the tail. It's unique to that plane."

"I wrote it down here. Do you have a computer where we can look it up?"

"Sure do. Let's go into my office." Ward led the way to a room at the back of the house next to a door that Carl estimated led to Ward's hangar. The room was small and had only one window. Ward sat down at his computer and got to a screen titled "Flight Aware."

"What's the tail number?"

"N422EB," said Carl. Ward typed it in.

"Okay," said Carl. "Two days before the morning he flew in, he flew from here to Flagstaff, Arizona. He stayed there, or at least the plane did, until 3:35 yesterday morning when he flew back here, touching down at six-forty-four."

"So he didn't leave Flagstaff except to come back here?"

"Not unless he turned off his transponder and didn't fly on instruments. Then Flight Aware wouldn't know where he was. Hardly anyone would turn it off unless they were doing something illegal, or going someplace they don't want anyone to know about."

"Like Mexico. Can you print the report for me?"

Ward did and handed it to Carl.

"Would Flagstaff have a record of when Pennstead landed and when he took off? I mean aside from arriving in Flagstaff from Sunriver and taking off to return here."

"Maybe. Unlike here, they have a tower. You can't land or take off without talking to them. They know who you are at the time but they may or may not keep a record of it."

"And Sunriver doesn't keep a record here?"

"Flight operations, the guys in that little building by the airport, they don't do flight control. Flight operations is here to sell fuel, service planes, and park planes on the ramp. By ramp, I mean the area where you can rent space and tie your plane down to the ground. The pilots don't even talk to them unless there's some special reason.

"A pilot is supposed to radio other planes in the area that he's about to take off or land on runway 36 or runway 18 so other planes in the area will look out for him. A pilot can even land at night with no one here at all. They punch 'Push to Talk' on their radio five times and the runway lights come on. But it's unlikely anybody else was coming in or taking off at 6:45 in the morning when Flight Aware says Pennstead landed."

"You mentioned two runways. When I drove past, I only saw one runway and a taxiway next to it."

"One runway. It's called 36 going north, short for 360 degrees on the compass, and it's 18 going south, short for 180 degrees."

"The planes parked outside all look clean," said Carl. "But Pennstead's plane was dirty when I saw it. The wheels were muddy and weeds hung from the sill of the right-hand door. The bottom of the airplane was scratched. Does that tell you anything?"

"I thought the plane looked a little worse for wear when he came in. That doesn't sound like Geoff Pennstead but your description would tell me the plane landed on a dirt runway or maybe a dirt road. I'd be thinking somebody was smuggling drugs in from Mexico. The DEA watches every legitimate airport in Mexico but they can't watch all the roads or dirt runways hacked out of the desert. Anyone who landed like that, though, was taking big risks. He could hit something or the Mexican police could pick him up. He'd have to be some kind of desperate."

"What do you know about Pennstead's personal life?" asked Carl.

"Not much. We mostly talk planes if we talk at all. Nice house. Cute little wife. He did have a land investment go sour down in La Pine but I don't know how serious that was for him. I think he's pretty wealthy."

Not any more, thought Carl. But he didn't say it.

Chapter 15

Liabilities

Carl found New 97 Partners online and looked up the owners. There were only two—Geoff Pennstead and Henry Kearnan. Kearnan's address was in La Pine, about eighteen miles south of Sunriver. Carl called him on the phone and introduced himself.

"I'm investigating the death of Geoff Pennstead and I need to talk with you about him. Will you be home this afternoon?"

"Geoff Pennstead? I didn't know he died," said Kearnan. "I talked to him last week. What happened to him?"

"Murdered."

"Well, I don't know if I have anything useful but I'll help you if I can. I'll be here this afternoon if you want to come down. Any time after one o'clock works for me. It's the log house once you get in here."

Henry Kearnan lived outside the city of La Pine proper, on land set off by itself to the southwest of the city, close to the county line between Deschutes County and Klamath County. His driveway, through a thinned-out lodgepole forest, was gravel. Carl passed a stable and a corral holding four healthy-looking horses. In the distance was fenced pasture with a dozen or so cattle in it. A barn, a small house, and a garage with five doors were board and batten, like the stables, and freshly painted the same dark brown. At the end of the driveway was a one-story house built with uniformly round red-colored logs. The buildings and fences were spotlessly maintained. The little lawn in front of the log house was neatly cut. The Kearnan ranch was a gentleman's ranch, built for the lifestyle, not for profit. It took a wealthy man to own a ranch like this one.

Henry Kearnan answered the door himself and stepped back to let Carl into the house. He was an inch taller than Carl with thinning brown hair. In his fifties, Carl guessed. He wore a clean but well-worn long-sleeved cowboy shirt with no decoration on it, blue jeans, and cowboy boots. His smile was reserved but seemed sincere. *A man like this,* Carl thought, *relies on the law to protect him and will scrupulously stay on the right side of it.* Of course, Carl cautioned himself, he could be wrong.

"I figured we could sit out on the porch," said Kearnan. "Do want a lemonade or a soda?"

Carl thought this might take a while and, he admitted to himself, he liked it here. "Lemonade if you've got it," said Carl.

"Marcie just made some." Carl followed Kearnan into the kitchen where the man got down two big glasses from a cupboard, stuck them in an ice dispenser in a double-door refrigerator, and filled them from a pitcher he lifted from a shelf inside the fridge.

The porch overlooked a lawn and a meadow sloping down to the Little Deschutes River, the only river or creek anywhere nearby.

"So how did Geoff die?" asked Kearnan.

"He was shot near his car on a road in Sunriver. I'd rather not say more until we understand the case better," said Carl. "We don't know who shot him or why. I'm looking for some background that might help. For starters, what is New 97 Partners and what's happening with it?"

"Did you see the news a while back about the bridge they were going to build in La Pine? It was going to take the main road, Highway 97, over the railroad so the road could handle more traffic and wouldn't have to slow down for the tracks. Anyhow, Geoff and I bought a good-sized parcel of land next to where the new section of road would go. Then they couldn't build the bridge and the whole project shut down.

"Our business, that's New 97 Partners, borrowed from Deschutes

River Bank to buy the land and we still had to pay back the loan. But the land wasn't worth developing anymore. Nobody would lease or buy it from us. I was ready to pay off the loan and call it a loss. But Geoff didn't want to do that. He said that no matter what happened to the road, the land was valuable and someday we could sell it off for a profit.

"He wasn't entirely crazy. Do you know that La Pine is the fastest growing city in Oregon? Granted, it is a small city but Portland State University says the population grew ninety percent in the last ten years and it's going to keep right on growing. So we kept making the payments on the loan.

"Well, six months ago I started getting notices that the bank wasn't getting full payments. I was paying my half but Geoff wasn't paying his. The bank said they were going to foreclose and take the property. I told Geoff we should let them do it. Take our losses and move on. But he wanted to keep the property and he didn't want his reputation to suffer from the foreclosure. He was trying to raise cash to prevent the foreclosure but he didn't make it. I got a notice that they did foreclose."

"When did they do that?"

It was the same day Geoff Pennstead was killed.

"What did you talk about last week, the last time you spoke to him?"

"He told me he was going to catch up on the payments. He had a way to get the cash. He didn't tell me how and I didn't ask. It was partly because I didn't a hundred percent believe him. But there was something in his tone that told me I didn't want to know. Wherever he was going to get the money, it bothered me. Like it sounded shady or risky or not quite on the up and up."

"No details? No hints?"

Henry Kearnan gazed off over the river. "Not a thing," he said. "Like I told you, he didn't want to tell me what he was doing and I didn't want to know. Sorry."

"So what happens to New 97 Properties now?"

"The bank will sell the property to pay off part of the loan and the court will demand the partnership pay what is still due. I'll pay off my part of it. You know, as his partner, I'll be liable for Geoff's part of the debt as well. I'll have to decide whether to go after his estate. If he was that desperate for cash, his estate might not be worth much. Do you know anything about it?"

"His widow is trying to figure that out. She doesn't know if she's got money or she's broke."

"It will all take time," said Kearnan.

Carl didn't think Kearnan was bothered much by the possibility he'd have to pay off Geoff Pennstead's part of the loan. The rich were different. The very rich were very different.

Chapter 16

The Return of the Prodigal

Leon had a golf game every Wednesday morning with three of his friends. One of them, Bob, now Bobbie, was a woman who used to be a man. Bob had been in the foursome for years before he made the transition. Every change along the way was a challenge for all of them. First the longer hair in a wave. The shaved calves below the woman's Bermuda shorts. Then lipstick and earrings. The body changes from hormones were subtle but they changed Bobbie's face enough to make you wonder what was different. Then breast augmentation and a series of other operations. Bobbie was willing to talk about the alterations. She welcomed each one of them. But the three men grew queasy learning about them, forced to recognize that anatomy they viewed as essential to their identity could be changed so fundamentally. They had never imagined so much cutting and folding and reversing. They secretly agreed they would rather not know quite so much.

"I can't imagine giving up my little squirter," Stanley had said. The men had frank discussions with Bobbie when she started the transition. They'd been friends a long time and the others wanted to support her if it made her happier. But as she became a woman, they treated her differently. They became more polite, considerate, and more protective of her. Stan made a joke one time about helping her find her lost ball. She took it in stride but the men stopped making jokes like that.

Bobbie played from the women's tees. In women's tournaments, she almost always won the longest drive. She didn't hit the ball quite as far as she used to but she could still wallop it.

"My chipping and putting is nothing to write home about," said Bobbie. "So I think the competition is fair." She had not yet won a woman's tournament. "Some of those women are very competitive," she told Leon. "Sometimes they are not as nice as men."

Stanley asked her once why she still played with the men's foursome that she had been playing with for years, not that the others weren't glad to have her.

"I was brought up to be a boy," she said. "All my teenage years, I struggled to do what boys do, act the way boys act. I should have been a girl and I wish I had been one. I would never go back. But that struggle to act like a boy was a challenge I sometimes met, like scoring a goal in a game you are not very good at. Or when you act in a high school play and play someone who isn't like you at all but you do it well. I miss it in a way. It's familiar. And I don't mind rising to the challenge sometimes."

So the men weren't always sure who they were playing with from one hole to the next— Bob who would outdrive everyone and curse a ball that went into a pond. Or Bobbie who would take extra care in lining up a putt then get sullen at four-putting the green. Sometimes she would talk more than the rest of them and sometimes she would go off into a world of her own. She expanded their horizons, though, and the men silently congratulated themselves that they could keep her as one of them and allow the four of them to enjoy the game together.

This particular Wednesday, they were playing Woodlands in Sunriver. The fourth friend couldn't make it and the starter asked if he could put a resort guest in with them to make up a foursome. They didn't want to play with a stranger but they had an unspoken agreement with the staff. If somedays the group solved a problem for the marshals then somedays the starter or the marshals would do them a favor. A favor like letting the group start on the back nine because they knew some slow foursome was finishing up on the front. In this case, the course was busy and the starter didn't want to waste an opportunity to slip someone into the schedule.

Leon, Stan, and Bobbie introduced themselves to the guest with feigned enthusiasm. If the guy turned out to be obnoxious, especially if he were rude to Bobbie, they'd all quit and go home. Walk-ons were sometimes walk-ons because nobody wanted to play with them. The man's name was Lester and he smiled back at them.

"Mr. Martinez!" Lester said when he heard Leon's name. "You may not remember me but I was in your art class back in 1992. You changed my life. I'm Lester Westlake. Mr. Martinez, I mean Leon, I'm so glad to see you again." Now that Leon heard the name, he did remember Lester—a troubled kid and a difficult student. He had sat in class as though he were in prison. Didn't talk to any of the other kids. Wouldn't touch any of the art materials or work on any of the projects Leon assigned. Other teachers said Lester acted the same in their classes, except for math. He wasn't a genius but it somehow kept his interest. Leon managed to catch his attention with some visual puzzles. A simple one was asking which of four drawings on circles within circles could you change into the Chinese symbol for Tao—a circle with a single curved line through it—by deleting some lines in the more complex drawing. Or drawing a pair of dice with three faces showing on each of them. Then drawing one more die that could not possibly be a rotation of one of the original die. It took more thinking than drawing but it did get Lester to put his pencil on the paper. After two weeks of that, Leon introduced him to de Chirico, an artist who painted manikins in very stark geometrical landscapes. Lester spent a few weeks imitating de Chirico. Not well, really, but he began to get a sense of the decisions de Chirico had made and the kinds of decisions that all artists must make. Lester actually became enthusiastic, eager to show Leon his latest work and talk about it. Other teachers said he was taking more interest in their classes as well.

In the history of art, Lester was attracted to some of the more grotesque images, like Goya's "Saturn Devouring His Son" and Renaissance paintings of San Sebastian shot full of arrows. Leon turned their conversations toward the artist's use of light and color and lines and discouraged talk about the subject of the painting. Lester did take to the new perspective, thank goodness, and his last project in the academic year was a sculpture of a girl, too abstract to tell whether she had her clothes on or not but he did a good job with her neck and shoulders.

"You turned my life around," Lester told Leon as they waited for their turn on the first tee. "I could have failed high school and wound up in a life that I hated." He'd gone to Oregon State and become an economist. He worked for an insurance company in Salem and was on vacation in Sunriver. Leon was pleased to hear this success but it was embarrassing to hear it in front of his friends. Leon was here to play golf, not to glory in old achievements.

Lester kept a certain distance from Bobbie for the first few holes and he rarely spoke to her. He watched Stan carefully to make sure, Leon thought, that Stan was what he appeared to be, a run of the mill heterosexual man. Lester closely watched how Leon and Stan interacted with Bobbie, mostly as they'd act with a woman that they'd known a long time.

"Do you know about the guy who was murdered a few days ago?" Lester asked the group.

Leon nodded. He was too close to that murder, and to Dara Pennstead, to talk about it with a man he hadn't seen for years.

"It was right near the house we are renting. The police came by to ask if we knew anything but we didn't have a clue. I was out playing golf when it happened and my son Tommy was buried in a video game."

"I think I went by there just before the poor man was killed," said Bobbie. "All I saw was a car pulling off to the side of the road. If I'd come by a minute later, I might have been killed myself."

"And Leon," Bobbie continued, "I was sure I saw Elizabeth behind me in your blue Toyota when I went past the water park. Did she say anything to you about seeing something on East Cascade?"

"Not a thing," said Leon.

"I think she must have stayed on Beaver Drive and didn't take

East Cascade. Some people think that's shorter but it really isn't."

"I'll ask her but I think she certainly would have said something after all the news about the shooting."

Robert Trent Jones Jr., the man who designed Woodlands, had laid the course out to take advantage of the gentle hills and worn-down lava outcrops available to him. A few of the holes had elevated tees and Jones had used the lava as obstacles in the middle of the fairways. On the fourteenth hole, Lester and Leon both hit into big grassy outcrop and helped each other find their balls. Leon couldn't hit his straight toward the green so he popped it back into the fairway with a sand wedge. Lester called his ball unplayable and threw it out onto the fairway where it rolled toward the green.

Waiting on the seventeenth tee, Lester told Leon he had a son who was as troubled as Lester had been as a teenager, but in ways that Lester didn't know how to deal with.

"He plays videogames all day. Or he's doing some Instagram or Tik Tok thing on his computer. He's not studying and he'll hardly talk to me. Shirley and I got divorced last year and I'm sure that hasn't helped. His mother says he acts the same way with her. I don't think he's forgiven either one of us. He doesn't act like he's into drugs but he has no friends as far we can tell."

"It's harder to be a kid than it ever was before," Leon said in sympathy.

"Leon, I know it's a big favor to ask," said Lester as they started up the eighteenth fairway, "but could you talk to Tommy? I know you are out of teaching and all that. But you did so much for me, and other kids too. I'm sure Tommy would get a lot out of talking to you, even one time."

Leon doubted one conversation would benefit Tommy. Leon was out of practice doing this sort of thing. Kids today were different from the kids Leon had taught. And Leon really didn't want to do it. Leon was done with all that. He'd earned his retirement.

"You were so good at helping kids," said Lester. "Not me alone but other kids too. You could change his life in an hour." Flattery, even when blatantly calculated, could have an influence. And flattery coupled with a challenge. "And if it doesn't help, you will at least have tried." So Lester wasn't going to blame Leon if Tommy went into a tailspin.

Leon would do it, he decided, but on his own terms. He'd make it as easy on himself as possible.

"One hour. You bring him to my house at a time that works for me and I'll do what I can do."

"That would be wonderful!" said Lester, even more excited than when he sank a long putt on Number 10. "I can't tell you how grateful I'd be." They exchanged phone numbers and emails and said they'd arrange a time.

They entered their scores in the pro shop and walked past the practice green to the café. The television showed a tournament on a course with palm trees and brilliant white bunkers. The players on the leader board were people Leon had never heard of. Lester and Stanley drank beer. Bobbie and Leon drank Arnold Palmers. Lester told them about walking onto a course in Baker City and playing golf with a member of the state legislature.

"Really nice guy. High energy and lots of enthusiasm. But not a very good golfer. Can't chip for beans. Leapt in his car the moment we were done. Had to go to a meeting."

Walking onto a course as a single and taking potluck for golf companions seemed to be a frequent event for Lester. Leon wondered why Lester didn't play more often with his friends, assuming he had them. Leon decided Lester might have turned his life around since he was a teenager but he still might not be a fully functioning adult.

Lester's son, Tommy, turned out to be no better than Lester used to be. Lester brought him to the Martinez house the next day and said he would be back in an hour. Leon and Tommy sat in the shade of the back deck with bottles of water from the refrigerator. Tommy's hair was long overdue for a cut and he had a general hangdog look about him.

Leon wondered how his father had gotten Tommy to come see him. The kid might still have some spark of hope in him that he could build on. The work would take more patience and attention than Leon had mustered in a long time and Leon tried not to show how equivocal he was about it. But he'd give it a shot.

"Your father says you're going through a rough patch right now. And not very happy about it. Is that about right?"

"I guess so," said Tommy.

"Well, the first thing I'd tell you is you are not the first person to feel that way. I've seen a lot of kids with a bunch of problems and a lot of feelings they had trouble with. At your age you're dealing with problems that you haven't been trained for and have no experience with. Like your parents getting divorced and I'm sure a bunch of other things. And with hormones out of balance on top of that, you can have a lot of feelings you have trouble handling. Feelings like fear of failure, frustration, worry, feelings of not being good enough, sadness, anger, hate, loneliness, fear that nobody likes you or ever will like you. The feelings can be worse than the real-world problems and they can get in the way of dealing with real issues. Feelings can paralyze you.

"And part of growing up is learning how to deal with your feelings. You have to learn a lot of that yourself. But the first step is naming your feelings and emotions. Putting words to them. Does that make sense?

"I guess so."

"Well, try it," Leon said. "Seriously. Try it for a couple of days and see if it helps. For instance, what are you feeling right now?"

Tommy stared at a vacant wooden chair with a cushion on the deck.

"Boredom," he said.

Was that really what he was feeling or was he trying to fend off Leon's inquiries? It didn't matter. Leon would accept it as stated. Leon paused for a moment so Tommy knew Leon was thinking about what he said.

"Good," Leon said. "And what does this boredom feel like?"

Tommy thought for a moment. "Like I want to get out of here. Like it's too much work trying to name my 'feelings' and it isn't going to help."

"And your feelings are nobody else's business?"

"Some of that."

"Fair enough," said Leon. What Leon didn't say was that he didn't really care what Tommy's feelings were and Leon was feeling a little frustrated and bored himself. "I don't need to know what your feelings are. But you need to know. Do you think you can do that?

"And when you get a grip on an emotion," Leon went on, "so that you can recognize it when it comes around again, try to understand where that emotion is coming from. What is setting it off? It won't always be the same thing. And you may not be able to do anything about it. But you'll learn. Understanding won't come quickly. It takes work."

Silence. Leon thought that was about as much as Tommy could take in one day. He stared off the deck, past the little lawn and the wild grass toward the golf course.

"Has anything happened recently, say in the last week, that bothered you?" Leon asked.

"No," Tommy said. "It's boring here." With all the things to do in Sunriver, Leon thought it would be hard to be bored. But teenagers. They can pass up opportunities when they are staring them in the face.

"Take a walk. Ride a bike. Go have a tennis lesson." Leon was getting impatient and trying not to show it. "Do you play golf?"

"No," said Tommy as though he couldn't imagine anything more boring.

"Your father plays golf," Leon said, "you could try a golf lesson. You might like it."

Silence and more gazing out over the golf course. The doorbell rang.

"Well," Leon said as Tommy and he got up, "you might think of what else you might do around here, at least to try something out. But more importantly I suggest you remember what I told you. Put words to your emotions. Don't worry about changing them yet. Just put words to them." Leon had given the same advice to his own son, Dan, fifteen years ago. But Leon gave it more lightheartedly then.

Dan was secure, motivated, and mostly happy. It was good advice but Dan would have been fine without it. Leon had doubts about Tommy, with or without his counsel. He saw Tommy to the door and turned him over to his father.

Leon decided he should never have agreed to talk with Tommy. It was painful. He was retired from having to do that sort of thing. And he doubted that he had done Tommy the least bit of good. His adult students, fortunately, never needed or asked for that kind of help. Except now, of course, Dara Pennstead.

Leon was too drained to pick up a brush and paint but too restless not to do something. He put his paint tubes in order and unpacked a new box of watercolor paper. He straightened the paintings on his studio walls. On his computer, he sorted photos he'd taken of scenes he had painted to help him remember them when he added the finishing touches later in his studio. He noticed something in one photo that he hadn't noticed before. It was the photo of the morning shadows at the crime scene on East Cascade Road. In the background in one of the houses that only appeared as a few gray lines in Leon's painting, the photo showed a man's head peering over the wall of an enclosed patio. Complexion and hair color undiscernible. Leon could not even be sure it was a man and not a woman. He would never have included that image in his painting—too far back, too indistinct, and too unimportant. But Leon could send the photo to Detective Breuninger and he might find it interesting. Leon hadn't been much help earlier and sending the photo would at least be a gesture of support for Carl and his investigation.

Leon fished Carl's card out of a drawer and sent him an email with the photo attached along with a photo of the painting he had promised to show Carl. He didn't follow up with a phone call. He doubted the photo would help and he didn't want to make too big a deal of it. He'd done his duty. He took the watercolor off the easel and slid it into one of the racks under the counter in his studio. The rack held dozens of his paintings. When the racks got full, he took some to the waste transfer station on the road to La Pine.

Chapter 17

His Brother's Keeper

Carl immediately recognized that the photo Leon sent him of Ben Crabtree's house was significant. Leon said he took the photo soon after he arrived at the crime scene, roughly 7:45 a.m. The time stamp on the photo was 7:43 a.m. At that hour, Ben had already arrived at Crane Prairie Reservoir to fish. Carl had confirmed that with one of Ben's fishing buddies.

Ben had told Carl he was the only one at his house. Yet Leon's photo contradicted him. Someone had peeked over the wooden back patio wall at about quarter to 8:00. Who was that and why had Crabtree lied about that person or not known about him? It was time to give Ben a second chance at a truthful answer.

Falling Star Loop looked much the same as it had when Carl last visited it. Lester Westlake's car was in the driveway of the house he had rented. The family renting number 71 was apparently out, at least the car was.

Ben Crabtree answered the door in a t-shirt and wrinkled Bermuda shorts. He'd shaved but he didn't look as snappy as the last time.

"Hello detective," he said when he saw Carl. He raised one eyebrow in a quizzical look as if he couldn't understand why Carl would be back. "Do you want to come in?"

"Sure," said Carl, "this should only take a minute." The front door led directly into a living room with only two windows but with a large TV tuned to a news channel brightening up the room. Photos of a family appeared on one wall and on top of a bookcase. The fabric on the sofa and chairs was light green, red, and yellow against a white background. This was definitely not a man cave. It looked like a happy place.

"Would you like some coffee?" asked Ben. "It was fresh about thirty minutes ago."

"Sure. No cream, no sugar." Ben turned off the TV and brought two cups of coffee from the kitchen. He sat in a stuffed chair while Carl sat on the two-seat couch. Ben picked up a remote and turned off the TV. Carl thanked Ben for the coffee and sat back in the sofa.

"Somebody was in your house the day of the shooting, about the time that it happened. Do you know who that might have been?"

Ben put a puzzled look on this face. "No one should have been here," he said.

Carl noted that Ben had not exactly answered his question but he let it pass for now. "A neighbor who has the key? A housekeeping service? Someone coming to make a repair?"

"Repairs? No. The housekeeping service comes when it fits their schedule. You could ask them but I don't think they came that day. The rental agent has a key but the house won't go on rental until September. I can't think of why they'd be here. How do you even know someone was in the house?"

Carl suspected Ben was hiding something while playing the concerned citizen. As helpful as he could be but having nothing to offer. Smart enough not to state something that Carl could easily check—like a repairman had come to fix the washer. Smart enough not to flatly state no one had been there. Smart enough to ask what evidence Carl had.

"We have a photo of someone looking over the patio wall that morning."

"Can I see it?"

"I don't have it with me," said Carl. In fact, it was on Carl's phone and he could have easily shown it to Ben. But it would be better if

Ben, and whoever he might be protecting, didn't know how good or bad the photo was. Ben would be more likely to reveal the truth if he thought the law could eventually figure out who the mysterious person was.

"Do you have an alarm system or a security camera?"

"Neither one. Sorry."

"Notice anything missing or moved? Burglary is pretty rare around here but it does happen." Carl thought Ben was weighing his options before he answered. Burglary could be a great explanation for the person in the picture. But it would draw even more attention to this house and what might have happened here. Ben would have to make up something that was missing and he could get snarled up in explanations. And why wouldn't the burglar take the big TV screen—transportable, easily sellable, and the single most valuable thing in the house?

"Nothing missing that I've noticed. Nothing valuable in any case."

"Okay. Thanks for your time. Give me a call if you think of anything else." Carl got up from the couch and put his mostly empty coffee mug on the counter separating the kitchen from the living room.

"I'll keep thinking about who could have been here," said Ben. "You sure about the time the picture was taken? An hour earlier or some other day, it could have been me."

"We're sure." Carl was sure. But it still left him with a question. When and how did the person in the house that morning get out of the house? He called Adam, the deputy assigned to watch the video from across the street.

"How much have you looked at so far?"

"Two-and-a-half hours, from 6:30 a.m. to 9:00 a.m. when the deputy left after knocking on the two houses I could see on the video and not getting an answer."

"I need you to look at the rest of the day. I'm especially looking for anyone leaving number 73 or any activity at that house at all. They may have come out a window or tried to conceal themselves some way. Keep a sharp eye out."

"I will, Carl, but I have to tell you I'm getting tired of watching trees and squirrels. Nothing much happens after that family leaves."

"Okay."

Carl didn't tell the deputy that he would want that camera monitored for days into the future. He had the strong feeling that Ben Crabtree knew more than he let on. He thought about getting a wiretap on Ben's phones—both his house phone and his cell phone. But judges were reluctant to issue a wiretap order without a lot more evidence than Carl had gathered so far. He had more suspicion than probable cause. He estimated that Jocelyn, the assistant district attorney, would not even agree to ask for a wiretap.

Dylan Crabtree got a call from Ben that evening.

"Bro, we've had some excitement here," said Ben. "A man got shot out on East Cascade and the Sheriff has been here twice asking me a lot of questions. I don't know a damn thing and I keep telling him I can't help him. I wasn't even here when it happened. But the detective told me they have photo of somebody looking over the patio fence after the shooting. I should have locked the damn door. Nothing seems to be missing, though, and I don't see anything that shows anybody was here. I'm going to get the cleaning service to come early. I don't like the idea of strange people in the house."

Silence on the other end of the line. Dylan was thinking. Ben went on.

"So how are things in Seattle? How's the job? Meeting any women?"

"Oh, you know. The job's okay." It was tiring to wrestle tires around all day, and hard work taking them on and off the rims. Dylan got more than his share of the most difficult jobs because the boss knew he didn't dare quit. But the work was out of the rain and his boss was fair most of the time. Dylan was being careful not to break any tools, machines, or the tricky tire pressure sensors. He torqued lug nuts by hand with a wrench to make sure they would hold without stripping threads. When the work was slow he was the first to take out the trash or pick up a broom and sweep the shop. "Some days are easy," Dylan went on, "and the boss doesn't mind if I spend some time with the books." Dylan was taking classes at night to get a college degree.

"I hope to get to Seattle in a couple of weeks," said Ben. "I'll let you know."

"It'll be good to see you," said Dylan. "It's been a while."

"Right-o."

Chapter 18

A Bad Impulse

Leon wished he had never painted the watercolor of the crime scene. He wished Dara had never called him. He led a comfortable life. He painted. He read. He played some golf. He spent time with his son and his son's wife and their daughter. He went hiking with Elizabeth. They went to concerts and art galleries and had dinner with their friends. Hell, simply keeping house with Elizabeth was a quiet pleasure as long as he wasn't making repairs or cajoling a contractor to come fix something. He wasn't crazy about shopping with Elizabeth but even that had its satisfaction. Elizabeth liked having him with her.

He put Dara Pennstead and Tommy Westlake out of his mind and went with Elizabeth to an outdoor art exhibit in the Sunriver Mall. Nothing Leon saw there surprised him but he had to hand it to the artists for trying. He and Elizabeth enjoyed the spirit of the art fair but they saw no one they knew. They walked back through the mall toward Elizabeth's blue Toyota parked in front of the grocery store. Elizabeth especially liked seeing so many locally owned businesses, not a chain store or a franchise among them. The little stores, in spite of their commercial orientation to tourists, reinforced the impression that Sunriver was a community unto itself.

A boy came out of a space between two buildings and turned in the direction of the grocery store. He was wearing a thick black sweatshirt that looked very hot on such a warm summer afternoon. His right hand was wrapped around something in the front pocket of the sweatshirt. It was Tommy Westlake, Leon realized, Tommy's jaw clenched in a determined expression. After years of teaching teenagers, Leon got the strong sense that Tommy was about to do something he shouldn't.

"Hey Tommy," said Leon in a firm but friendly voice. "How are you? What are you up to?"

Tommy stopped and turned around, flustered and rapidly getting angry at being interrupted on whatever his mission was. "Nothing," he snarled. Leon looked at the lump in the sweatshirt and the way Tommy was holding it. Leon was afraid it was a gun. He stepped in front of Elizabeth.

"It's Mr. Martinez. How are things going after our talk?"

"Don't you stop me," said Tommy. He pulled a pistol out of his sweatshirt pocket and pointed it shakily toward Leon.

"Don't make a big mistake here, Tommy," said Leon sternly, as though Tommy were an unruly student about to paint dirty words on a school wall. "You don't have to do this." Without taking his eyes off Tommy, he could sense people moving away behind him and to either side. He heard someone gasp and a woman telling a child to come along quickly. Behind Tommy though, a tall man, who looked like he'd played football in his youth, came towards Tommy from the door of the bookstore. He carried a thick coffee table book in one hand.

"The whole world is a mistake," said Tommy, not seeing the man. "One big fucking mistake. And everybody in it is a bunch of hypocrites." He raised the gun and tried to steady it, more to fend off Leon's talking to him than actually aiming it. "I have things to do," he said and began to turn away.

The big man raised the book above his shoulders and slammed it down hard on Tommy's head. The man tossed the book aside and grabbed the hand with the gun in it, sweeping it down so the barrel pointed toward the ground. Tommy staggered and the man ripped the gun out of his hand by the barrel. Leon stepped around Tommy and wrapped his arms around him from behind, pinning Tommy's arms to his side.

"We need to call the police," commanded Leon.

"My wife is calling them now," said the tall man. He gently placed the gun on the ground and held it down with one foot.

"Let me go! Let me go!" Tommy shouted. "You can't do this. I know my rights."

"You gave up your rights when you pulled that gun," said the man.

Leon knew this wasn't true. Tommy would have some rights. But for sure Tommy did not have the right to walk away from threatening to shoot someone. This was not a playground dustup. Elizabeth stood in front of the boy, ready to bash him with her fists if he showed any sign of hurting Leon.

"Assault! Assault!" yelled Tommy. "They're robbing me. Help me. Help me. Let me go." He squirmed as much as he could but Leon held him even tighter.

People who had kept their distance came closer to see what the fracas was all about. Leon kept his eye on one man who looked to be debating whether he should interfere.

"The police are on their way," Leon shouted to the man. "We'll have them sort this out." The man relaxed and stood in place for thirty seconds. After deciding whether or not to get in the middle of what looked less and less like a robbery, the man turned and left.

"Please let me go," Tommy now pleaded, trying to turn his head to look at Leon. "I promise to never do this again. I want to forget the whole thing."

Leon didn't answer and didn't loosen the bear hug he had around Tommy. His arms were getting tired, though, and he hoped the police would show up soon. Tears began forming in Tommy's eyes but he didn't stop trying to break free.

Officer Katy Maples rushed up from the direction of the grocery store. She had her hand on her gun but didn't pull it from her holster.

"Where is the gun?" she demanded.

"Under my foot," said the big man.

"Keep it there," said Katy Maples. "Don't pick it up. Are there any other guns here?"

"Not that we've seen," said Leon.

"Hands forward," Maples commanded Tommy. Tommy only squirmed. Maples grabbed his wrists one at a time and put handcuffs on them so quickly it looked like a magic trick. "You're going to stay right here, right?" she asked. "If you try to leave, you'll be breaking the law. Do you understand?" Tommy had presumably broken much more serious laws than fleeing the police. And she hadn't told him he was under arrest or even that she was detaining him. But her speech had the desired effect. Tommy nodded his head and stayed put.

"Do I need to handcuff either of you?" she said to the two men. "I need you to stay here."

"I'll stay," said Leon.

"I'm here," said the other man. "My shop's right there."

"You'll want to talk to me too," said Elizabeth. "I was here the whole time." She stood pressed against Leon now, his arm around her shoulders.

Another officer arrived and Katy told him she had detained the two men, Elizabeth, and the boy. He held Tommy by the arm while Katy dealt with Leon, the tall man, and Elizabeth.

"Step away from the gun," she told the big man. "I'm going to pick it up." She expressly pointed her body cam toward the gun as the big man stepped back. She pulled nitrile gloves and a plastic bag from her vest. She picked up the pistol, a Glock G48 Black, with the gloves on, then ejected the magazine, pulled the slide slowly and caught the round that spun out of the top of the gun. She slid the slide back and forth again and found nothing in the chamber but daylight coming through the barrel. The gun, magazine, and the one loose round went in the plastic bag that dangled from her hand as she spoke.

"Can you step over here a minute," Katy said to Elizabeth, "and tell me what you saw?"

Leon wanted to tell the story. He thought he could explain it better than anyone. But the officer had her way of doing things and he would be patient. As he watched the two women talk, it occurred to him why she started with Elizabeth. The officer had no idea what had happened, who was at fault, and who she was going to wind up arresting. Elizabeth looked like the person least likely to be at fault here. Not involved but clearly present.

Elizabeth said she didn't know how her husband recognized the boy. But she was very clear that the boy, Tommy, had pulled the gun out of his sweatshirt and pointed it at Leon. She repeated what the boy said about hating everyone and how everyone in the world was a hypocrite.

"I think he was planning to shoot a group of people at random," said Elizabeth.

"How did the gun get under that man's foot?"

"The man came out of that bookstore there and hit the boy over the head with that book that's on the ground over there. Then he yanked the gun out of the boy's hand. The man put the gun down and put his foot on it. That was when my husband pinned the boy's arms back. Or maybe it was before. I'm not sure. I was so worried about my husband."

Elizabeth was anxious, thought Leon, but not hysterical. Her account was something Katy could rely on. Leon and the big man, interviewed separately, confirmed Elizabeth's story. Katy turned to face Tommy.

"Look at me. I am arresting you for menacing under Oregon Revised Statute 163.190. I am going to read you your Miranda rights and then take you to jail in Bend. The most important thing for you right now is not to say anything." Tommy didn't look like a fountain of information. Katy began, "You have the right to remain silent…."

Chapter 19

A Family Heirloom

Leon and Elizabeth went into the grocery store together and they stayed together with the cart the entire time they were in the store, like shipwrecked sailors clinging to a plank in the middle of an ocean. They'd been reminded that either of them could be taken away in an instant. There were people in the world who would do them harm without a second thought.

"I hate guns!" said Elizabeth to the windshield when they were back in their car. Leon drove carefully home. The familiarity of their house and the routine of putting away groceries made them feel secure. Elizabeth washed her face and called Sarah Chatham, a lifelong friend, to tell her what happened. Sarah was smart and practical. Her expressions of sympathy would be sincere but brief. Sarah would help Elizabeth develop her own thoughts about Tommy Westlake, the threat to Leon and herself, Leon's heroics—brave, thoughtless, surprisingly clever, or just damn lucky—and what resolutions Elizabeth might make going forward to keep herself safe and her mind functioning in a rational way. Sarah was an attorney, semi-retired, who would have time to drop what she was doing to talk with Elizabeth.

Leon retreated to his studio. It was by the grace of God that no one had been shot. Leon had a distant relationship with God, like one might have with a second cousin one rarely saw. Long before

Leon was born, when his family was driven out of Spain by Franco and the Fascists, the Catholic Church had strongly backed Franco. Since then the Martinez family had flatly renounced all organized religions. Still, Leon had decided, most people, including himself, needed to believe in God whether or not he really existed or even resembled the God they imagined. Sitting in his chair, he briefly thanked God for saving Elizabeth and himself.

It was time to get back to routines that assured him his world was on an even keel. It was not a time for trying to be creative. What routine task might quiet his mind?

Leon could clean his shotgun, something he did every six months whether he used it or not. He had not, in fact, fired it for several years. He used to go bird hunting east of Bend with his friends and with Dan. Most of bird hunting, and maybe the best part of it, was traipsing through the sagebrush, shotgun pointed down but at the ready, finding nothing for hours but anticipating every second the rush of wings and the rise of a pheasant, quail, partridge, or grouse. Wild turkeys made a good meal. Chukar were the most physically demanding because they escaped up steep slopes where it was hard to follow them. The ground and sky went on forever in the desert and the weather, in the chill of the morning or the lashing of a thunderstorm, made no allowances for the hunter or his mission.

And the dogs loved bird hunting. Sniffing along the ground hoping to scare up a bird. Proudly finding a downed grouse. The men and the dogs understood each other. They shared a common goal. The enthusiasm of one buoyed the enthusiasm of the other. Leon had put down his last dog five years ago.

Leon's shotgun had belonged to his grandfather and Leon had a great affection for it. It was a twelve bore two-barrel side-by-side made in Spain in the 1920s by a Basque company, Aguirre y Aranzabal. Leon kept it in excellent condition. Elizabeth wanted it out of the house.

"You never go hunting anymore," Elizabeth said over and over. "Some of your friends can't walk nine holes of golf, much less go hunting. Dan is much too busy with his family and his work to go hunting with you."

Leon quietly insisted he might go hunting again. He wanted to leave the gun to Dan. And he rationalized that he kept the gun for home protection.

"The person you're most likely to shoot is yourself, or maybe me, not some burglar," said Elizabeth. She read him statistics from the newspaper that showed the rate of suicides using guns kept in the home were higher than the rates of home invasions.

Leon protested that neither he nor Elizabeth were likely candidates for suicide or for getting into any kind of argument where he'd touch a gun. "It's a precaution," he said. He kept the shotgun in a special wall rack on his side of the bedroom closet. It was loaded so the first trigger pull would fire birdshot. That ought to disable and discourage any intruder. It would hurt like hell and throw the intruder off balance. Not to mention telling the interloper that Leon had a shotgun and could fire it again. The second trigger would fire buckshot. At the short range across the bedroom, the buckshot would almost certainly kill whoever it was.

A pistol in his bedside table would give Leon a quicker response to an intruder. But Elizabeth would have liked that even less than the shotgun. And Leon would have to aim more carefully with a pistol, something hard to do if awakened from a deep sleep in a room with the lights off. Finally, if he missed with a pistol, the bullet would go right through a plaster wall and could still kill somebody in the next room. Shotgun pellets would embed themselves in the wall.

Leon loved the shotgun as he might love a work of art or a family heirloom. Yet, he conceded, you couldn't tell where a gun would wind up or what harm it might do. Maybe Elizabeth was right. Maybe he should sell the shotgun or surrender it to the police. He would think about that while he took the gun out and cleaned it.

He brought the cleaning kit from a drawer and laid it on a counter in his studio. He broke the gun open and backed a cartridge out of each barrel. Something, he saw immediately, was very wrong. Both the cartridges were buckshot. Leon's mouth opened in disbelief as he checked and checked again. The cartridge on the right should have been birdshot. Had Dan borrowed his shotgun for a hunt and loaded it wrong when he put it back? Dan would have asked before he borrowed it. Dan would likely have a key to the house but he would have picked up the gun from Leon and handed it back to him, not simply walked off with it and deposited it back in the closet.

Elizabeth would never have touched the gun. The only other person with access was the lady who cleaned their house once a week. She wouldn't even go into Leon's half of the closet. Leon had to dust and vacuum that part of the closet himself. The woman lived a quiet life with her husband. What use could she have for a shotgun?

The only explanation left was that Leon had misloaded the gun himself. He was a careful man and, if he was relying on that gun to deal with an intruder, it was absolutely necessary to load the gun the same way he had always done. How could he make such a serious error? If he'd made that mistake, what other mistakes might he have made and not even recognized? Was his brain starting to go? If he was losing it, Elizabeth surely would have noticed. Did she decide not to tell him? Or had she told him and he'd forgotten? It didn't seem possible.

Had the gun been fired? Leon peered through the barrels but couldn't tell. They looked clean. He threaded a clean cloth through the end of his brass cleaning rod and ran it through the right-hand barrel. It came back with faint black and gray smears on it. Same result with a clean swab down the left-hand barrel. The results were not definitive, thought Leon, but it looked like the gun had been fired since Leon last cleaned it. It simply wasn't possible that he took out his gun, fired both barrels, reloaded, put it back without cleaning it, and then forgot that he had ever done it. He wasn't that looney.

Well, he decided, he'd ask Dan before he asked Elizabeth and the cleaning lady. He'd eventually figure out what happened. He cleaned the gun carefully, inside and out, checking that the last swabs he used came back clean in both barrels. He checked and double-checked that he loaded birdshot in the right barrel and buckshot in the left. Then he put the shotgun back in the rack and put the cleaning kit away.

Whether someone else had used the gun or he couldn't trust his own memory, the gun had become less predictable. He would give the gun to Dan if Dan would take it. If not, Leon would find a buyer who appreciated how unique and beautiful it was. A good gun to a good home.

Chapter 20

The White Car

"I saw that white SUV again," said Shanti when she called Carl. "It was parked across the street from my house last night and then it drove away. I've been studying SUV's since we talked before. It was a Toyota RAV 4."

This was progress, thought Carl. It was great that Shanti had narrowed the car down as far as she had. But Toyota RAV 4's were the most popular car in Oregon and white was the most popular color. Why couldn't it be a bright red Ferrari?

"I'm sorry I didn't get the license number but I'm pretty sure it was the same man driving it."

"How sure?" Carl wondered how the man, who could have only seen Shanti for a few seconds when he passed her the other way on Cottonwood Road on the morning of the shooting, could have found her.

"I think he must have seen the sign on the side of my car. It's a sign for my yoga studio. It sticks on my door with magnets. It doesn't have my address on it but he could have looked that up."

"When did you see him?"

"Last night at about ten. I closed the drapes while I was cleaning up the yoga studio. It's in the front of my house. Then I turned off the lights and opened the drapes to get the sun in the morning. He was parked across the street with his lights out."

"I'll get the Bend police to keep an eye on your house," said Carl. "Call 911 if you see him again and tell the 911 operator I said it was important to identify the car and the driver. Do you have a gun?"

"No," said Shanti. "Wouldn't think of it. I teach peace. I live peace."

"Isn't there a story in yoga about a warrior going into battle who discovers his chariot driver is a god? The god tells him to go ahead and fight?"

"Arjuna was a prince. I am a yoga instructor," said Shanti. "He had his place in the world and I have mine." Carl thought about the RAV4 driver. What was his place in the world? Shanti paused for a moment, then went on, "And you have your role too, detective, for which I am grateful." She was more philosophical than he was, Carl thought, but she was not necessarily more naïve.

"One more little thing I should tell you, though," Shanti said. "It's bothered me that I didn't tell you back at McDivot's. Elizabeth Martinez asked me not to mention it and I'm sure it's irrelevant. But telling you is the right thing to do. She and I got to the golf course at the same time. When she drove into the parking lot, her trunk was open. The lid was bumping up and down. She said it was probably illegal to drive like that and she'd just as soon I didn't mention it. So I didn't. She said she must have forgotten to latch it."

"I'll make a note of it. But don't worry about telling me. I might have stopped her if I'd seen her on the highway, to tell her to close the lid. But I can't give her a ticket if I didn't see it and I'm certainly not going to track her down at this point."

"Okay, I've done my duty," said Shanti with a laugh in her voice. "Thanks for listening."

"Call 911 if you see that man again."

"Will do."

Chapter 21

A Second Chance

Lab technicians were not known to be excitable. But the voice of Bob Fielding from the crime lab had actual exhilaration in it.

"Guess what, Carl!" said Bob.

"What?" said Carl, half feigning and half feeling excitement himself. He was sitting in his cubicle at the Sheriff's Department headquarters in Bend, scanning a printout of six hundred and sixteen white Toyota RAV4's registered in Deschutes County, trying to think of ways to sort and rank them for investigation. It was a dispiriting prospect.

"We have a boy in juvie for threatening to shoot people at the Sunriver Mall. The Sunriver Police think he was on his way to shoot up the whole grocery store." A sad story, thought Carl, but why was Bob so eager to tell him about it?

"The gun he was carrying?" Bob went on. "It's registered to Geoff Pennstead."

Carl sat up straight in his chair. "Well, that is exciting," said Carl. "Do we know how the kid got the gun?"

"Not so far. That's your department, not mine. But if you want to talk with him, he's in Juvenile Hall with his father and his lawyer waiting to meet with the district attorney."

"I want to be there. What's the boy's name?"

"Thomas Westlake. Wants to be called Tommy."

"I know that kid," said Carl, finally getting excited himself. "His father is renting a house right on top of the Pennstead murder. The kid said he didn't see anything but it sure looks to me like he did. I've got to go talk to him pronto."

Carl called juvenile hall. The assistant district attorney, Jocelyn Nelson, was set to meet with Tommy in fifteen minutes. Carl left his desk and walked seven hundred feet past the adult jail over to juvenile hall. Jocelyn was in an interview room waiting to talk to Tommy. Jocelyn wore a dark blue suit and short dark hair. She could be ice cold when the occasion required but sociable when the pressure was off. Today she was somewhere in between thoroughly professional but managing a smile when she saw Carl.

"What's he charged with?" asked Carl.

"Right now it's menacing with a firearm. But he may have had bigger things in mind, maybe going in to the Country Market, the grocery store, and shooting people at random."

"Like the East Side Safeway shooting in Bend," said Carl.

"A half-baked imitation of it," said Jocelyn. "He only had a pistol. Not that he couldn't have killed people with it. Fortunately he was stopped before he fired a shot. And he didn't wind up killing himself. We can't show yet that this Tommy Westlake did, in fact, plan a mass shooting. The Sunriver Police are searching the rental house he was in for diaries, videos, web postings, and whatever, to see if anything will indicate the boy's thoughts before he took the gun to the mall."

"I need to know how Tommy Westlake got the gun he was arrested with. It belonged to my murder victim."

"You can ask," said Jocelyn, "but I don't think he'll tell you out of public-spiritedness. His attorney is going to want something in return and I'm nowhere near ready to negotiate. I haven't even decided what to charge him with yet."

"How about some kind of general consideration for helping us on this one issue? Tell him the sooner he tells us and the more he tells us, the more you'll take that into account when he's tried and sentenced."

"I can try. I've worked with his attorney before. It's Craig

Hathaway and I think he'll trust me to come through. But promising leniency means we're giving something up on our side. How much is this information worth to you?"

"I'll tell you, we're floundering on this murder case. Nobody saw the shooting. We have no suspects. We haven't found the weapon—it was a shotgun, not this pistol. We found drugs at the victim's house and we don't know how they fit in. I think Tommy either saw the shooting or knows much more about it than he's told me so far."

"How do you know Tommy didn't kill Pennstead himself?"

"Can't be sure but the shotgun was fired from about five feet above the ground. Tommy Westlake is barely five feet tall."

"Okay, Carl. I hope this turns out to be worth it."

Craig Hathaway, Tommy's attorney, knocked on the door and ushered in Tommy and his father, both of them glowering.

Jocelyn introduced herself and asked the Westlakes if they remembered meeting Carl. Lester said yes and Tommy looked at Hathaway who nodded back to him. Tommy said yes as well.

"You are charged with menacing with a deadly weapon," said Jocelyn in an even tone, as though she were telling a student which homeroom he was assigned to. "More charges may be coming or the charges may change. We have security camera footage and multiple eyewitnesses. I think you will be found guilty if this case goes to trial but you should listen to your attorney, Mr. Hathaway. He can give you his opinion on the likelihood of a guilty verdict if he hasn't already. Since you have no prior arrests or convictions, the court has a lot of room to decide what becomes of you if you are found guilty—whether it's probation, a fine, or time in detention. In making the decision, the judge will consider, among other things, how cooperative you have been not only in your own case, but in another matter."

"Hold on a minute," said Craig Hathaway. "It's much too early to be talking about the sentencing. My client hasn't even had a bail hearing, much less a trial and a conviction. What's the value of a vague promise for leniency? Who says you won't drop the case anyway or he'll be acquitted?"

"The timing is critical," said Jocelyn. "Tommy might help Detective

Breuninger solve a different crime, a murder. We would very much take that help into consideration when making our sentencing recommendation for Tommy. Of course, if Detective Breuninger finds the murderer without Tommy's help then any deal on leniency is off the table."

"What do you want Tommy to tell you?" asked Craig.

Carl answered. "How did he obtain the gun? What was he doing and what did he see or hear before, during, and after the shooting on East Cascade? Everything he knows about it."

Jocelyn added, "Very little of what we want Tommy to testify about is directly relevant to Tommy's own case. We've got video and witnesses showing that Tommy brought the gun to the mall. He can't deny he had it. A trial would hinge on whether he threatened people with the gun and I think it is very clear that he did. Have you seen the video I authorized the court to show you?"

"I watched it," said Craig without further comment. "I need to discuss your suggestion with Tommy and his father."

"We'll be around for fifteen minutes," said Jocelyn. "If you need more time than that, give me a call and we'll arrange a time to meet."

Carl and Jocelyn found an empty interview room to wait in. Jocelyn had emails to read and a phone call to make. Carl sat patiently until Jocelyn paused in her whirl of activity.

"What do you think Craig will recommend?" he asked.

"He'll make sure they understand the deal but I don't think he'll recommend either way—whether to take it or not," said Jocelyn. "I'm betting on the father. He'll see that Tommy will probably be convicted and he'll want to do whatever he can to keep his son out of jail."

"I want the kid to talk," said Carl, "but I'm not sure how much difference it will make. Are we giving away too much?"

"The sentence is up to the judge. He may be lenient whether I recommend it or not. Or he may completely ignore what I say."

Craig Hathaway stuck his head in the door.

"We'll take your offer," he said.

"Does Tommy need a break before Carl questions him?"

"He says not. He's amped up. He'll be glad to get it off his chest."

Carl sat across from Tommy in the interview room with Tommy flanked by his father and Craig Hathaway. Jocelyn sat beside Carl.

"Okay, Tommy, why don't you tell us in your words everything that happened the morning of the shooting on East Cascade?"

Chapter 22

What Tommy Knew

On the morning of the murder, Tommy was alone in the house, he told Carl and Jocelyn. His father had left for a golf game. The father, Lester Westlake, said he left right around 7:00 a.m. Tommy had been sitting on a stool in his kitchen eating a bowl of Honey Nut Cheerios when he thought he heard a gunshot. He was not experienced with firearms, except in movies and videogames, but he said it sounded more like an explosion than a sharp snap. It didn't sound like firecrackers.

Tommy got up immediately to see where the sound came from. He went out the front door of the house facing Falling Star Road, and, seeing no people or moving vehicles, ran around the side of the house to look through the trees toward East Cascade Road. Up the road to his right, a man was lying on the road whose head was "messed up." Further up the road was a silver Mercedes sedan parked off to the side. Then a white SUV came along the road from Tommy's left, going full speed, and ran right over the body before continuing up the road.

Tommy ran to the man lying in the road. "To see if I could help," he said.

Carl thought Tommy was attracted to the excitement of a real-world murder but Carl wrote what Tommy said. A pistol was lying on the road near the man. Tommy picked it up by the grip and put it in the kangaroo pocket of his sweatshirt, still holding onto it.

Tommy ran to his house but looked back toward East Cascade to check whether anyone had seen him. He saw a green SUV come along the road from the left, from the direction of Beaver Drive, and stop. *That would have been the man who called 911,* Carl thought. After a few minutes a police car arrived from the right and Tommy went back inside his house so no one would see him.

Tommy hid the gun under his bed but he got it out frequently to look at it while his father was out of the house or sleeping. Carl asked him what he thought about while he was looking at the gun but Craig Hathaway, Tommy's attorney, cut off the question before Tommy could answer.

Tommy could not describe the drivers in the white SUV, or the green SUV—not even whether they were big or little, male or female. He didn't know if there were passengers in either of the cars. He hadn't looked at the license plates. From the time he went outside his house to the time he got back to it, running both ways, he hadn't seen any other cars except the Mercedes. He hadn't seen any people except the dead man.

Carl had hoped for more but did have two new pieces to put in the puzzle. The first was that Geoff Pennstead had brought a loaded gun with him to the crime scene. Given the medical examiner's finding that Geoff might have had something in his hand when he was shot, he was likely holding the pistol. Why hadn't he fired it when his killer pointed a shotgun at him? Maybe Geoff didn't think the killer would actually pull the trigger. Maybe his killer thought Geoff was going to shoot first.

The second thing Carl learned was that a white SUV, very possibly the white RAV-4 that Shanti Sargeant saw on Cottonwood Road and again outside her house, was driven by someone desperate enough, or vicious enough, to run over a dead body. Carl would bet the driver was also the person who remotely shut off the gas in Pennstead's car and then shot him.

But why did that person want to stop Pennstead? Was Geoff carrying the money he'd told Kearnan he was going to take to the bank?

If so, how did the shooter know that? Did he plan to shoot Pennstead or only scare him with the shotgun?

And why a shotgun? Because it looked more intimidating? Because a pistol could be identified by the markings on the bullet but a shotgun could not? Because the shooter knew he wasn't a good shot and a pistol might miss?

Carl tried to imagine how the scene might have played out. If the shooter was the driver in the white SUV, that person would have had to either run back to his car or back up his car so the car could first appear to Tommy, not next to Pennstead's body, but coming fast from the left.

Yet Tommy had not seen any of that. He'd only seen the SUV run over Pennstead's body and drive off.

Tommy's statement did raise the priority of finding the RAV4 that Shanti had seen leaving the area. Carl would find some way to prioritize the list of owners and ask the Sheriff to have deputies interview as many of them as possible. The citizens would resent being asked where they were on a given date and time. It was nobody's business. And, of course, the car owner who had actually run over Geoff Pennstead would say he was nowhere near Sunriver on that morning. Carl knew trouble would expand like a balloon if the press learned about it. All but one of the people on the list were innocent. The list sounded like something the secret police would have in another country.

But someday, somehow, a name on the list would match up with some other clue, some other scrap of information. And that might crack the case wide open. The SUV driver might be the shooter or he might at least have seen the shooting. And Carl had something to hold over that person when he found him. Abusing a corpse was illegal in Oregon. Running over Geoff Pennstead's body in the light of day was a clear instance of abuse.

The law seemed a little irrational to Carl. No one was actually injured. But abuse did not square with the "generally accepted standards of the community" and that was enough to make it a felony.

Chapter 23

Race for Glory

"Dad, I hope you can do me a big favor." The call was from Dan and it had been a while since Leon's son, with his own self-sufficient life, had asked his father for anything. Leon and Elizabeth saw Dan and his wife, Amy, frequently, and sometimes babysat four-year-old Emma who adored them. Dan and Amy lived in a newer Bend neighborhood called Northwest Crossing.

"Dad, I've been training to swim in the Cascade Lakes Races next week. The problem is they can't find enough people for the safety patrol—you know, people in kayaks to help swimmers if they need it. If they don't get enough kayaks, they'll have to cancel the whole race. I'm hoping you can help out. It's this Saturday morning up at Elk Lake. Have you got time to do that?"

"I have the time but I don't think I'd know how to rescue anybody."

"It's not like anybody's going to drown. It's just that somebody might need to hang onto the kayak and rest. And if somebody really is in trouble, you wave your paddle in the air and the motorboat will come help out."

"You sure about that? I thought they didn't allow motorboats on Elk Lake."

"They make an exception for the race. Anyhow, can you do it? I'll come down and pick you up at 8:00 a.m. We can put your kayak on top of my car. They're serving hot dogs and hamburgers after the race and then we come home."

"Okay," said Leon, "love to do it. Is Amy coming?"

"Not this time. Emma has a playdate. How about Mom?"

"I'll ask her."

Leon and Elizabeth had two kayaks hanging from pulleys in the garage. The kayaks hadn't come down the last two years and Leon would have to get an annual boat permit before he took one of them up to Elk Lake. He was pleased and excited to spend time with his son, to support all the swimmers, and be out on the water again in the mountains. He would need his life vest, his hat with a wide brim, and plenty of suntan lotion. He would wear swimming trunks under a long-sleeved fishing shirt and bring swimming goggles in case the kayak tipped over.

Elizabeth said she'd as soon not go.

"You go and have a good time. But it will take all morning to watch two short races where you can't tell one swimmer from another until they come out of the water. Sometimes not until they're standing in front of you. Wish him well for me."

Leon sat down to read the local paper, *The Bulletin*, after the call from Dan. He read the paper every day. Some of the stories were very much the same—moving the homeless to better locations, the eternal conflict between water for farmers and water for fish. On a happier note, the local high school sports teams always did well in statewide competition. The girls' North Bend Little League team were champions of the entire West Coast Conference.

Leon only read the obituaries of people he knew. That was happening more often now, as teachers he'd known reached the end of their years. On this day, the paper ran an obituary of Geoff Pennstead. Earlier articles had been about his murder. The obituary was about his life, mostly about his career. Leon guessed the words had been written by someone who worked with him. Dara wouldn't have her act together or take the time to write an obituary, though she might have helped.

Before Pennstead had become a private investor, he had been at Deschutes River Bank, the same bank that Elizabeth had worked for.

He had risen in the ranks of the bank in Portland but had spent several years in the seventies as branch manager in Bend. That was back when the bank had only one local branch. Later, when Elizabeth became branch manager and then regional manager, she grew the bank to three Bend locations.

Leon checked the years Pennstead had been in Bend. They covered the time of an event that neither Elizabeth nor Leon had mentioned for over forty years. Leon had put the man's name out of his mind long ago. But it was a small branch back then and Geoff Pennstead had to have been Elizabeth's boss. Geoff Pennstead was the manager who had coerced her.

Elizabeth was a teller back then, the best and most diligent teller they had. She had gone through all the training to become a loan officer. Geoff had encouraged her, even mentored her. He had a habit of putting his hand on her back while they were looking at a ledger together but he stopped doing that when she told him it bothered her.

At her annual review, Elizabeth anticipated he would tell her that her promotion had been approved back in Portland. He asked her to come into his office after the bank closed. His office was the only one that had a door and blinds that could be pulled down. The review was positive, even glowing. Best of all, her promotion had been approved and only needed Geoff's signature to become official. The two pages finalizing the promotion lay on his desk.

"One more thing you have to do," he said. "You have to give me a blow job."

"You're kidding."

"I'm not. A few minutes and you're out of here with a new position and a big raise. Otherwise you're not. It could be another year. Maybe longer."

This was back in the 1970s. The "Me Too" movement did not exist. The law, bank management, and even her colleagues at the bank would tell her she'd have no luck complaining about Pennstead's behavior. Everyone in authority would say it was a case of "he said, she said" and they would do nothing. Pennstead would say Elizabeth made the whole thing up. He never threatened her, never propositioned her. She was simply angry that she didn't get the promotion she wanted.

Nonetheless, Elizabeth thought rapidly, if she declined, she would always be a threat to Geoff. She could wait for her moment, wait for him to proposition some other woman who was foolhardy enough to speak up. And then she could strike. The problem would be that Geoff would know she was a threat. He would seize any opportunity he could to hold her back, to even get her dismissed.

Elizabeth presented a kindly exterior to the world. It was sincere. She wanted other people to be happy, to generally get what they wanted. She was better with clients than Geoff or anyone else in the branch. But she had a calculating heart, a banker's heart.

She would take the promotion. And someday, somehow, she would make Geoff Pennstead suffer for it. She would get her revenge.

"You'll never tell anyone. And you'll never ask me for anything like this again." Elizabeth bored her eyes directly into his.

He smiled, not a smug smile of victory, but the friendly smile of having concluded a business deal good for both parties.

"Agreed," he said. On the credenza behind his desk was a washcloth and two glasses, one full and one empty. He'd thought of everything.

"Sign first," said Elizabeth. He did sign but he kept the document on this desk.

"Lock the door," said Geoff. When she turned back from the door, his pants were down to his ankles and he'd turned his chair sideways to make room for her. She didn't look him in the face.

As he grew more animated, he reached for her breast and she pushed his hand away. He pressed his hand on her head and she let it be. It was almost over.

She stood as Geoff lay back in his chair, slowing the rhythm of his breathing. Elizabeth snatched the paper from his desk, looked Geoff in the eye, and spat the contents of her mouth into his face. He laughed.

"Congratulations on your promotion," he said as she walked out the door.

Leon was the only person Elizabeth had ever told. For days she scrubbed her face frequently, brushed her teeth six times a day, and washed out her mouth with Listerine. Leon was upset too, wandering around the house aimlessly, forgetting what he was doing. But he comforted her, hugged her, kissed her, and took her to bed.

He was sure the boss's name was Geoff Pennstead. Had Elizabeth finally exacted her revenge? It was hard to imagine. Should he even ask her? She'd be terribly hurt if she learned her husband suspected she would be capable of murder. If he was ever going to ask her, it wouldn't be now.

Dan was going to swim in both events on Saturday, the 500 meter at 9:15 a.m. and the 1500 meter at 11:30. The 1500 meter was the official Oregon Open Water Championship for the distance.

Both race courses were triangles, starting and ending at the same point at the south end of the lake. Dan and Leon jammed their car between rocks and trees where they wouldn't block any other car and slid the kayak off the roof. They carried the kayak down to the gray-brown sand and gravel beach and left the boat there while Dan went to check in.

Leon wished he could paint the brightly lit scene before him, though he'd already seen far too many paintings of forested lakes with mountains in the background. Elk Lake stretched away from him a mile and a half to the north. South Sister towered beyond the lake, snow fields still swooping down from the crater at the top. Air-filled buoys to mark the course rode high in the water, like giant yellow and red pumpkins in a field. The swimmers and spectators, over a hundred of them, were sitting on towels or beach chairs or else milling on the shore, some wearing no more than their bathing suits though the air was cool, and others wrapped in towels or huddled in oversized sweatshirts. If he were to paint the scene, the green of the trees, the blue of the water and sky, and the black and white of South Sister, it would be offset by the bright buoys and the riot of colors in the coverings of the swimmers.

The water was sixty-eight degrees but swimmers were already out in it, warming up for the race. The single kayak on the lake wasn't enough to watch all of them. Leon strapped on his life jacket and dragged his boat into the lake until the water rose to his knees. He sat down in the kayak and lifted his legs in. He and Elizabeth used to go on paddle excursions five times or more each summer, on the Cascade Lakes and on the Little and Big Deschutes. Their kayaks, including this one, were long and slim, built for speed across flat water. Because they were narrow, they were tippy. If a swimmer needed a rest, Leon would loudly urge him or her to hang onto the bow of the kayak, not the side. If a swimmer needed serious help, Leon would probably wind up in the water with him.

He paddled onto the lake, farther out than the other kayak. He didn't think swimmers needed to come out so far to warm up but swimmers were far from shore, oblivious to whether a kayak was near enough to help them if they needed. They assumed they wouldn't need any help and they were probably right. There was something primitive about swimming alone in a cold mountain lake that was like being on foot in the desert. Away from all the inventions of civilization, away from other people, a lake swimmer was little different from his or her ancestor doing the same thing a hundred thousand years earlier.

Two women were treading water and talking. Their voices carried over the water and Leon could hear every word. He paddled away from them so he wouldn't be eavesdropping.

People were gathering on the beach and Leon headed back to shore. The volunteers running the race held a briefing for the swimmers. The man with the motorboat ran a briefing for the safety patrol, a group of eight people who had not been trained, tested, or qualified but who had simply signed up and brought a kayak.

"The first rule," said the man who led the safety patrol, "is don't become a problem yourself. Don't tip over. If you get dehydrated or tired, come back in. Don't get too close to the swimmers unless they're struggling or they ask to rest. If they need help, call it in on the radio." The man passed out walkie-talkies and briefly explained how to use them—on, off, and push to talk. He assigned positions on the race course in the same order the group was standing around him on the beach. Leon got the first position on the middle leg of the race, the leg that did not begin or end on the shore but went from buoy to buoy between the outgoing leg and the return leg. He got back in his kayak and paddled out a hundred yards where he could watch the beginning of the 500-meter race. The swimmers went off fifteen seconds apart in order of the seed time they had entered when they signed up for the race, fastest first.

Even with a swim cap on Dan, at six-foot-four, was easy to spot in the line on the shore. Leon watched him run into the water and dive. After that it was hard to make anyone out among the black swim caps, the splashing water, and the churning arms. Leon turned his kayak toward his assigned position. He could paddle much faster than the first swimmer could swim. He passed the turning buoy and faced the kayak around to wait for the swimmers. The first four around the buoy were men but the fifth was a woman.

"Good for her," said Leon to himself. He saw Dan go past neck and neck with another man. He hoped Dan had closed the fifteen second gap with the man in front of him and not the other way around.

"Hey, kayak number 3, get back in position," he heard over the radio. "You need to be back by the buoy." Leon had unconsciously followed the swimmers. The man was right but Leon knew the problem wasn't serious. He was still watching all the swimmers he was supposed to. He was sure the voice came from the other man watching this leg of the race. The man wore a ranger type hat and had a yellow kayak with multiple pieces of equipment and sacks of supplies strapped to it. The man took himself very seriously. Leon paddled back toward the turning buoy.

The winning time was four minutes fifty-five seconds. The last swimmer finished in less than twenty minutes. Dan said he thought he had done well but the individual results wouldn't be posted for another half hour. He and his father sat on a log overlooking the lake. Leon had serious questions he wanted to ask Dan, about whether he borrowed the shotgun, about what Dan's mother might have done, about the law and what his mother should do now. For that matter, what Leon should do now. But now was not the time. Leon would wait for the drive home.

"Well, I'm going to go warm up again," said Dan after a while. He talked with some other racers on his way to the water.

Officials held another briefing for the safety patrol before the second race and Leon was assigned the same position again but on the longer course.

"This will be a mass start," said the man with the motorboat. "The men will start first and they are supposed to sort themselves out on the beach so the faster swimmers are in the front. The gun goes off and it's every man for himself. We'll have the motorboat nearby in case anyone gets injured or starts breathing water. After that, the field should spread out. Then the women will start together the same way.

"The swimmers have been reminded not to hit or hinder each other," the man told the kayakers. "You're not a policeman but if you see one swimmer interfering with another, tell them to cut it out. And report them when you get back in here." The swimmers had identification numbers on their arms written with grease pens.

Leon watched the start again, this time a much bigger splash of water as dozens of swimmers hit the water, four, six, or eight at a time. He had plenty of time to paddle out further to his position. He remembered not to follow the swimmers but to stay in position. The swimmers were surprisingly spread out after having started in two huge groups. One man, standing out from all the rest, was swimming butterfly and seemed intent on finishing the whole 1500 meters with it.

One woman, in the middle of the pack of women, stopped suddenly after rounding the first buoy, appearing to adjust her goggles. She began again but swam awkwardly, turning her head high to the side with every breath. Leon watched her carefully, trying to determine how much trouble she was in and whether he should approach her to help. After five strokes, he saw she didn't have her goggles on at all. She was trying to swim without putting her face down in the water. The strap holding her goggles on her head had broken and she couldn't repair it. He could help her, though she might be disqualified if anyone saw him doing it. No matter. She wasn't leading the pack and must be in the race for fun, though she wasn't having much fun at the moment. He maneuvered his kayak across her path and dangled his own goggles barely above the water where he thought she would see them. She changed course to swim around his boat. He goosed the kayak a few feet forward and she gave him an angry look until she saw the goggles and stopped.

"Don't touch the boat," Leon reminded her. She paddled toward him.

"Thank you," she said before she took the goggles and smiled a bright smile at him. She was a young woman with a narrow face. No longer looking at Leon, she tread water while she put the goggles on and pulled them tight. "Thanks a million," she said and gave him another smile. "What a difference."

"Good luck," he said and backed the kayak away. She put her head down, gave a kick, and swam past him. With a cap on her head and her face streaming water, he doubted he could recognize her again. But she was wearing a green and yellow swimsuit. He might get his goggles back at the end of the race.

Leon kept his station until the last swimmers passed him then followed them around the course. Far ahead he could see the man doing the butterfly all the way to the end of the course.

The woman came up to him as he beached the kayak and handed his goggles back to him.

"Thank you," she said again.

"You're welcome," said Leon, "glad I could help. Good luck." She went off to join whoever she'd come with.

Dan came in fifth among men age 30 to 34.

"Not bad for a hard-working husband and father," said Leon.

"I can't complain," said Dan.

Leon fished a dry towel from the kayak and handed it to his son. They stayed long enough to get hot dogs and lemonade with the other swimmers and volunteers. They strapped the kayak on top of Dan's car and slowly maneuvered the car out to the highway.

Dan drove Leon and the kayak downhill the forty minutes to Leon's house. Dan might get distracted or even upset when Leon finally asked his questions and told him what he knew. Leon began as they passed Devil's Lake.

"Did you happen to borrow the shotgun this spring?"

"Dad, I haven't been hunting in years. I would have told you if I borrowed it."

"That's what I thought," said Leon. "Unless I'm losing my mind, somebody borrowed it, shot both barrels, and put it back in the closet without cleaning it. It's the strangest thing."

"Wasn't me," said Dan, not expressing surprise or concern. He was like that.

"Have you seen any signs of my getting Alzheimer's?"

"No, Dad, I have not." Dan laughed. "Has Mom? Or you?"

"Aside from this gun, I haven't noticed anything. Your mother hasn't mentioned anything special."

Leon had wanted to share his concern about Elizabeth's conceivable connection to Pennstead's murder. But he could not bring himself to tell Dan about Elizabeth's long-ago incident with Geoff Pennstead. It's not the sort of thing a man needs to hear about his mother. Leon abandoned his plan to tell Dan about his worries for now.

They drove silently a mile past an area that had been burned six years earlier. When they got to healthy forest, Leon had resolved to talk with Elizabeth. But Elizabeth was out when he got home. Dan helped Leon unload the kayak. He declined the offer of a shower but took a Gatorade with him on his drive home to Bend. Leon showered and changed his clothes to go pick up Gabriel and Maria Isabel at Redmond Airport.

So far this summer, the weather had been beautiful. Warm, sunny, and clear—the kind of weather that made people want to visit Sunriver. A few days had a smoky haze from forest fires far away—in Washington or Canada or on the other side of the Cascades. But never enough smoke to keep golfers off the golf course or stop hikers from climbing the mountains. The smoke from distant fires had disappeared entirely for Gabriel and Maria's visit.

"We saw green fields as we were landing," said Gabriel. "I thought you said it was forests to the west and desert to the east. I didn't expect to see so much green."

"Irrigation," said Leon. "The water comes in canals from the Deschutes River. Before the railroad and the lumber companies came here, people thought the future was in agriculture. The lumber mills are gone but farming and ranching are still here."

Leon never hinted at remembering the week in San Francisco with Maria and neither did either of his guests. But Leon remembered that week both tenderly and guiltily. He wondered if Maria thought of it as well.

Even in the midst of passion, she'd kept a place for Gabriel. On the second morning, naked and warm, Leon had trailed his kisses down slowly from Maria's neck to her shoulder to her chest above her breasts, each of which he licked until she moaned. He descended further down her rib cage to her stomach and belly, kissing across her pubis from one side to the other. He stroked her thighs and pressed them outwards to reveal the channel where his kisses would please her most.

"No," Maria said softly, not yielding to Leon's pressure. "That is for Gabriel. It is what he can do. Give me your cock."

What had he saved for Elizabeth? Nothing. Well, that wasn't true. He had saved his heart. He had saved his commitment to love her until he died.

Gabriel and Maria were good guests. Elizabeth and Leon, as always, were good hosts. The refrigerator was stuffed with choices. Towels were abundant. Dinners at home and out were all good. They canoed on the river and rode through the woods on very gentle horses. They visited Benham Falls on their way to Bend and the High Desert Museum. Their tour of the Cascade Lakes was capped with a ride up the chairlift at Mt. Bachelor. Mountain bikers flew down the slope beneath them at what seemed a terrifying speed.

Chapter 24

Sleeping in Seattle

Dylan Crabtree went to work at the tire shop the day after he returned to Seattle. His black eye was healing but was still noticeable. He was tired and his vision was not back to one hundred percent. But he was especially careful and the boss was glad to have him back.

Another tire man told Dylan that two men came looking for him while he was away.

"Tattoos up the ying-yang," the fellow employee said. "The boss told them you weren't here but they didn't want to believe him. Kept looking toward the back of the shop. They hung around in the parking lot until the boss told them to get out of here. Said they were bad for business. I don't know what they said to him but one of them made a move like spitting into the air. After a minute or two, they went away."

Dylan knew who they were, guys he knew in prison, one of them a cellmate. Dylan had kept on good terms with them back then. It was good policy. But he wanted nothing to do with them now. Their trajectory would lead him back to more crimes and then to prison. His trajectory, he hoped to God, would be in a better direction.

When he saw Alma the next Tuesday, he didn't know whether to tell her about the two men. If they made trouble for him it would be better to have told Alma ahead of time. But even mentioning them would cause Alma to have more doubts about him, to make her more vigilant, more restrictive, and more likely to recommend his probation be cancelled for something else that might go wrong. He decided to tell her and hope she would understand. And he hadn't actually talked with them.

Dylan had missed only two of his night school classes and he asked one of his accounting classmates what he had missed. She was a woman his age who had never said anything in class but appeared to be diligent about taking notes. Her name was Marilee—short hair, plainly dressed, and no make-up. As if she were hiding her femininity. They found a copy machine and she gave him three pages of notes from the week before. Neither of them wore a wedding ring.

"It's important I do well in these classes," said Dylan. "I want to get a business degree so I can be a manager somewhere. I work for Les Schwab Tires and got this black eye from work." He didn't want Marilee to think he'd been in a fight.

"I'm working for a business degree too," said Marilee. She said she was a cashier at Safeway and wanted to do more.

"Do you want to get a cup of coffee?" asked Dylan.

Marilee took a moment to answer. "I don't think so," she said. "I'm getting a divorce and my head is not in a place to be spending time with men. Any men."

"Too bad. Can I ask you again in a little while?"

"Maybe. I'll let you know."

The class would only meet two more times.

"Can you give me your phone number?" asked Dylan.

"No," she said. "But you can give me yours. And then we'll see."

They were both damaged goods, thought Dylan. She didn't know he was an ex-con and he'd have to tell her. But even the hope that Marilee would call, that they would talk, that they might form some kind of relationship, meant Dylan was on the track to be a human being again.

Dylan's cellmate and another tattooed wonder came to the tire shop two days later. Dylan made a beeline for the restroom where the superintendent found him.

"No visitors at work," said the boss, "you know the rules. No phone calls and no socializing. And your buddies keep eyeing the tool chest like they might see something they like."

"You gotta help me here," said Dylan. "Please. I didn't ask them to come and I don't want anything to do with them. Can you tell them I don't want to see them? Tell them to leave and not come back. You've got them on the surveillance camera, right? Tell them you'll arrest them for trespassing."

"I don't want to get involved with all that. Going to court. Trying to prove this or that. Telling the owners we've got to hire lawyers. Hell no. They're your friends. You tell them to get lost."

"They're not my friends. They're ex-cons on probation. If you say you'll call the police, they'll be scared to death."

"Okay. We'll try that. But if they keep coming back, then you're the source of the problem. There have to be consequences."

"Just tell them you'll call the police."

The shop had four garage doors at the front that stayed open in all but the worst weather. There was a red line on the floor across each doorway and a sign that said "Employees Only Beyond This Point." The boss told the men they had already broken the rules, that standing in the parking lot while not here on business was trespassing, and that if they came back, he would call the police. They left.

Dylan went back to work. That evening Marilee called him.

Chapter 25

An Evil Light

I should have started shooting the second they stopped me. That's what Tommy Westlake kept thinking. *I should have shot Mr. Martinez, then Mrs. Martinez, then anybody else who tried to stop me. Then I should have run to the coffee place. People were sitting outside and waiting in line. Some of them were too old or too fat to run fast. If I had any bullets left, I could have gone into the grocery store. Then I'd stand outside and wait for the police. I wouldn't have any bullets left but people wouldn't know that. They'd be scared. The police would try to sneak up on me, hiding behind corners of buildings or cars in the parking lot. I'd take careful aim at one of them and then they'd shoot me. Maybe a sniper. Maybe all sorts of guns all at once. Then they'd find I had no bullets. They'd been scared of nothing. Just me standing there, out in the open, with an empty gun. What a bunch of idiots.*

They'd handcuffed Tommy and taken him to jail. He'd had a psych evaluation. He knew how to act like a normal kid. He swore he never intended to hurt anyone. He simply liked having a gun. The police searched the house his father had rented and found no more guns, no angry notes, no descriptions of mass shootings. The court released Tommy into his father's custody with a strict warning not to go anywhere near a weapon. They recommended he see a psychologist. In other words, they treated him like a child.

What would Lara Croft do? She'd find another weapon. Even

more deadly. Tommy could be creative. He could think. He searched the house. There were knives in the kitchen but the biggest knives were gone. His father must have hidden them. There were tools for the fireplace. There were his father's golf clubs. There was a shovel in the garage but no axe. You could kill a person with any of these things but probably only one, maybe two, before somebody fought you. That would take time. Besides, you'd look ridiculous trying to kill people with a shovel. That would be proof you needed a psychologist. Or maybe a whole new brain.

His father's car. He could drive it at high speed into the water park. All those people in bathing suits, lying in the sun, thinking the world is safe for them. That the world was made for them. That troubles were far away. Or maybe rev the engine and drive right across the lawn by the resort during a concert. One minute you're sitting on the grass enjoying the music and all of a sudden, reality comes crashing in on you, people screaming, bodies flying, and these tons of steel cutting through the crowd and headed right your way. You try to get up and run but you're not fast enough. It's too late. A quick hard lesson in how cruel life can be. How other people can't help you. Too busy looking out for themselves. How even God can't help you. It would take someone like Tommy to teach you that lesson. Someone who saw the truth. Someone who saw how rotten the world truly was.

But, if he were being truthful, and the one thing Tommy thought he could cling to was his willingness to face the truth as he saw it, he had never driven a car. It wasn't that hard. But he could mess it up. Something simple—like steering too sharp or not turning enough. He would have to learn while he was doing it. Simply backing out of the driveway. How exactly do you know how much to turn the wheel?

He sat in his father's car and stared at the dashboard. He knew what most of the buttons and switches did and he could figure out the others. It was like a video game. But the wrong button could ruin his whole plan. He lifted the trunk lid and looked in. The battery was sealed. He couldn't get at the acid inside. A tire iron was under the floor mat with the spare tire. But that would be as stupid a weapon as the shovel. There was a box of flares for marking an accident or a breakdown. That was no help. Were people going to stand there while Tommy lit a flare and tried to burn them to death?

Maybe he could burn down a house. Or the lodge at the resort. Or the so-called "Great Hall" that was built out of logs. People were supposed to love it because it was so old, built before Sunriver ever existed. People would be shocked if he burned it down. People would be sad. People would be mad. They'd be upset. But they wouldn't be scared. He wanted people to be scared.

People were scared of fire. But in a building, they could always run outside. What they were really scared of was a forest fire. Forest fires were on the television all the time, newspeople guessing how big each fire would get and where it would go. People drove past burning trees to escape, flames swirling around their cars. What if a big fire came to Sunriver and burned it to the ground?

But, Tommy figured, the fire couldn't start in Sunriver. Someone would see it when it was small and call the fire department. And the fire station was in the center of Sunriver. They would get there in five minutes and put the fire out. Of course, you could start fires at night and run from house to house lighting them. But still, the fire might not get very far before the fire department came. And most of Sunriver would sleep through it. No fear. No mass panic.

What Tommy imagined was an enormous forest fire racing toward Sunriver, growing and growing before anyone noticed it. It should start in the forest west of the river where no one would see him light it or stop him. Somebody would see the smoke soon enough and call the fire department. So it couldn't be a small fire. A single truck could put out a small fire. It needed to be big and it needed to start big. It should start in multiple places at the same time or close to the same time. It needed to get up into the trees, not just creep along the ground burning pine needles.

How long before they sounded the sirens? Sunriver had five sirens on towers spread across the community. Tommy looked it up online. And the county would send text messages to everyone in the area who had registered for them. That would be mostly residents but some of the tourists as well. Would the text say get ready to evacuate or would it say evacuate now? Tommy signed up to receive alerts so he could tell how seriously people were taking the danger. If they got to "evacuate now," some people would go crazy. They would leave their houses wide open and drive much too fast on the curvy Sunriver Roads. There would be crashes. Injuries. Panic.

If it was big enough, the fire would jump the river and burn Sunriver, at least part of it and maybe even all of it. Houses and cars burning. People, the slow ones, the stupid ones, the left behind, could die. People, happy and ignorant the day before, would flee. By car, by bike, and on foot, smoke all around them getting thicker, not knowing whether the flames would catch their feet, singe their socks, leap to their shirts, their hair, their mouths, their eyes.

They might blame Sunriver, or the fire department, or the forest keepers, or lightning, their own plans that brought them here, some sin they had committed, or the bad luck that had dogged them all their lives. But they would know some force, perhaps a single individual, was out to get them. Someone or something they had betrayed, or slighted, or simply ignored when they shouldn't have. That something was powerful. That something had calculated its revenge and that revenge was happening now.

Tommy had the flares and he had the bicycle his father had rented for him. The air was dry and the forest was dry. Oregon already had five forest fires going, all started by lightning in remote areas.

A wind from the west would help. It would blow the flames across the river and into Sunriver. In the summer, the wind was from the west more than half the time. Tommy looked it up. And the next day would fit the pattern—wind from the west at six miles per hour.

Tommy got up at five a.m. and ate a bowl of cereal by flashlight. He didn't want to wake his father up. He didn't wash the bowl or flush the toilet so there would be no sound of running water. With fifteen flares, two energy bars, and a bottle of water in his backpack, he left the house at five thirty. He pedaled west though Sunriver down to the pedestrian and bike bridge over the Deschutes. It was called the Cardinal Landing Bridge and it was about a mile north of the airport. He'd never ridden the bike that far before but he'd studied the maps carefully. He'd memorized the forest roads, closed to vehicle traffic, on the other side of the bridge.

He didn't completely trust his memory and there were no signs for the roads. As he climbed the rise through the forest on the far side of the bridge, he had to guess what road he was on.

And the forest was not what he'd imagined. The trees were spaced apart and the lowest branches were ten feet off the ground. He'd expected thick vegetation with fallen trees and dead branches littering the forest floor. There were patches of manzanita, bitterbrush, and wild current but most of the ground was bare with a scattering of pine needles. Nonetheless, here and there, in clearings in the trees, there were slash piles—enormous piles of dead trees and trimmed branches—as if someone truly wanted bonfires. The forest service planned to burn the slash piles on cool wet days with men and equipment all around them to control them. Summer days, like this one, were much too hot and dry for burning.

Tommy decided to light every slash pile he could, one after another. He would ride through the forest to every pile he could find. The fires would get so big, he thought, they would catch the standing trees on fire too. It would be too much for the firefighters. The fire would get bigger and bigger before they could stop it.

But where was the wind? The air sat self-satisfied in the forest. A caterpillar could have outrun it. Should Tommy wait for the wind or get cracking? He'd come this far. If he didn't act now he didn't know what would happen. His father would discover him gone and ask him what he'd been up to. If his father simply returned the bike to the bike shop, Tommy would miss his chance entirely. He had to go now and hope his plan would work.

Where to start? Tommy couldn't see Sunriver through the trees and he wasn't sure where he was. He knew he had come south from the bridge. So he should start from where he was and work north. He could ride his bike over the forest floor if he went slowly and watched out for rocks, sticks, and sudden depressions in the dirt.

Tommy had never lit a flare before. What a waste if he couldn't get it to light. He'd studied the directions on the box. It seemed simple but the people who wrote the instructions often didn't tell you something important. Something they thought was obvious but it wasn't obvious at all.

Break the cap off the end of the flare. Turn the cap around and strike the rough top of the cap against the end of flare. Which end the directions didn't say. Tommy would try both. Strike away from yourself. Some idiots, Tommy supposed, would light themselves on fire. Keeping the flare away from you, place it on the roadway between your car and the oncoming traffic. Or, Tommy thought, stick it in a brush pile and stand back.

The flame at the end of the flare was very sudden, very red, and very bright. They spit metallic-looking sparks straight out from the end. Tommy wanted to examine the flame, even admire it. But the light hurt his eyes. He inserted the flare in the slash pile where it rested across two branches. The twigs above the flare ignited almost immediately but the flames from the flare didn't reach any higher. Tommy doubted the fire would really catch. Other little branches started to flame. But the fire was still small, like lighting a fire in a fireplace with paper and kindling in the house his parents used to have in Portland.

The fire got bigger and bigger, slowly at first and then quickly. Tommy could feel the heat. He backed away and admired the flames, gaining altitude every moment. He stood back further and admired his work. He could feel the heat from the fire building and he had to keep backing away. He remembered he had work to do. He had to tear himself away. Onto the next slash pile. He had faith now. Once the flare was placed, or even tossed into the next pile, he would be gone.

Chapter 26

A Fast Retreat

Rosalia's concert was wonderful. Elizabeth couldn't follow the Spanish lyrics but she said she enjoyed it.

"Too much rap," said Maria. "Even I can't understand it all. But it was amazing."

Gabriel, who played guitar professionally, said Rosalia had taken flamenco in a whole new direction.

In the Spanish fashion, they went for drinks and a light supper at Duda's Bar after the concert.

The next day would feature a hike in the Cascades, following a trail up Tyee Creek from Devil's Lake. The trail went all the way to the top of South Sister, the third tallest mountain in Oregon. They wouldn't go anywhere near that far. They'd turn around at the tree line or even earlier if they'd had enough.

In the morning, the four had breakfast at the Sunriver Lodge so they wouldn't have to cook. Gabriel and Maria would treat. They'd gotten coffee but their food hadn't come yet when Leon first spotted rising smoke. The restaurant's big windows looked west over a lawn, a pond, and a manicured green for putting practice. Beyond the green lay an unkempt field, then the airport's single runway and trees that marked the shores of the Deschutes River. Beyond the river, the land rose unevenly for a dozen miles through a pine forest to the base of Mt. Bachelor. The smoke Leon saw rose not far beyond the river and now a second pillar of smoke was getting started north of the first.

As soon as Leon pointed it out, Elizabeth lifted her cell phone and called 911. She gave her name and location.

"I can see smoke rising about a half mile west of the Sunriver Airport. Two columns of light gray smoke. The smoke is blowing east toward Sunriver. Sky is clear. Temperature here was seventy-three degrees twenty minutes ago." The operator said something to Elizabeth and Elizabeth said goodbye.

Three columns of smoke were visible now, the first one rising several hundred feet already. Others in the restaurant and people on the putting green were turning to look at it. Elizabeth's call to 911 might have been the first call but it would be far from the last. Their waitress paused pouring coffee to look out the window.

"We need to leave," said Elizabeth, "immediately. Please cancel our order."

Leon was surprised but he was sure Elizabeth must be right. She'd figured out something that he hadn't.

"I've already told the kitchen to start it," said the waitress pleadingly.

"Then we'll pay for it," said Elizabeth.

"I'll get your check."

"No time for that." Elizabeth paused for a quick calculation. "We'll give you a hundred-twenty-five in cash. You keep the change. Leon, have you got that much cash?" Leon stood up and handed the waitress a hundred and thirty. "Let's go," Elizabeth urged. Leon took a quick sip of his coffee. One other table was getting up and leaving but most people were content to watch the smoke or even to ignore it.

"Are we leaving because of the fire?" Gabriel asked as they rushed out of the restaurant. "It's a long way away."

"It's getting bigger," said Elizabeth, "and the wind is carrying it this way."

"We're going, we're going," said Maria. "But can you explain this to me? The flag on the golf course is barely flapping. How can the fire possibly get here that fast?" Now the foursome was hustling through the lobby of the resort, headed down the steps for the front door and the parking lot.

"The wind will be faster higher up," said Leon. "And it can carry burning branches into Sunriver. They could start fires all over the place."

Sunriver's five sirens went off as they walked through the parking lot to their car, Elizabeth leading the way. Leon unlocked the car remotely and opened the two doors on the passenger side. Elizabeth slammed herself into the front passenger seat.

"Get in, get in," said Elizabeth. "I'll shut the door."

Leon went around to the driver's door and their guests climbed into the back, clearly puzzled at the urgency and responding more out of respect for Elizabeth than any fear of danger. Leon did look carefully behind him before backing out but then accelerated through the parking lot. He turned left toward the main exit from Sunriver and got about five hundred feet before stopping to let three cars come in on the right from the Sage Springs parking lot. He could see Elizabeth, with her lips pressed tight, didn't want him to be so polite. But, Leon felt, no matter how important hurrying mattered, it mattered as much for the other people as it did for the four of them. Emergency or not, or especially in an emergency, you had to show consideration for other people. You had to be fair.

The cars ahead of them were bunching into a solid stream, moving slower than the twenty-five miles per hour speed limit. The sirens had not stopped wailing since they started.

"This was what I was afraid of," said Elizabeth. "Everybody is trying to get out of Sunriver at the same time. This is just the beginning. It's going to get worse. I hope we started in time."

"Let's turn on the radio," said Leon, "and see what they tell us." The radio started with classical music before Leon changed it to AM and to KBND. They listened with frustration and instantaneous boredom to a commercial for Lowe's before the local news began with a story about the fire, already named "The Conklin Road Fire."

"Conklin Road is the road we took to Benham Falls," said Leon.

"The cause of the fire is unknown but is suspected to be arson," stated the woman on the radio. "The Forest Service, the Oregon

Department of Forestry, and local fire departments are responding. Sunriver Resort, Upriver Ranch, and Caldera Springs are at evacuation level two. That means 'Get Set.' Residents should get set to evacuate on a moment's notice."

Two Deschutes County Sheriff's patrol cars passed them going the other way, lights flashing and sirens churning. Traffic slowed to a crawl until they passed Beaver Drive coming in near the shopping center.

"Looks like the Bay Bridge at rush hour," said Maria.

"The traffic is going to get much worse before this is over," said Elizabeth. "Most people haven't even gotten out of the house yet."

"The radio only said to get set," said Leon. "Sunriver holds at least twenty thousand people in the summer with only two regular exits and one emergency exit. If the fire department goes to level three and tells everyone to leave, it's going to be gridlock."

The radio went to a commercial and a weather forecast before the announcer repeated the earlier news on the fire. Then she added, "If you are in the Sunriver area and you're getting ready to evacuate, remember the five P's—People, Pets, Pills, Photos, and Papers."

"Who would forget their pet?" asked Maria.

"Not many," said Leon. "I read most people won't go back for the other things if they forget them. But they will go back for pets they forgot or couldn't find. Then get caught by the fire."

Leon's car, an Acura SUV, had finally made it out to the traffic circle on South Century and they exited to the south toward home. Traffic moved better in this direction as most other drivers exited east toward the main highway. An even layer of light gray smoke now tainted the bright blue sky above.

"Sunriver is now at Level 3 evacuation," said the announcer on the radio. "Anyone in Sunriver should leave immediately, according to the Sunriver Fire Department. Surrounding communities are still at Level 2. If you are in Upriver Ranch or Caldera Springs or anywhere else in the area, you should get ready to leave."

"I'm sure glad we're out of there," said Gabriel. "You sure knew what you were doing, Elizabeth. I wonder about the other people in the restaurant? And our waitress?"

"I think they'll mostly get out," said Leon, "if they don't stop by the place they're staying first. And, of course, the evacuation is a precaution. Even if they don't get out, the firefighters may stop the fire before it does a number on Sunriver."

"Can you imagine if they dropped their children off somewhere," said Maria, "or don't know where their children are?"

Leon turned up the radio when the woman announcer came back on. "We have breaking news on the source of the Conklin Road Fire near Sunriver. The Forest Service says that even prior to a full investigation, they believe the source of the fire was arson. At least one individual set fire to slash piles that were built for controlled burns by the Forest Service. The Forest Service and the Deschutes County Sheriff are searching for the arsonist and continuing their investigation."

Two fire engines from the La Pine Fire District screamed past as Leon turned into Upriver Ranch. There were no other cars between the front gate and the Martinez house. Golfers were still on the course, ignoring graying sky and the sirens they heard in the distance. Upriver Ranch had no sirens. The Martinez house was just as they left it.

"No hiking today," said Leon, "at least not until we're sure we're all safe and our house is safe. Sorry about that." He didn't mention how sorry he would be if the house were gone.

Chapter 27

Disaster Preparedness

When they stepped from the driveway to the house, Leon and Elizabeth and their guests saw a curtain of white smoke rising against the background of the Cascades. The smoke was blowing east, much more of it over Sunriver than above their own heads. Below the smoke and far in the distance, a low-flying plane dropped a long spray of red liquid.

"The fire will probably never get here," said Leon. "It would have to jump the river and head south. But we might as well be ready."

"Wallets, medicines, pills, and clothes," said Elizabeth. "We should keep our cell phones with us and be sure to pack the chargers. Bring your laptops. We'll put some food in a cooler."

"Your jewelry," said Leon. Elizabeth's jewelry wasn't expensive but she had accumulated it over forty years. Some pieces meant a lot to her, including gifts from Leon on five and ten-year anniversaries. Leon had an eye for beauty and her friends complimented her especially on the necklaces on the rare occasions she got to wear them.

"Your jewelry might have better odds staying in the safe here than riding around with us in a car," said Leon.

"I'll divide it in two. Some stays, some comes with us," said Elizabeth. Leon knew most people wouldn't want to divide it. And they would have a hard time deciding which to take and which to leave. But Elizabeth could do it without hesitation. She saw the problem. She knew the solution. And she would act. "I'll wear my wedding and engagement ring," she said. "Bring some of your paintings."

Gabriel and Maria had far fewer choices to make. They simply packed the bags they had brought to Oregon with them.

"We still haven't had breakfast," said Elizabeth. "I started the coffee and we'll have an omelet and toast in a few minutes when you're done packing."

"I think we'll have time," said Leon. "We're probably safe here, not in the path of the fire. And they don't want us to evacuate because the roads are jammed already. You could take Elizabeth's Camry," he told Gabriel and Maria. "You don't have any reason to stay except you'll sit in traffic for a long time if you go. It's different for Elizabeth and me. We need to sort things to take with us and I want to wet down the house with a hose."

"We talked about that," said Gabriel. "We'll stay. We're probably safe and we'd rather be with you. We'll jump in the pond if we have to." The pond on the Upriver Ranch golf course was less than a hundred yards away. "And anything we can do to help, just let us know."

Leon could barely fit a fraction of his paintings in the car. And he would have a hard time choosing. If he had weeks to choose instead of minutes it would still be difficult.

"It would be simpler not to take any," he said.

"Take some," said Elizabeth.

A half hour later, Elizabeth had sorted her jewelry and packed suitcases for Leon to put in the car, leaving room for Gabriel and Maria and their luggage. She found Leon sitting in his studio, only two paintings pulled out of the storage racks, now leaning up against the door. The smoke-filtered sunlight coming through the window was eerie, like the light during a solar eclipse. Elizabeth turned on the lights.

"You pick them," he said. "Pick the ones you like." Elizabeth started through the storage racks left to right, pulling out each painting about six inches and, with rare exceptions, pushing it back in again. She couldn't possibly see the whole painting when she made each decision and Leon was surprised she acted as though she remembered them all, some she hadn't seen for decades. Suddenly one painting made her hesitate and she pulled it all the way out of the rack. It was the plein air watercolor of the killing on East Cascade. Elizabeth, still bending over with her hand on the painting, turned her head to Leon.

"You were there?" she asked.

"Yes," said Leon. "The road was blocked off and I went to investigate."

"So you weren't there when it happened, when the man was shot."

"No way. The tarp was already on the body when I got there. Should we keep it?"

"Hell no," said Elizabeth slamming it back in the rack. "And if the fire doesn't get it, I'll burn it myself." She went back to pulling out paintings and putting them back. Leon began wrapping the art she had already picked in big sheets of brown paper for protection. He tied each package shut with twine.

It alarmed Leon that Elizabeth knew where and when that picture was painted. The road and the lodgepoles could have been dozens of places in Sunriver. The tarp could have been there for road construction or something else.

Maybe she recognized the car, Geoff Pennstead's car. The car had been in the newspaper and the television news. Or maybe the truth was what Leon had feared earlier. Elizabeth had been there when Geoff Pennstead was shot. Maybe, incredible as it seemed, it was Elizabeth who had shot him. As soon as this fire was over, and their guests were gone, he needed to talk with Elizabeth about getting a lawyer.

Leon put the paintings in the back of his SUV. Clothes, jewelry, medicines, and other odds and ends went in as well, leaving room for Gabriel and Maria in the back seat with their luggage on their laps. Lunch was already packed and in the car for the hike they had planned to take. Elizabeth put more makings for sandwiches in a paper bag and put them in the back. Leon and Gabriel could roll up the garage door manually if the power went out.

"I hope this is all for nothing," said Elizabeth. "I hope they stop the fire before it gets anywhere near here."

"I'm going out to wet down the house," said Leon.

"In all this smoke?" asked Elizabeth.

"I'll wear an N95 mask we bought for Covid. And an old pair of Dan's swimming goggles to keep the smoke out of my eyes. If it gets too bad, I'll come inside."

"You did think ahead," said Elizabeth. "Remember if you start coughing it's time to stop. Don't try to be a hero. Smoke can kill you and I don't want you coughing around the house for days afterward."

The air was gray outside the house now and Leon could barely see the Upriver fairway a hundred feet away. When he opened the outdoor faucet and grabbed the nozzle at the end of the fifty-foot hose, he was relieved to see the water pressure was still good. Wetting down the horizontal surfaces was his first priority. Burning embers from the fire would fall off the walls but they would rest on the deck, the windowsills, and the one balcony. They'd sit there long enough to set the house on fire. The roof was concrete tile and wouldn't catch. Leon watered all the decks and sills he could reach with the hose from the first faucet. Then he disconnected the hose and moved it to three other faucets to complete his counterclockwise circle of the house. He went around again to wet down the vertical surfaces. No trees or shrubs were planted up against the house.

KTVZ had chartered a helicopter to shoot video of the fire. To Elizabeth, Maria, and Gabriel, watching on television, the helicopter seemed to be above the lodge with the camera pointed west. All it could show was the putting green outside the lodge and a lot of smoky air. Then from top of the frame, a burning pine branch fell straight down into the pond by the green. The television showed that short segment over and over.

"The Sunriver Fire Department, along with Bend and La Pine fire departments, is putting out spot fires all over the resort," said an off-camera male announcer. "Some residents are helping with their own hoses but the fire department is directing people to evacuate and not stay to fight the fire themselves. Residents should leave the hoses out where the fire fighters can use them but turn the faucets off. Don't leave the water running."

After a commercial break and five minutes of other news, the helicopter was much higher in the sky and, Elizabeth guessed, about two miles south of Sunriver. She and the others had heard its blades whirring as it flew overhead. The smoke cloud was clearly defined in the video now. It rose in a long line west of the river and then flattened toward the east, toward Sunriver and Highway 97.

"The terrain and the weather are ripe for fire," said a spokesman for the Forest Service who appeared in a room with a podium on the television. "Humidity is low. Temperature is warm and rising. The fire is now about four miles wide. The Forest Service is building control lines at the north and south ends of the fire to prevent it spreading to the side. Wind at the ground level is blowing east about five miles per hour and is pushing the fire toward the Deschutes River where the Forest Service expects it to halt. A hundred feet above the ground, the wind speed is twenty miles per hour and the biggest danger now is that burning branches will land in Sunriver and start fires."

After more commercials and news, the television showed another reporter, a woman, standing in gray pine forest with ash-covered ground behind her. Smoke rose from a stump to her left. "I'm here with Doug Scofield, the head of a Forest Service Crew working toward the fire from Conklin Road. Doug, what can you tell us?"

"We're mopping up behind the fire so it doesn't start up again from embers in stumps or fallen logs. This area is burned over but it could burn again if the fire comes back this way. A cold front is coming in later and that can make the wind unpredictable."

"So is it better to fight the fire from behind like this instead of the front?"

"Safety first. You don't want a fire crew to get trapped between the fire and the river. And the river is a better control line than anything we could build. The air tankers are dropping retardant on the forest between us and the river and they may drop more on the trees on thirty acres of forest on the other side of the river."

"Is there a reason they wouldn't do that?"

"It's not up to me," said Scofield, "but they don't want to pollute the wetlands and the river if it isn't necessary. The fire retardant is like liquid fertilizer and it can throw the ecology out of whack."

"And this fire was started by an arsonist?"

"For sure. That's not official but I'd say it's obvious. The Forest Service thinned out the woods this year and left the trimmings in slash piles. The plan was for controlled burns when it got cooler in the fall. Setting those piles off in August was a maniac's dream."

"Have they caught him?"

"No but they will. He started the fires with highway flares. We found a cap from one of the flares and it has fingerprints on it. If they're not his, they belong to somebody he knows."

KTVZ went back to the studio, stating once again that Sunriver was at Level Three evacuation and the surrounding areas were at Level Two.

Leon came back in from outside and watched the TV over the heads of the others. A shot from a helicopter showed long lines of cars trying to leave Sunriver. They were bumper-to-bumper from deep in the resort all the way out to Highway 97.

Chapter 28

Flight I

Ward Beacham and his wife were still asleep in their house when the Sunriver warning siren woke them. Ward went into his office to check for messages on his cell phone. Deschutes County had sent them a Level 2 warning—the "Get Set" warning—to be ready to evacuate at a moment's notice. Ward thought it must be a mistake, like the "This is not a drill" warning to all of Hawaii in 2018 to seek immediate shelter because of an incoming ballistic missile. Typical government screw-up.

The morning sun shone brightly through Ward's office window and the air outside was clear, a good day for flying.

But when Ward looked out another window, to the west, black smoke was rising above the forest across the river.

"I'm going to open the hangar door while we still have electricity," Ward told his wife. Utilities were underground in Sunriver but the fire could still find a way to cut them.

"We should follow our plan," said Marilyn. She'd insisted they keep fire extinguishers in every room and rehearse their response to a forest fire.

Marilyn gathered up their keys, their prescriptions, a laptop, and a few of their favorite framed photographs, especially the one of their son. They had many more photographs backed up online. She placed everything by the door to the hangar for Ward to help her load onto the plane. They had carry-on bags ready with toiletries and two days' clothes in them.

Together, Ward and Marilyn took pre-cut plastic sheets out of a cabinet in the hangar and laid them over the beds and the living room furniture. If the house burned down, they wouldn't be of the slightest use. But if the house filled with smoke, the plastic might save the furniture from being impossible to clean. Even if a fire truck poured water into the house, the furniture might survive.

Ward stepped out his front door with binoculars to check the progress of the fire. A white RAV4 came up River Road, emerged from the smoke, and parked in Dara Pennstead's driveway next door. A burly man with a beard stepped out and looked over at Ward.

"Do you think the fire's going to get here?" asked the man.

Ward glanced over at the forest once more. Smoke rose across the entire horizon, from across the river to several miles north.

"I wouldn't bet against it," said Ward. "And if the fire does get here, you want to be gone."

"I won't be long," said the man. He turned to knock on Dara's door.

"And tell Dara she needs to get out of here," shouted Ward. The smoke suddenly thickened and Ward sneezed. He turned to go inside his house. Marilyn didn't have a mask on and he told her she'd need one soon. He locked the front door behind him and walked straight through the house to the hangar.

Chapter 29

The Devil's Due

Dara Pennstead had imagined killing her husband for some time. She hadn't decided if the idea was a daydream or the start of a plan. But it kept coming to mind. She didn't hate him. They actually got along. And she didn't have another man, or a different life, waiting in the wings. It just seemed the natural thing to do. She was barely fifty, energetic, and still attractive. She worked at keeping her figure. Geoff wasn't a bad man but he was seventy-seven years old. He'd kept his golf game but his strength, his balance, and possibly his mental sharpness were beginning to slip. He stooped more when he walked and he sometimes forgot what she told him five minutes after she said it. They never danced anymore. Sex was out of the question.

He was wealthy, at least some of the time. When he wasn't, he said it was a cash flow problem. Trips to Paris one year and cold cereal for dinner the next. Dara could never put a number on how much money he had. He showed her his will, though. Percentages of his estate would go to his children from an earlier marriage. Some would go to charity. But fifty percent would go to Dara.

Dara needed a script for murder, like the musical score for a song. And the script had to include her getting away with it. No "Frankie and Johnnie" or "Miss Otis Regrets She's Unable to Lunch Today." Not quite "Mack the Knife" either. She only thought about killing one person, not making a career of it. But a good script for murder never quite came together.

Had it occurred to Geoff that his wife might kill him? Dara thought it probably had. He was smart, God knew. He probably thought she would never get her act together to do it. Geoff was the answer to a prayer when they married. Dara was working as a waitress in Bend and her singing career, such as it was, was fading. Geoff had a big house in Sunriver and a house in Palm Springs for the winters. He had a plane to fly back and forth between them. Dara was singing at a hotel restaurant the first time he saw her and, as often happened with her male listeners, too often in fact, he fell in love with her on the spot. Her voice kindled romantic notions in men, particularly older men, emotions the men had forgotten they'd ever had. But Geoff was more level-headed than the others when they talked. His imagination did not cloud his vision of her. He could see who she was, where she was in life, and he still liked her. Their affection for each other, aided by calculations they both understood, led them to marry.

Romance had faded. Dara's future looked like playing maid and nursemaid to a weakening man.

To fill what was missing in their marriage Dara sometimes lengthened her shopping trips to Bend with a stop at the house of a man she met before she married Geoff. His name was Dave Pasciuti and he was thirty. He was a bartender who sold small quantities of cocaine to people he met in the bar. Sometimes he sold cocaine to women who came to his house, or he gave it away, and then he had sex with them. Sex and cocaine went well together and the women didn't mind that Dave was forty pounds overweight or that his beard hid a face like a bear. Dara bought cocaine from Dave and stayed for rock and roll in his bed. She would take a shower and then go do her shopping at Newport Avenue Market. She never took any coke home with her.

The reasons Dara didn't seriously plot to kill her husband kept shifting—a lingering affection, a fading commitment to the promises she'd made, the unknowns of how guilty she might feel later, and the fear that her life might not really be better afterwards—that she'd become a different person, a murderer, for no progress at all. What would happen if she attempted to kill Geoff and she failed? Geoff could divorce her and leave her penniless. Or use his money to convict her of attempted murder. Or make her life miserable in some other way. Even if she succeeded in killing Geoff, there was the risk she would be found out, arrested, tried, convicted, and spend the few good years she had left in jail. Out of the frying pan, not-that-awful, into spending twenty-four hours a day cooped up with dregs of society.

This was not a good time for Geoff to die anyway. It was a peanut butter and jelly year. No trips to Paris or even to Portland. Geoff had sold the house in Palm Springs and taken out a second mortgage on the Sunriver house. Not a good time to be inheriting Geoff's estate.

At Dara Pennstead's house, the day of the fire started with smoke climbing high in the sunny sky across the river. At the top it spread out, shining as white as new snow. It was pretty. Dara thought of painting it. Her cell phone buzzed before she took one step toward the closet where her watercolors were. The alert on the phone warned all of Sunriver to prepare for evacuation.

She gathered up her CD's, her jewelry, her wallet and three purses, Advil and Tylenol, and as many clothes as she could fit in her car. She took two of Geoff's watches, one of them a Rolex, along with cuff-links that appeared to be gold. She scoured the house for anything else of value and found nothing more.

"Why wait?" she said to herself. "I should get the hell out of here." Then she thought of leaving the house empty. The police and fire department would be overwhelmed. It would be the perfect time for a burglar to break in and take whatever was left behind. And if the house were truly threatened, she wanted to be there to persuade the firemen to save it before the others. It was her only home and maybe her only remaining asset. Was it insured or had Geoff scrimped on the insurance payment? The firemen would listen to the pleas of a small helpless woman. Well, they might. If they could save some houses and not others, why not save hers?

Geoff always told her their neighborhood was more vulnerable than others in Sunriver. To the west, across the river, it was all national forest, no houses that needed to be saved. Their neighborhood was off by itself at the end of River Road, farther west than any other houses in Sunriver and the first to be hit by a fire coming from the forest. On top of that, River Road was the only road to and from the neighborhood. Dara pulled a few CDs back out of her car, poured herself another cup of coffee, and sat down to wait for the fire or the firemen, whichever came first.

She was lost in Blossom Dearie singing "Teach Me Tonight" when her doorbell rang. It might be the police checking on her. They no longer stationed anyone outside her house twenty-four hours a day, though they drove by frequently. She could call 911 if anything suspicious happened.

The person she saw through her peephole was, to her surprise, Dave Pasciuti, her cocaine dealing friend. He'd never been to her house before. She'd always met him in Bend. Did Dave care enough about her to come express his sympathy for Geoff's death? Or even, God forbid, deepen their relationship? Maybe he thought an older woman, recently widowed, would shower money on him. Or had he simply come to sell a little cocaine and indulge in drug-fueled sex? She was not in the mood for any of it but she was curious. It was a strange time for him to come. Didn't the smoke make him think twice about coming to Dara's house? What kind of friend was he and what kind of friend did he want to be? She combined a half smile and quizzical look and stepped aside to let him in.

"Are you making house calls now?" she asked. "If you got any drugs, you need to turn around right now and leave. The police are watching this house."

"I don't have any drugs. I am out of that business starting a week ago. It's fentanyl. It can be in anything. People are dying. Not only junkies. Weekend users. Party users. I don't want to be the guy that sells something that kills them. And I've stopped using myself. It was time to grow up anyway. I've decided to have a life."

"So no more bartending?"

"Only until I find something else. A career where I can make some progress."

"Big change!" said Dara.

"I'm lucky to have gotten away with being a kid for so long."

"Is this the effect of a new girlfriend?"

"Not yet. It's on the agenda. Got to start looking beyond the women I meet at the bar."

"Is this goodbye? Aren't I part of your old life?"

"If you want to stay friends, I'm all for it. It's not like you led me astray or anything. You should lay off the cocaine yourself. Drugs are much more dangerous than they used to be."

"Good advice," said Dara. "We'll see. So if you're not here for drugs and sex, to what do I owe the honor of this visit? Did you know that Geoff died? It's been in the news."

"I knew as soon as it happened," said Dave. "I'm sorry it took me so long to come see you. It must have been a shock. I mean, you must have known he would die before you did. He was so much older. But getting murdered. That's gotta blow your mind."

"It's a mess. The mortgage is behind and he owes people money."

"I'm pretty sure Geoff had a boatload of cash on him when he died," said Dave. "Cold hard cash. And that's what I came to see you about."

Dara's neck tensed immediately. But at least Dave didn't seem angry or threatening. "How do you know anything about whether Geoff had cash or not?"

They sat in the living room. Dara turned on the lights, strange in the middle of the day. It was getting darker and darker outside as the smoke got thicker. Dave leaned back in his chair.

"Tell me," said Dara

"Geoff knocked on my door. He told me he needed a contact. He had a cash flow problem with all the business deals he was in. He needed cash, a lot of it and quick."

"How did he even know who you were? How did he find you?"

"He had a private detective follow you."

"Oh," said Dara. "I thought he never knew." She did care what he thought. Yet he should not have been so suspicious. If he had trusted her, he would have been happier.

"He had the idea he could use his plane to smuggle drugs into the country and make some quick money. He wanted me to put him in touch with people. I told him I was small time and I didn't know people like that. And I told him people like that were scary. It would be dangerous merely to know their names. But he said he wanted a contact. I gave him the name of a guy I knew in Arizona. I said I didn't know if the guy could help or not. And I told him to be careful.

"A week went by," said Dave, "and Geoff called me. He said he'd talked to people who had talked to people and they had a plan. I told him I didn't want to know anything about it, not a word. He said he had a little problem. He was so short of funds, he needed money to fuel up the plane and get it down there. He didn't need a lot of cash, he said, because he wasn't going to buy and sell the merchandise himself. He was getting paid for bringing it in, a drug mule with an airplane. It would be a big fee and he would pay me back for the fuel plus twenty percent as soon as he got back to Oregon. He needed three thousand dollars for the fuel. I don't have that kind of money in my checking account so I met him at Sunriver Airport and charged the fuel to my credit card. That way at least I knew the money was going for fuel and not for something else.

"While we were fueling I dropped an Apple Air Tag, sealed in modeling clay, into the fuel tank so I could see where the plane went. Mostly I wanted to know when it was coming back so I could be sure to get my money. I was afraid Geoff would pay off his other debts and forget about me. I mean, the other debts were enforceable in court and mine wasn't. And his other creditors could shut down his business deals and take his house. Your house. I had no recourse. Do you know what I mean by recourse? I couldn't go to court. I didn't have even a piece of paper saying I'd loaned him the money. He could say 'See ya later' and I'd be sunk.

"Geoff left it vague about where and when he was going to pay me the money he owed so I wanted to catch him before he gave the cash to his big creditors—the bank and whoever else. I would have met him at your house as soon as he landed but I didn't want you to know Geoff had found me. So I rigged his car to where I could stop it where I wanted. He told me he had a big payment due in Bend the day he got back and he would be rushing to get it to the bank. I stopped his car on East Cascade. I was lagging behind him so he wouldn't see me and I sent the signal to stop the fuel pump when I knew he was in the right place, a stretch of road with no houses close by. He stopped exactly where I planned. But there was another car that stopped behind him, a blue Toyota.

"I hung back waiting for the other car to pass but it didn't. I figured some other bastard had found out about Geoff and the money and whoever it was planned to rip him off, probably for all he had. Then I saw that Geoff was out of his car with a gym bag in one hand and a pistol in the other, waving it around and pointing it at the driver of the second car. I didn't want any part of that. It was much more serious than I'd bargained for. That kind of action is part of why I'm getting out of drugs. I turned to back up so I didn't see what happened for a few seconds. But when I stopped and looked forward, Geoff was lying in the road with his head blown off and the other car was driving away with its trunk open.

"All I knew was I didn't want to be there. So I stepped on the gas and skedaddled. I'm sorry, I think I ran over Geoff while I was leaving. But I'm sure he was long gone already. His head…"

"Don't," said Dara. "I've heard enough about it already. Thank God they didn't make me identify the body."

Dave stopped his story. He wasn't sure what to say next. But he had come for a purpose. "So I never got the money Geoff promised me and I need it."

"Well, I need it too and I don't have it. If Geoff had any money after that trip, he took it with him. Whoever shot him must have it."

"He might have left some here," said Dave. "Have you looked? Could we look now? Maybe start with a tool chest in the airplane hangar."

"We can," said Dara. "I'd love to find some moolah stashed away. But you know we may get evacuated any minute. And the police have already searched the house for drugs. If Geoff squirreled any money away somewhere, I think they would have found it."

"Let's look anyway," said Dave. His voice sounded strained.

A knock sounded on the door.

"Here it comes," said Dara. "Mandatory evacuation."

Chapter 30

Reversal of Fortune

Tommy Westlake heard the sirens the very second he lit his eighth flare.

Now they're scared, he thought. He placed the whooshing flare into the brush pile and stood up. He imagined people waking up in their beds wondering what was going on. Others were on their way to golf or tennis or swimming, thinking they were going to enjoy their day. Now they knew something was wrong with their world, that some outside force would upset their day, their plans, maybe even their lives, even if they didn't know what it was yet. They would find out soon enough.

Tommy mounted his bike and charged through the woods to the next slash pile. Surely he would find homes for all the flares before anyone showed up to stop him. They'd come up Conklin Road, which paralleled the river about a mile to the west of it. They would be driving fast with lights flashing, probably with a siren to let him know they were coming. But he was a hundred yards from the road and could get behind a tree or a brush pile or simply lie flat on the ground while they passed. He rode through the woods, looking over his shoulder when it was safe to take his eye off the ground in front of him. He lit the next brush pile on the east side, the side away from the road.

When the last flare kindled the last fire, Tommy stood back from the pile and watched the flames grow, slowly at first, then reaching the top of the stack and then suddenly setting the entire pyre alight. He watched the flames leap into the empty air. Then looking south, he saw a roiling gray mass of smoke towering in the sky. It was immense. It was threatening. It was by far the biggest thing Tommy had ever created, the biggest effect he had ever had on the world. The sirens in Sunriver went on and on. The smoke cloud grew bigger and bigger. Tree branches, bright orange with fire, rose up in the smoke and drifted to the east.

I should be happy, he thought. He expected the joy of vengeance, the power of instilling fear in hundreds of people, the sure knowledge that he had seized their lives and shaken them like a dog with a rat. No one in Sunriver would be doing what they wanted. They would be doing what Tommy wanted.

Yet Tommy had overlooked something in his calculations. He had the power to light the fires but he did not have the power to stop them. He wanted to frighten people but he had not considered that the fire, once out of his hands, could flatten the forest, gut people's houses, and even possibly kill people, including children. He hadn't thought his vengeance would go that far. He didn't want that. He was more powerless than ever.

The fire was no longer Tommy's tool. It was its own force of destruction—completely indifferent to any rules or any sense of right and wrong. He was horrified. He wished he could take it all back. He wanted to go back to the house and have a normal day, whether his father ignored him or not. He wanted to go play video games. He wanted no one to ever know he had unleashed this destruction.

The forest around the last brush pile was still unburned. If he rode fast, he estimated, he could get to the Cardinal Landing bridge ahead of the fire. He could ride home from there and pretend he had never left. If his father was still sleeping, Tommy could wake him up and they could escape the fire together.

He rode southeast as fast as the uneven forest floor would let him. If he didn't come out at the bridge, he would walk or ride parallel to the river until he came to it. He could even swim across the river if he had to. People didn't swim in the river for fun. It was too cold. But Tommy could do it if he set his mind to it. Lara Croft could swim.

Tommy coughed once to clear his throat. He couldn't see far ahead but the land still sloped down and he was sure he was headed in the right direction. His eyes began to sting and he coughed again. The bicycle's front wheel hit a dip that Tommy hadn't seen. He went over the handlebars and rolled onto a soft bed of pine needles. He wasn't injured. He left his bike and started walking. His eyes hurt so much, he kept them shut and navigated from the peeks he took every ten seconds or so. He was coughing continuously. This had all been a big mistake. It was time to start the game over. It was unfair, he thought, that he could not pause the game while he thought about it.

Through the smoke to his right, he caught a glimpse of red and yellow. A line of flames, less than a foot high, stretched away from him. The flames leaned downhill in a gentle breeze. The line did not appear to be moving yet the ground was black on the uphill side and untouched on the side toward the river. Tommy could walk faster than the flames advanced, especially if he could stop coughing.

With his eyes closed, Tommy walked straight into a tree. The bounce knocked him to the ground. He thought of lying there a while to gather his strength. But he couldn't stop coughing. He had a terrible sore throat and gasped to breathe. He got to his knees and struggled to stand up. He couldn't stop coughing long enough to balance. He started to crawl but even that was hard work. He wasn't sure he was going in the right direction. He needed to rest. He needed to breathe. When he toppled over, he wasn't sure what position his body was in.

What would Lara Croft do now? Tommy thought as he lay there, no longer coughing. It was the last thought he had before he died.

Chapter 31

Flight II

They loaded the plane together. Marilyn brought two bed pillows with them. Ward didn't ask why she'd take up so much room with pillows they could replace at Walmart. At least they didn't add much weight. The two seated themselves and Ward started the engine. He took a last look around the hangar. In spite of being a big empty space, he had an affection for it. To own that kind of space, you had to have succeeded in life, especially if you're going to dedicate that space to something like an airplane—something few people had and hardly anyone truly needed.

When he got the plane outside, Ward pushed a remote to shut the hangar. The electricity was still working. He listened for broadcasts from nearby planes on the Unicom channel. A Cessna was about to take off going south on the single runway. While Ward taxied over to the airport, he saw the shadowy figure of the Cessna taking off above him. He asked the pilot if he saw any obstructions on the runway. The runway was over a mile long and Ward couldn't see to the other end of it. Ward's Epic E1000 needed only half the distance but it was the correct procedure to check that the runway was clear.

"Nothing on the runway," came the reply. "I saw elk standing in the meadow at the north end. They're nervous with the fire. You better look out for them."

Roger," said Ward. "Thanks." He broadcast that he was taxiing north halfway up the taxiway then taking off going south. He repeated his takeoff plan when he turned onto the runway and reported, for anyone who was listening, that he'd seen no deer or elk on the southern half of the runway. Hearing no other radio traffic, he revved his engine and accelerated.

Ward and Marilyn could see their own house, still intact, as the Epic rose into the air. There was another car in front of Dara's house, now, a black sedan. Dara and a different man, taller and thinner than the man in the white SUV, were walking from the house to the car, the man holding onto Dara's arm. Dara's arms were pulled back in a funny way.

"I think her arms are tied behind her," said Marilyn.

"I think you're right," said Ward. "I'm calling Detective Breuninger. Dara's in trouble." Ward thought of turning around for another look but decided it was too dangerous. He'd have to fly low enough to see through the smoke. He could run into another airplane or into a helicopter that had come to fight the fire. Or he could run right into a burning branch lifted by the heat and the wind. He continued to climb to the south, not turning until he was clear of the smoke.

Ward scanned the sky around him and above him. A DC-10 was descending toward the forest to drop fire retardant. He saw no other planes but he did see three helicopters with bags hanging on cables beneath them. One was over the river picking up water. Ward set a north-northeast course for Redmond Airport. He and Marilyn would stay in a hotel there until they knew when they could return to their house, if they could return to it at all. They could sleep on their own pillows and that was very important to Marilyn. If they couldn't go back right away, they'd fly over to Portland, buy some new clothes, and see some of their friends.

Chapter 32

Menace

The knocking on Dara's door had changed to a heavy pounding as she went to open it. The smoke outside was worse than before. A man in a brightly colored shirt and neatly pressed pants stood in the doorway with a scowl on his face.

"Are you Mrs. Pennstead?" he demanded.

"I am. And who are you?"

"Name's Che and I need to come in." He pushed past Dara and slammed the door behind him. He didn't look like a Che. He didn't look Mexican or Cuban or from that part of the world at all. He had blond hair that grew past his ears and his face could have been from anywhere in Northern Europe.

"Where's the two kilos?" he demanded. He drew a pistol from under a windbreaker and pointed it into the living room as he entered. "Who are you?" he growled at Dave.

"Paul Bunyan," said Dave. It was the first name he could think of and he immediately regretted his choice.

"Let me see your wallet." Dave pulled his wallet out of a back pocket and handed it to Che.

"You're Dave Pasciuti. I want to see you too. Now where's the coke?" Dara did not know who Che was but she did know what he was talking about. It was the package of drugs Carl Breuninger had found in a seat pocket in the plane.

"The Sheriff took it," said Dara. "I don't have it."

"Don't you hold out on me, bitch." He pointed his gun at Dara's face. Her knees threatened to give way beneath her. Then she got angry.

"They gave me a receipt," she said. "They said somebody might come looking for it. And they check this house all the time."

"The police are dealing with the fire and the smoke. I saw them on the way in. They don't have time for you, lady. Show me the receipt. It better be legit."

"It's in the top right-hand drawer of the desk in the corner. I can get it for you."

"Let's all three of us go over there and you open the drawer. If I see a gun in that drawer or an alarm goes off, I'll shoot you where you stand."

"There's no gun," said Dara.

Dara stood up and led the way to the desk, Dave behind her and Che behind Dave. They all knew how this had to work. They had to stand where Che could keep an eye on Dara, Dave, and the drawer at the same time. Dara opened the drawer slowly and lifted out a white sheet of paper. It was a Deschutes County Sheriff's Department form for receipt of evidence, in this case "approximately two kilograms of a brown powder that appears to be cocaine." The description said it was contained in a one-gallon Ziploc that was wrapped in Saran Wrap and taped. The form was signed by Detective Carl Breuninger. Che read it carefully, folded it, and slid it into the side pocket of his jacket. He was clearly pissed, more than he had been before, but he was trying not to show his frustration to Dave and Dara.

"So where's the money?" he asked.

"What money?"

"Don't play stupid with me, you tart. The money your husband got paid for carrying the coke."

"You know my husband was killed, don't you? If he had any cash, somebody took it. I've never seen it. I'm flat broke."

Che's pistol went off with a bang that echoed loudly in the room.

"Ow!" yelled Dave. A red stain spread on his canvas shoe with a black hole in the middle of it. His face was contorted in pain.

"That's for starters," said Che. "A lot worse is coming if I don't see the money. Give me your cell phones," he said. "Slowly. One at a time." They each pulled their phones out of their pockets and handed them to him. He stuffed them into his pants pockets, the bulges disrupting the sharply dressed look he cultivated.

"Put out your other foot," Che commanded Dave.

"No, no, no, no, no," said Dave. "I don't know anything."

"You're a teaching opportunity," said Che and shot Dave in the other foot. Dave screamed.

"Now, little lady, where is the rest of the money?" He pointed his gun at her feet, then her knees, then her chest, and finally her eyes, as if deciding where to shoot.

"It's at a friend's house," she said. "He lives in Upriver Ranch."

"What's his name?"

"Leon Martinez."

"Take me there."

Chapter 33

Follow the Money

Che pulled Dara's wrists behind her and strapped a zip tie around them. He pulled her sideways by her left arm, throwing her off balance and almost to the floor. On their way out of the living room, Che turned, as if it were an afterthought, and shot Dave Pasciuti one last time. Dave grunted a low moan and keeled over in his chair.

Che dragged Dara out the front door, almost off her feet, and made his way to his car, a late model black Cadillac sedan with gray ashes on it. Both of them coughed. Che pushed Dara into the passenger seat of his car and slammed the door. As he walked around to the driver's side, Dara lurched forward and reached for the door handle with her hands behind her back. It was hard to get in position and get the right grip. She pulled the handle and tried to back out the door. But Che was in the car now and he yanked her toward him. He stretched across her and pulled the door shut, then pushed a button on his door. Dara could hear all the doors locking. So much for that idea. She wasn't getting out of that car until he let her out.

Che turned the air conditioning on full blast and flipped a switch to recirculate the air. They were still coughing but it wasn't getting worse. The air they were breathing was clean.

Che backed the car out of the driveway, jammed the gear into drive and accelerated blindly out River Road. If something suddenly appeared in the smoke ahead of them, Dara thought, Che wouldn't be able to stop before he hit it. Fine for him, she thought. He had the steering wheel ahead of him and he'd even put on his seat belt. But she had no seat belt and her hands were behind her.

"Slow down!" she said, as though she were talking to a careless friend or her husband, not a stranger who had just shot Dave in front of her eyes. "You can't see anything out there." Che didn't reply but he did back off the speed. *He's vicious,* Dara thought, *but he isn't stupid.* And he heard what she said—more than she could say for some men.

Flames blazed high up in the smoke to the right of her. The flames came from the trees above the airport's parking lot. The lower-level flame further back was the flight operations center itself. It was a wooden building. She couldn't see the hangars north and south of the operations center. They had steel walls and steel roofs. They wouldn't be burning.

A thousand yards further along the road, Che jammed on the brakes. The car stopped ten feet short of a horse madly shying away from the car and pulling desperately on a halter held by an anxious young woman. It was the last horse in a line evacuating the stables and being led to the airport where the ground would not burn beneath it. The wrangler wore a hat and a bandana soaked in water. The woman calmed the horse and led it off the road. She glared angrily at Che and Dara as they passed. If she saw the plea for help in Dara's eyes she ignored it.

The car barely caught the sharp right turn in River Road as it went around the end of the airport. Che stormed forward again until they got past the Nature Center. A car was stopped ahead of them with its hazard lights blinking. Beyond it was a whole line of cars with their lights on, none of them moving.

Che wrenched the steering wheel to the left and accelerated, driving on the wrong side of the road. Everyone was trying to get away from the fire, not drive toward it. But Che was not the first one to think of driving the wrong way in the other lane. After passing ten cars, he was forced to a stop behind another line of unmoving cars.

Che took his gun and hid it in his belt under his windbreaker. He got out, walked forward, and rapped on the window of the car ahead of him.

"What's the hold up?" he demanded. He was ready to shoot whoever was causing the problem. "We've got two lanes. And nobody is moving an inch."

"It's the roundabouts," said the man. "They're only one lane. If this doesn't get better, we're going to pull off the road and start walking." A very worried-looking woman sat in the front seat. Two young children, a boy and a girl, sat in the back seat with a black Labrador retriever that tried to stick his nose out the driver's window and get a good sniff of Che.

Che came back to the Cadillac and got in, staring at the windshield ahead of him.

"Look," said Dara, pointing with her head past Che out the side window on the driver's side. The deck of a house was on fire, one-foot-high flames rising from a single spot, like a campfire in the wrong place. The flames looked as though they could easily be extinguished with a few buckets of water or a series of well-placed boot stomps. A handyman could repair the damage in a day. But the flames were starting to climb the house wall. A man, presumably the owner, came out of the house and tried to smother the flames with a green plaid wool blanket. He was too late. The flames had reached the eaves and the roof began to burn. Dara could see flames inside the house as well, like fireplace fire that escaped. A firetruck drove into the short driveway. Two men jumped out but the driver stayed in the truck talking into a microphone.

Instead of fighting the fire, the fireman pulled the man with the blanket away from it and retreated down the driveway to the road. The firetruck backed up to the road as well. Out of seemingly nowhere, a helicopter appeared above dragging a red canvas bucket below it. It jockeyed for position before the bucket opened and dropped the contents on the fire. Almost all the fire on the outside of the house went out immediately—the roof, the outside wall, and the deck. The firefighters rushed back, putting on face-covering breathing masks with large lenses for eyes. They picked up a garden hose, turned on the faucet and rushed through the front door. One fireman carried the hose and the other carried an axe and a white fire blanket.

If Dara could get out of the car while Che was distracted by the firemen, she might be able to escape. If she ran toward the fire truck, the driver could radio for help. Anybody seeing a fleeing woman with her wrists bound would certainly call 911 or maybe even rescue Dara themselves. She thought she could count on Che not to shoot her when the firemen and all the people in their cars were watching. But she couldn't reach the door handle without half standing up. Che would notice and yank her down before she even touched the lever.

Che turned away from the fire and stared intently ahead for ten seconds. He pulled out his cell phone. He searched Google Earth for an aerial view of Sunriver. He scrolled to where his car was stopped.

"What is the address?" he asked Dara in an accusatory tone. She hesitated, buying time though she knew it was pointless. She was, at best, putting off the moment when Che would shoot and kill her.

"Lone Pine Drive in Upriver Ranch," said Dara.

"What's the number?"

"I don't know. But I can recognize the house."

Che looked down at his phone again, scrolling slowly up and down, left and right.

It would take hours to get there in this traffic. Dara found some consolation in that, even if she had to spend those hours in the company of a horrible man with her hands tied behind her. She'd seen men like this when she sang on the road professionally—sometimes handsome, sometimes hideous, but always sharply dressed. Lots of hair but well styled and cared for. Big stone in a ring on their finger. Didn't dance but leaned on the bar waiting for some woman who wanted something different, something exciting, or simply a man with money to spend. A woman who wanted to take a risk, to go with a man who looked dangerous. And the men were dangerous. They were criminals, always risking being caught but acting as though they were so smart, so powerful, so connected that the police never scared them. Their biggest worry was not the police. It was disappointing the bigger criminals they worked for. Or being the target of some rival criminal. Yet they projected absolute invulnerability. They had to. And they had to largely believe it themselves. Some would be in and out of jail for years. Some would overdose. Some would wind up shot dead in a public bathroom. Dara stayed away from them no matter how handsome they were.

Dara was a smart girl, at least in handling men. She had lots of experience. How could she get him on her side? Or trick him into making a mistake that would get her, and Leon for that matter, out of this jam?

"What's your name, again?" she asked.

"Che," he said firmly. He still didn't look like a "Che." He looked American—low rent criminal but with some brains in his meat locker. If he was an addict, he had a secure and steady supply. But he was tough and single-minded. He was not interested in her good opinion of him. And his real name wasn't Che.

She couldn't charm this guy or flirt with him. She couldn't offer him sex either subtly or straight out. He got all the sex he needed from women a lot younger and more desperate than Dara. At least more desperate up until now. Fake Che had a gun and she had her hands bound.

"I'll make you a deal," said Dara. "You take the money but you don't hurt me or my friends. We'll say we were blindfolded. I'm sure my friend has napkins or something we can use. We say we never had eyes on you or your car. You hardly said a word and we can't recognize your voice."

Che, or whatever his name was, took a minute to respond. Traffic was moving now, albeit slowly.

"Sounds good," he said. "Let's agree on that. But no funny business."

"Okay," said Dara. She did not believe him for a second. He agreed only in order to keep her calm and cooperative. Once he had the money, he would kill them all. And, she knew, he didn't trust her either. But at least they were talking. What could she offer him? What could she threaten him with? Dara began to sing.

Singing would not make Che fall in love with her. But it might make her more human in his eyes—a person who harbored the same emotions he did, a person he could sympathize with. A person he wouldn't shoot the way he'd shot Dave.

She sang one of the few songs she knew in Spanish. It was called *Cuando Vuelvo a Tu Lado*. If Che was a Spanish name and Che could pretend to be Latin, Dara could pretend to speak Spanish. At least, she knew, she pronounced the words correctly. The melody would be familiar in any case, the same as *What a Difference a Day Makes*. But the meaning of the song was totally different.

If the song had any effect on Che, it was hard to see. At least he didn't tell her to stop. He looked intently at his phone, scanning back and forth and then carefully tracing a new route. He put the phone down and sharply turned the car around, scraping a bush by the side of the road. He drove back a hundred feet, past the line of cars in the other lane, and charged across the road into a meadow. Driving much more slowly now, and watching carefully for holes and ditches, it took ten minutes to get through the meadow and onto a golf course. Dara recognized the long seventeenth hole of the Meadows. Che sped south to the green, onto the eighteenth hole, and past the lodge. He kept going through the front nine on cart paths and fairways. When they got to the south end of Sunriver, another line of cars waited to exit through a gate the police had opened onto Spring River Road, the road that ran between Sunriver and Upriver Ranch. It was an emergency exit, not a regular exit. Rather than get in line, Che drove through the trees to a space directly opposite the gate. He jammed his way in front of a red Kia whose driver leaned on his horn. Other horns immediately joined in the protest.

Che still had to wait for the cars plugging the gate to get through it. As he sat there with a look of cold calculation on his face, a man in hunter's camouflage got out of the fourth car behind and walked up to the Cadillac with a rifle in his hand. Che rolled down his window, pulled his pistol from under his jacket and stuck the muzzle one inch out the open window where the man could see it. The man halted, pointing his rifle down into the dirt.

"Back off," Che shouted. The man stood and thought a moment, then backed away twenty feet before turning and walking back to his car. Che lay his pistol down in his lap and lifted his phone.

A solo policeman at the exit was directing traffic to the right, blocking left turns with his car, arguing with drivers who wanted to go left. The left led toward US Highway 97, two lanes in each direction. But turning left meant going past the main exit from Sunriver which was jammed. The road to the right went toward the mountains. People didn't want to go that way. They didn't know for sure the road went south of the fire and they wouldn't trust the policeman who was directing them that way. They didn't know, or had forgotten, that in less than a mile in that direction, another road branched off that headed directly away from the fire.

Che didn't mind going right. After fifty yards, he crossed the road into a dirt road with a metal gate that led into Upriver Ranch. The gate was locked, as Che expected, but it was within walking distance of the Martinez house on Lone Pine Road. Or it would be in walking distance if they weren't overwhelmed by smoke while they walked. In fact the smoke was thinner here and Dara could see some blue sky above the haze. Straightening out his body above his seat, Che drew a long jackknife out of his front pants pocket and opened it as he sat down. He bent Dara forward with one hand while he reached behind her with the knife to cut the zip tie from her wrists. He pulled her arms around in front of her and, before her arms could relax for a minute, he grabbed a new zip tie out of his jacket pocket and strapped her wrists again. At least her arms hurt less in front of her than behind.

Next he slipped two blue surgical masks out of his other pocket and deftly put one on Dara, sweeping back her hair to put the straps around her ears. He put the other mask on himself and got out of the car. Dara got her door half open before Che was around the car, squelching any thoughts she had of running away. He pulled her out and stood her up. Hidden from view by the car, he quickly took his jacket off and wrapped it over her wrists, manhandling her arms left and right in the process.

"Don't let this fall off," he said. He led her firmly to the gate, not letting her stumble or drag her feet. "You're going to climb through the gate and I'm going to be right behind you."

What was he going to do if she didn't climb through the gate? If he shot her, he'd never find Leon's house. Cars were going by and the policeman was only fifty yards away. Dara stood beside the gate and made no move to go through it.

Che sighed and reached in his pants pocket again for his knife. He opened it with a flick of his thumb.

"Would you like to lose an earlobe?" he said. "Or will it take a whole ear to get you moving?" Dara looked in his eyes with all the hatred she could summon but she put her two hands on one of the crossbars of the gate and slid her leg, her body, and then the other leg between the bar and the one above it. Che climbed up the gate in an instant and leapt over it.

"Let's go," he said but didn't grab her arm. "Keep up or I'll start cutting."

The forest here was a mix of lodgepole and ponderosa. Sunlight, filtering through the smoke, made it look like evening on another planet. Sirens and horns in the distance were muffled by the smoke and trees. A helicopter was somewhere out there, its blade noise rising and falling as it surveyed the fire from above. A noisy airplane flew overhead and went away again.

They came to a paved road that the map on Che's phone said was Lone Pine. The road was quiet, no traffic at all. It was a dead end that served the houses that were on it and went no further. The owners had either left to avoid the fire or they were hunkered down inside.

"Which way?" Che asked.

"Left," said Dara. "Can you untie my wrists? They hurt and it makes it hard to walk." Che pulled his jacket off her wrists and put the jacket on himself again. He sliced the zip tie with a flick of his knife. He didn't let the zip tie fall to the ground. He put it in his pocket. He was threatening to kill her, Dara thought, but he didn't want to litter.

They walked fast past three houses when Dara realized Lone Pine was the wrong road. She'd only been to Leon's house twice for art class. The classes were usually held at the Sunriver Lodge or at a gallery in the Sunriver Mall. She remembered what his street looked like and Lone Pine wasn't that street. She'd better tell Che before they got to the end and she hadn't pointed out a house.

"This is the wrong street," she said. "It must be the next one over." Che snatched her arm and his eyes glared deep into her own.

"Are you messing with me?" He didn't bring out his knife again. Yet.

"No, no," Dara answered. "I was wrong, that's all. That's it. I'm sure it's the next street. I'm sure I'll recognize it." They cut through a yard, across a fairway, and around the end of a pond. Dara thought of dashing the few feet to the water, diving in and swimming away from shore. She'd gone snorkeling and scuba diving with Geoff in Belize and she knew how to swim underwater. A TV show had demonstrated that water slowed bullets down so much they couldn't hurt you after a foot or two. She wasn't sure of it. Maybe Che didn't know how to swim. Or maybe the pond was shallow near the shore and he could dash in after her. One sure thing, though. The water would be cold, even on this summer day. She was still making up her mind when they left the pond behind.

At least it was the right road when they got to it. Maybe she could go to the wrong house and hope no one was home. Che wasn't stupid, though, and she had tried his patience already. She was beaten down, dominated, afraid for her life and afraid of being hurt. She desperately hoped that Leon, wise and caring Leon, would somehow find a way to destroy this awful man. In any case, Che would soon be more Leon's problem than her own. That was cowardly of her, she knew, but she was exhausted.

Chapter 34

Race for Redemption

The Deschutes County Sheriff's Department and the Sunriver Police Department were overwhelmed trying to evacuate Sunriver. Traffic was slow, cars full of anxious people. Some who had had their vacations spoiled were more upset than homeowners who stood to lose their house and everything in it. Some people were depressed and some were angry. Some were excited and some were impatient. Fortunately, so far, no accidents were serious enough to block traffic.

All the Sunriver exits were jammed—the north exit out Cottonwood Road, the main exit out to South Century, and the emergency exit to the south that opened onto Spring River Road. The Sunriver Police and deputies from the Deschutes County Sheriff's Department were directing traffic, mostly trying to stop people from driving the wrong way in the left lane where they would block fire engines, law enforcement, and ambulances from getting where they needed to be.

The wind had risen and the fire had intensified. In spite of the sirens some people were not checking their televisions or their cell phones. Some renters did not take the warnings seriously. Some homeowners wanted to stay with their homes and fight the fire if it came. Police and deputies went door-to-door checking that houses were empty or the people in them were leaving. Officers and deputies told everyone if the warning changed from "Get Set" to "Go Now" then evacuation would be mandatory and they could be arrested for staying. The threat of arrest was mostly empty. Law enforcement did not have time to arrest anyone.

"If the fire gets closer," the doubters were warned, "we won't have the manpower to come back for you. We're not going to risk other people's lives because you didn't get out when you should have."

Police officers and sheriff's deputies were committed to checking house by house. Some people, sick, old, or children at home alone needed help leaving. Pets left behind were a particular problem. They couldn't be told to leave. They wouldn't get in a police car or they panicked if they were placed in one.

With four thousand doors to knock on, the Sheriff assigned all the personnel he could find to work their way through Sunriver, including Detective Carl Breuninger. It wasn't in his job description but the department needed him and he might actually save someone's life. He was given a neighborhood toward the north end of Sunriver where a few homes bordered the Deschutes River. They were bigger houses than most and it took longer for people to answer the doorbell, or for Carl to be sure no one was home.

He'd done five of the twenty houses he was assigned when he got a call on his cell from Ward Beacham. As Ward and his wife were escaping the fire in their plane, they'd seen a man holding Dara Pennstead by her arm outside her front door. It looked like she had her hands bound behind her. There was a black sedan in the driveway that Ward had not seen earlier. Carl radioed dispatch to say someone else would have to check the other houses around him and he needed backup at Dara Pennstead's house on River Road.

It would be a long way around through multiple circles to get to Dara's by road. Traffic would be backed up to a standstill. But a dirt road, closed to the public, ran along the river from the neighborhood Carl was in to connect to River Road near the north end of the airport. Carl drove through a wire fence to get on the road and bounced along a half mile to the other end, breaking through another wire fence without slowing down. He was driving a sheriff's department pickup truck with push bars on the front. The bars protected the front of the truck but the department would have to pay to fix the scratches in the paint.

Carl figured the man who kidnapped Dara had come looking for the cocaine left in Geoff's plane. Dara had the receipt Carl had given her for the two kilos but a drug dealer might not be satisfied with a piece of paper, no matter how official it looked. The man, assuming it was a man, might harm or kill Dara out of anger or to demonstrate the merciless strength of the dealer's gang. If Carl cornered him, there could be a gun battle or a hostage situation. The Sheriff's Department would have a hard time assembling a swat team with so many resources committed to the fire.

If Carl met a black sedan coming the other way on River Road he would stop it, draw his gun, and take cover. If he didn't see the sedan, he would check Dara's house.

River Road had no cars on it going either way. Carl cycled his car's siren as he raced by the airport and approached Dara's house through the smoke. A deputy's patrol car was on the scene with Deputy Shane O'Connell standing beside it. He had been on this road checking that residents were evacuating. Next to his car in Dara's driveway sat a white Toyota RAV4. Carl snapped a quick photo of the car and its license plate with his phone. He would look up the license number later.

"Waiting for backup," said the deputy when Carl stepped out of his car.

"That's me," said Carl. "We need to go now."

Carl and Shane drew their guns as they approached the house. Both men were wearing bullet proof vests. They stood on either side of the front door and Carl rapped the door with his knuckles.

"Sheriff's department," shouted Carl. No answer, no sound of activity in the house.

"Open the door or you're resisting arrest," said Carl. He doubted his threat would stand up in court but it might serve in the moment.

No answer. It was a sturdy door and it would take a battering ram to break it open. But Carl tried the door latch and found it unlocked.

He went through the door first, his gun pointed in front of him. Shane followed close behind. When Carl swung his gun into the living room, he saw a heavy man with a beard slumped forward in a chair. Both the man's shoes were bloody and there was blood on his shirt as well. The man's hands hung empty off the front of the chair. He didn't look up but he was breathing slow breaths.

"Watch behind us," Carl said to Shane. He radioed the County Sheriff's Department dispatch and identified himself. "We need an air ambulance here," he said and gave Dara's address. "One man wounded and bleeding in the chest and the feet. Apparent gunshot. They can land the helicopter on the tarmac behind the house." He didn't explain why the house had tarmac behind it. The dispatcher could see a map of the location on the terminal in front of her. The helicopter pilot could also navigate to the house through the smoke and talk with the other helicopters in the area to make sure they all kept their distance from each other.

"Air ambulance on the way," said the dispatcher.

"I have to ask this man some questions now in case he passes out. Then I'm going to lay him on the floor and put pressure on the chest wound."

"Lay him on his side so he can breathe easier," said dispatch.

"Right," said Carl.

Carl knelt down next to the man.

"Anyone else in the house?"

"They left," the man whispered.

"Who?"

"Dara Pennstead and some guy with a gun. He shot me."

"Where did they go?"

"To find somebody named Leon. He has the money."

"What's your name?"

"Dave Pasciuti."

"Is that your RAV4 outside?"

"Yes?"

"What do you know about Geoff Pennstead getting shot?"

No answer. Dave was getting weaker. He wanted the man in the sheriff's uniform to help him but, foggy-brained as he was, he knew for certain that he didn't want to talk about Geoff Pennstead.

"A Medevac is coming," said Carl. "I'm going to help you lie on the floor. You'll be more comfortable and you'll breathe better." Dave was too weak to complain. Carl and Shane pulled him off the chair and gently laid him on his side on the floor, his back up against a sofa. No sucking sound came from the wound and that was good news. The bullet had not punctured a lung. Carl pulled a pillow over the bullet hole in Dave's chest and pushed on it. That would slow down the loss of blood.

Another deputy had arrived and Carl told him to search the house along with Shane. They came back to say no one else was in the house.

"Take over here and keep pressing on the wound until the ambulance gets here." Carl moved aside and let Shane take over. Dave was breathing but barely conscious. "I'm going to the Martinez house in Upriver."

Carl radioed the Sheriff's Department to request deputies at Leon and Elizabeth's house. Carl didn't know the house number but he'd been there before. "It's the fifth house on the right on Owyhee Road," he told dispatch.

"We don't have anybody to spare," said the dispatcher. She was on the edge of the anxiousness dispatchers could usually rise above.

"It's life and death."

"It's life and death if we don't get Sunriver evacuated." She was getting exasperated. Carl was irrelevant to the big problem she was trying to help solve. On another day, he would have been the department's top priority. Today he was a distraction.

"I'm going," said Carl. It might take two hours to drive through Sunriver on roads now jammed with traffic. The bike path along the river, barely wide enough for his truck, would be much shorter. Carl followed the path to a road close to the emergency gate to Spring River Road. Cars inched along Spring River and forty cars waited to get out the gate. Carl ignored the gate and aimed his truck at the wooden fence that ran beside the road. He revved the engine with his left foot on the brake pedal. He released the brake and slammed on the gas. The car shot forward, bouncing over the rough ground and bitterbrush. When it burst through the fence, the airbag inflated and slapped Carl hard in the face and chest. He sat stunned for a few seconds and then recovered.

Across Spring River Road was the locked maintenance gate into Upriver Ranch with a black sedan parked in front of it. Carl broke through the wooden fence beside the gate, this time bracing himself for the blow from the steering wheel. He had visited the Martinez house on an earlier case and knew exactly where it was. He navigated to it over roads, fairways, and cart paths. He parked out of sight of the house and approached it on foot.

Chapter 35

The Tipping Point

Leon and Elizabeth had packed Leon's Acura. Gabriel and Maria had helped. One of Leon's paintings now had a hole in it from the rush. They were watching the news on television, a strange thing in the middle of the day. They were getting jumpy. They couldn't start anything, whether painting, or reading, or laundry, because they could get interrupted at any moment by an evacuation order.

"There's more coffee," said Elizabeth, "and more bagels. Shall we play some dominoes while we wait?"

Leon took down a leather case of dominoes from a shelf in the room and set it on a square game table with four chairs around it. Gabriel, Maria, and Elizabeth moved to the table feigning enthusiasm

The front door, unlocked, swung open and bounced off the doorstop with a cracking sound. A man with a shiny shirt stepped in with one arm around Dara Pennstead's shoulders, the opposite hand holding a gun to her head.

"What on earth?" demanded Leon.

"Are you Leon Martinez?" the man insisted.

"Yes I am," said Leon.

"All of you," said the man, "sit down the couch where I can keep an eye on you." He clearly didn't mean Dara because he still had a tight grip on her, and he flicked the gun toward the others to emphasize his command. The couch was built for three people and it was going to be crowded.

"Now!" shouted the man. "And turn that damn TV off."

Leon slowly reached for the remote on the coffee table in front of the couch and pressed the off button. The two men sat closest to the front door and closest to the man with the gun, as if to protect their wives. They faced the blank television screen but their eyes were on the man. He dragged Dara farther into the room to face them all, making the gallantry of the men pointless.

"Who else is in the house?" asked the man.

"No one," said Leon, then second-guessed himself. If the man thought someone else was in the house he would act more cautiously, ask more questions, move more slowly. But when the man discovered Leon had lied, the odds of his shooting somebody would go up. Leon did not correct himself.

"I want the cash," said the man.

"What cash?" said Leon.

The man pointed his gun at Maria and fired. She jerked back against the couch. Her head snapped forward, then back, then fell forward again, her chin resting on her chest.

"What have you done?" yelled Elizabeth. "There was no need for that. What kind of animal are you?"

Leon, deafened by the blast of the pistol, could barely hear her.

The man swept his gun to the right and rested his aim at Elizabeth.

"Where is the cash?" shouted Che. "Don't make me ask again."

"Che, Che, Che," Dara yelled. "It's in his golf bag. I put it there."

"The bag is in the garage," said Leon, "but there's no money in it."

"There better be," said Che. "Let's go, all of us. Stay together."

"You lead," he said to Elizabeth. "Don't get out of my sight."

Leon and Elizabeth got up but Gabriel slid over to Maria and put his arm over her shoulders. He rolled her up to a sitting position and looked her in the face. Her eyes were wide open and her face was slack. There was no response.

"She's done for," said Che. "And you will be too if you don't get up." Gabriel held Maria in his arms and gave no sign he'd heard what Che had said.

"Let me get him," said Leon, as though he were an associate of Che's and helping him out. He stepped over to Gabriel and took one arm in both hands, pulling gently at first and then more firmly. "We'll call an ambulance," Leon told him. "That's the best chance we have." Gabriel was so confused he accepted Leon's words. There was no way Che was going to let them call an ambulance. And Leon did not think that an ambulance would help Maria. Gabriel let Leon lead him over to the hallway that led to the garage.

"Keep together," commanded Che. He came along behind them, one hand on his pistol and the other on Dara. He followed them into the garage and carefully scanned the room.

"The bag is right here, next to the wall," said Leon.

"Show me," said Che. "And get the money out slowly."

"In the long side pocket," said Dara.

Leon bent over and unzipped the pocket. Che moved closer, still with his gun to Dara's head. Leon pulled a fat manila envelope out of the bag, folded in half lengthwise and wrapped tight with transparent tape. Written on the envelope were the words, "Property of Dara Pennstead. Return when asked."

"Open it," said Che.

"I'll need a knife," replied Leon.

Che considered this for a moment. He let go of Dara. "None of you move," he said as he reached in his pocket, pulled out his jackknife, and handed it to Leon. "Don't get any ideas. Open it on the car hood."

It was odd, Leon thought, how Dara was looking open-mouthed at the car, Elizabeth's blue Camry, as though it were the strangest car in the world.

Leon, the art teacher, was familiar with knives and paper. The knife was extremely sharp. He slit the envelope open lengthwise and dumped out stacks of cash in paper wrappers.

"Are you going to count it?" asked Elizabeth. She was making fun of Che. And if that made him mad so much the better. "Now take the money and get out of here. We won't call 911 and the police are too busy to worry about you. They probably have too many calls to answer already."

Che didn't say a word. He aimed his pistol at Elizabeth, holding it out at arm's length. Leon instantly stepped in front of her. When he heard the shot, he expected pain and a quick collapse. He would find himself on the floor, staring at the cement, and quickly losing consciousness. But the pain he felt was only in his ears. The sound of gunshot had echoed off the hard walls of the garage. Che was no longer standing in front of him. He was crumpled on the floor, his gun still in his hand.

Dara burst into tears. Leon was dazed but relieved to find Elizabeth clutching him while he supported his weight on his own two feet. Gabriel was still standing but huddled into himself. There was another person in the room now, appearing as if by magic. He wore a tan shirt and pants with a heavy black vest. He pointed a pistol at Che on the floor. The new man's arms were tensed but his eyes, surprisingly cool, surveyed the room. Leon recognized his teeth, straight across and even. It was Carl Breuninger.

"Anyone with him?" asked Carl.

It took a long search through the caverns of his brain for Leon to come up with the simple answer. "No."

"Any more weapons?"

"His knife," said Leon. "I still have it in my hand. Shall I put it down?"

"Place it on the floor," said Carl. "Any of you hurt?"

Dara had collapsed to her knees, her hands to her face, sobbing.

"Not here," said Leon. "But our friend, Maria, was shot in the living room."

"Yes," said Carl. "This and the living room are crime scenes. Why don't you all go sit in the dining room while I sort this out. Do not discuss. I repeat. Do not discuss what just happened here. I'll need statements from each of you. Let's get out of the garage now. Deputies are on their way to secure the house."

"Just get this money out of my house," said Elizabeth. "And this woman."

"As soon as I talk to her," said Carl. "In the meantime, wait in the dining room. No talking." He took pictures to show where Che, his gun, and the knife were lying. He took more pictures of the money and the envelope. He put a glove on and put the gun, the knife, and the money in separate evidence bags. He holstered his own gun and checked for Che's pulse to be sure. There was none.

Chapter 36

Who Knew What

Two deputies had arrived and Carl directed them to separate the witnesses. Leon protested that he wanted to stay with Elizabeth and Gabriel.

"We've all had quite a shock. We need to be together, especially with Gabriel. The poor man's wife has just been killed. We promise not to discuss what happened here." Carl let the three of them stay together at the dining room table while he called the Sheriff. A woman deputy took Dara down the hall to the guest bedroom while Carl called his boss. Gordon Knapp's assistant answered the call and tried to tell Carl the Sheriff was busy keeping on top of the fire and investigating who started it.

"Tell him it's important and I'll be brief," said Carl. The assistant put the call through. "I had to shoot a perp," Carl told Gordon. "You'll get a full report but I wanted you to know right away. The guy's dead. He shot and killed one person and he was about to shoot three more. It's part of the Geoff Pennstead case. He was alone. No suspects on the loose."

"Witnesses will back you up?"

"I'm sure they will. I saved their lives."

"Is the media going to find out anything that will cause a problem?"

"I smashed two fences and scratched up the front of the car but no other collateral damage. Nobody else hurt, threatened, or put in danger. All proper police practice."

"Written report by tomorrow?" asked the Sheriff.

"You got it."

Carl was angry at the people he had to interview. One or more of these people, maybe all of them, had known about the money and hadn't told him about it.

And how did Dara Pennstead even know Leon and Elizabeth? What was their relationship and how did the money fit into it? Aside from that, how did a young man, now dead and dressed like a cartel enforcer, wind up in the Martinez garage?

Who to interview first? Gabriel, the houseguest, was an emotional wreck and he probably knew less than anyone. Dara was emotional, probably dazed, and the person most likely to fabricate even when she was rational. Carl liked Leon, even trusted him, and Leon might remember some detail that others overlooked. But for a clear and honest description of events, Carl decided Elizabeth would be the best bet.

And Carl was right, up to a point. She gave Carl a thorough and detailed chronology of events between Dara and Che's sudden arrival and Carl shooting the man dead—who was where, who said what, who did what, and even what order they all walked into the garage. She had never seen the man before and she'd only seen Dara once or twice when she was singing in Bend. To be thorough, Carl asked Elizabeth whether she knew Geoff Pennstead.

"As it happens," she said. "Forty years ago, he was a manager in the branch of Deschutes River Bank where I started out. Then he moved to Portland and left the bank. I hadn't heard anything about him until he was in the news for the shooting."

Leon's description of what happened at his house was consistent with Elizabeth's. He had no idea there was cash in his golf bag or how Dara knew it was there. The only way it could get there, he thought, was if Dara, or someone, had put it in the bag while it was sitting in the rack at the Woodlands golf course bag drop after he'd finished his game. He'd had a beer with his friends before he brought his car around to pick up the clubs and take them home. Carl could ask the guys at the bag drop if they saw her.

Carl asked only two questions of Gabriel—whether he'd ever seen the man who shot his wife before or whether he knew anything about him. Gabriel said no. Carl expressed his sympathies then brought the three of them—Gabriel, Elizabeth, and Leon—together in the dining room.

"My interview with Mrs. Pennstead will take some time and the crime scene investigator will need to be here for several hours. We've called two hearses but I don't have an estimated arrival for them. Have you got a place you'd rather be than here? They've got the fire under control and they've called off the mandatory evacuation in Sunriver. You could wait outside the house but there's still smoke in the air."

"We were getting ready to evacuate. We're packed and ready to go," said Leon.

"We can't come back to this house until that garage is washed and scrubbed like an operating room," said Elizabeth. "You'll have to lock up the house for us, detective. We're going to be gone for days."

"Understood," said Carl. "I'll give you the names of companies that specialize in crime scene clean-up and biohazards. There isn't a lot of blood but we don't know what germs or drugs are in it. And of course, you want to remove all traces of what happened. The companies are very thorough."

"We could stay in a hotel," said Leon.

Elizabeth overrode him. "We'll go crazy cooped up in a hotel room. And we can't inflict ourselves on Dan and Amy. We should stay with Sarah." Sarah Chatham was Elizabeth's childhood friend who lived on Mirror Pond in Bend. "And I'm sure she won't mind putting up Gabriel. She has plenty of room."

"I'll only stay one night," said Gabriel. "I need to go home and make arrangements."

"Anything you want," said Elizabeth. "Come stay with us one night at Sarah's and we'll take you to the airport in the morning."

"But we don't want to put Sarah and Bud in danger," said Leon.

"Do you think we're in danger, Carl?"

"You need to be careful but no, I don't think you're in danger. We'll tell the media that the Sheriff's Department has confiscated the drugs and money the man was sent to bring back. I'll ask Mrs. Pennstead if this Che ever said your name over the phone or if he might have sent a text about you but there is no reason he would need to do that. Whoever he worked for must know about Dara Pennstead and we're going to increase our protection around her."

Dara was in a spare bedroom and Carl could hear her singing softly to herself while he talked with the others. She'd started with a sad song, "Am I Blue?" and was on to happier songs, "It Might as Well Be Spring," and "The Sunny Side of the Street." She was practicing the familiar, trying to reassure herself. She was on to "Pennies from Heaven" when the others left and he went to interview her in the guest bedroom. The woman deputy who had been sitting with her was glad to see Carl. She whispered to Carl that she would rather be investigating the crime than babysitting. And Dara's old-fashioned songs were not on the deputy's playlist.

Carl sat in the one wooden chair in the bedroom while Dara sat on the side of the single bed she'd been lying on.

Dara told Carl the man called himself "Che" and she pronounced the name with a sarcastic laugh. She was still upset. Carl could understand. The man had held her captive in his car for over an hour, shot two people in front of her eyes, and she fully expected he would shoot her. She was mad about the bruises on her arm and furious that Che had pressed a gun to her head. She said she'd gotten some rough treatment in her life and she thought that was over when she married Geoff. She would have killed Che in a second if she could have.

That danger was over now, Carl told her. Che was dead and Carl was there with two other deputies. "Did the man tell you where the money came from or how he knew you had it?"

"I didn't know the money had anything to do with Geoff," she said. Carl thought she was lying but he let it pass for now. "This Che thought I had the coke you found in the plane. I showed him the receipt you gave me. Then he wanted the money he said his business associates paid Geoff. Business associates, my ass. I told him I didn't know about any money but then he shot Dave Pasciuti and I told him about the money I'd put in Leon's golf bag. I was afraid he would shoot me. You'll want to know where all that money came from. I'd like to know too. Somebody left it in a gym bag at my back door in the middle of the night. I have no idea who did that or why. It was in Geoff's gym bag when I found it. Somebody must have taken it or found it when Geoff was killed and decided it belonged to me. I'm grateful, I guess, but I don't know who would be good enough, or generous, or rich enough to do that."

"And you didn't think to tell me about this money that mysteriously appeared?" asked Carl.

"I thought the money was Geoff's and now it was mine. At least whoever left it thought I should have it. And I sure as hell needed it. I thought if I told you about it, you'd take it away. I guess if I'd known I'd almost be shot over it, I would have called you."

Carl was not surprised at Dara's story. He didn't let on how frustrated he was.

"The whole time he was with you at your house, in the car, and here at the Martinez house, did this Che call or text anyone or did anyone call him?"

Dara thought about it for minute. "I don't think so," she said. "He looked at a map on his phone while we were driving to Leon's house. He might have texted someone but I didn't see him do it. He definitely didn't talk to anyone." *That's good news,* thought Carl. It meant Che's confederates probably didn't know about Leon and Elizabeth Martinez. If the Sheriff kept their names out of the press, they should be safe.

"How do you know Dave Pasciuti and what was he doing at your house?"

"He was a bartender where I used to sing," said Dara. "He said he'd loaned money to Geoff and he came to ask me to pay it back. I told him I didn't have any money. When this 'Che' showed up, he shot Dave in the feet to scare us into giving him drugs or cash or whatever. When he took me outside to show him the way to Leon's house, he shot Dave dead. He was so casual about it. Poor Dave."

"He survived. At least so far. He's on his way to St. Charles if he isn't already there. Dave told me you'd gone to the Martinez house."

"You saved my life," said Dara. "All of our lives. Except for that poor woman on the couch."

Carl asked dispatch to arrange a hotel room in Bend for Dara. She protested that she wanted to go home.

"I can't allow that," said Carl. "Your house is a crime scene. And it's for your own protection. Che may not be the last thug to show up on your doorstep."

"At least let me get some things."

"Make a list and we'll have a deputy bring them to you."

Carl watched Elizabeth, Leon, and Gabriel leave in Leon's car for Sarah Chatham's house. Gabriel was reluctant to leave Maria behind, now with a blanket over her, but Carl gently led him to the car.

Carl drove Dara to the hotel in Bend himself. He left one deputy to wait for the hearses and lock up the house. He got another deputy to meet him at the hotel and keep an eye on Dara. Breuninger had a long evening ahead of him writing up reports on the incidents of the day. In a couple of days, he'd have to sit through a hearing on his officer-involved shooting. He'd done his duty, risked his life, and saved three people. But it was still going to be a pain to sit through an onslaught of questions, all aimed at making sure he hadn't done anything wrong.

Before he went back to headquarters to write reports, Carl wanted to talk with Dave Pasciuti in the hospital in Bend—assuming Dave wasn't too far gone on painkillers and sedation. The doctor on the case told Carl over the phone that Dave could talk for a bit but he would tire quickly. He'd tell Dave that Carl was coming. Dave would recover from his wounds but he wouldn't be walking or serving drinks behind a bar for at least two months.

Chapter 37

Confessions and Repentance

Carl found Dave Pasciuti tilted up in bed in a private room. Some friend had already gotten Dave an attorney to stand by his bed through the interview. The attorney, a haggard man of about forty whose suit needed to be cleaned and pressed, might tell Dave not to say anything. Or he might have enough brains and confidence to let Dave answer some of Carl's questions and place himself on the right side of the law.

"You're not a suspect," Carl began. "You're a victim and a witness. But I'm going to read you your Miranda rights anyway."

"We'll waive the reading," said the attorney. That was a good sign.

Carl tried to act friendly and sympathetic but it was difficult. Carl strongly suspected Dave could have prevented this whole disaster, from Geoff Pennstead's death to the near death of three other people. Carl would bet Dave was somehow involved in Geoff's drug smuggling. Even after the smuggling, when Geoff was shot, Dave should have come forward to tell the Sheriff what he knew. He obviously knew something. He was almost certainly the driver of the white RAV 4 that Shanti Sargeant and Tommy Westlake had seen. And Che hadn't shot him for target practice.

But Carl got more than he expected from Dave. Dave said he'd loaned money to Geoff to fuel his plane but he wouldn't say why he did that. He went to Sunriver Airport with Geoff and paid for the fuel directly. While the gas was going in, Dave dropped an Apple AirTag into the gas tank. Dave was concerned about getting his money back and he wanted to know when Geoff got back to Sunriver. Dave's attorney would not let Dave talk about how he knew Geoff Pennstead or whether Dave knew anyone in Arizona.

Dave said he tracked Geoff's trip all the way. The plane's transponder was on when Geoff took off from Sunriver and Dave could follow it online with Flight Aware until Geoff landed in Flagstaff, Arizona three hours later. Dave hadn't given him money to refuel in Flagstaff but somebody must have, unless Geoff had some cash hidden away after all.

Three hours after Geoff landed in Flagstaff, the AirTag told Dave that the plane was in the Sonoran Desert in Mexico. In another two hours, the AirTag said Geoff was back in Flagstaff. Or so Dave said. Dave's iPhone purely reported where the AirTag was last detected. It didn't keep a record of everywhere the AirTag had been.

With his attorney's permission, Dave used his iPhone to show Carl he could identify the plane's current location, still in the hangar at the Pennstead house.

Carl suspected that Dave, eager to get his money back, was the one who cut off the fuel in Geoff's car. But Dave would not admit it or admit that he was anywhere in the area when Geoff was killed.

"If you saw him get shot, or saw a likely killer at the scene," said Carl, "you'd be doing us a big favor and it won't be forgotten."

"My client has nothing to say about that," said Dave's lawyer. "And you have nothing to offer. My client is not charged with any crime. He is a helpful citizen."

"Geoff Pennstead smuggled drugs. Your client helped him commit that crime by loaning him gas money."

"My client said he loaned money to Pennstead but he never said he knew what Pennstead was going to do with the money. I'm not sure you can even prove Geoff Pennstead smuggled drugs. You've got nothing. And Dave has been very helpful to you." Carl had to admit the attorney was right about that.

Dave would not say why he went to Dara Pennstead's house but he did describe what happened once he was there and Che showed up. From that point on, Dave's story matched Dara's, except that Dara thought Dave was dead when Che took her from the house.

Ash coated everything in Sunriver—houses, cars, trees, roads, and golf courses. Pool filters ran for twenty-four hours a day to get the water clean again. The smell of smoke hung heavy for a week. Some people were still suffering from smoke inhalation and some had gone to the hospital. But no one had died from the fire itself except the boy who had started it. Firefighters found his body during their mop up operation. Tommy's body hadn't burned and his father reclaimed it.

Twenty houses were destroyed beyond repair, including eight at the end of River Road. Dara's was spared. Carl told the firefighters it was a crime scene that needed to be preserved. All over Sunriver owners had to rebuild their decks or patch charred roofs. Newly bare black branches had to be cut down. The forest floor in many places would still be black after winter snow came and went. But new grass and the leaves on the currants and bitterbrush would soften the landscape when spring came.

The riding stables had burned to the ground and the horses were moved to a barn east of Bend until the following summer. The large steel hangars at the airport had survived along with the planes inside them. But the little wooden flight operations building had burned to the ground. The airport never officially closed though no planes landed during the fire.

The fire department saved the marina, the restaurant by the river, and the Nature Center. It helped that they were all right next to river.

The forest west of the river was desolate, bare trunks of trees sticking up like a well-spaced collection of telephone poles. The Forest Service was quick to cut down the trees near the water so they would not fall in the river. But planning for the rest of the land had not even started. Sunriver residents wanted the ugly trees logged and new seedlings planted. The Forest Service might even make money on the timber. But environmentalists wanted to let nature restore the land the way it naturally would after a fire.

Dara's house was unlivable without a deep, deep cleaning. It smelled like a trapper's cabin after a long wet winter and absolutely everything, from the sheets to the silverware, was covered in a thin black layer of soot. The local housecleaning companies, who usually cleaned not-very-dirty rental houses once every week or two between renters, couldn't keep up. They pulled in workers from the entire Northwest, some of whom helped themselves to whatever took their fancy inside the house.

Dara stayed, worried and bored, in a hotel in Bend. It was a two-hundred room hotel that catered to conventions as much as to tourists. No large group was coming in for ten days and they had rooms available even in the middle of summer. Dara's room on the second floor had a balcony overlooking the river. She spent her days on the phone prodding lawyers and accountants to untangle Geoff's finances. They kept finding more places Geoff owed money. But also more investments—some solvent, some broke, some readily sellable for cash, and some that would take years to sell. Dara struggled, not knowing whether she was rich or poor, whether she could keep the house or would have to go back to living in a cheap apartment and working as a waitress, harder work than ever now that she was older.

Chapter 38

Revelation

Sarah Chatham's house on Mirror Pond was a ten-minute walk from where Elizabeth grew up in Bend. Its east-facing terrace looked out over the pond, a dam-widened stretch of the Deschutes River. Downtown Bend rose behind the trees across the water. It was the ideal place, Leon thought, for Elizabeth to recover from having her home invaded and a man shot dead in their garage. The Bend Police cruised past Sarah's house several times a day and Carl Breuninger called or stopped by to see how they were, always hoping, they knew, that Leon or Elizabeth would remember something that would give Carl a new clue, a new line of investigation.

Bud, Sarah's husband, tried to talk about art with Leon, but his knowledge was limited and his interest, sincere but awakened for the first time, led to questions and comments he knew were stupid when he asked them. But it was friendly conversation, a reassurance that most of life was not about crime or violence. Bud tried to talk with Elizabeth about business, the economy, and the stock market. But Elizabeth had been a banker and Bud had sold heavy machinery to saw mills. They started repeating the same conversations.

"Sit on the terrace and read a good book," said Sarah. "That's what I like to do when I have the time." Sarah was a semi-retired attorney, the partner nominally in charge of the small office in Bend, a branch of a large firm in Portland. She walked to her office most mornings and came home for lunch with Bud, and now Leon and Elizabeth. Sometimes she went back to the office in the afternoon. Sometimes she worked at home and sometimes she didn't work at all.

Elizabeth was reading a two-volume history of Oregon. Leon was reading a book on the arrest in China of the artist, Ai Weiwei. Elizabeth put down her book on the second afternoon and looked out over the pond from where they were sitting on the deck. It was a hard look, a look of concentration and tension, not a look of appreciation for the beautiful summer day in front of her eyes.

"I need to talk to Sarah when she comes home," said Elizabeth, "and I need you to be there."

"Over cocktails?" asked Leon.

"Might as well, though this won't be relaxing." It was late afternoon and the shadow of the house, edging toward the pond, kept them out of the heat.

Elizabeth wished that Bud was not there when Sarah joined them in the big wicker chairs with fat green cushions on the terrace. But she could hardly shoo her friend's husband away. Fortunately he had the sense not to say anything as Elizabeth told her story and Sarah listened carefully.

"There are things I haven't told Detective Breuninger. I didn't think they would help and I didn't want to get mixed up in this murder. But now we are mixed up in it, thanks to that woman bringing that money into our house." Elizabeth surprised Sarah with the harsh tone in her voice. But Elizabeth dropped it and went on.

"And I think I owe it to Breuninger to tell him what I know, even if I don't think it will help. So I'm looking for two things. First, whether you think I should tell him anything at all. And second, and I'm sorry to ask for your legal advice, I want to make sure I do this properly and don't get myself in trouble."

"Ask away," said Sarah. "We'll get a criminal attorney involved if we have to."

"I was there when Geoff Pennstead was shot. I'm sorry, Leon, that I didn't tell you this before. I didn't want you to worry or push me to call Carl. I thought this would be simpler if I pretended I didn't know anything. And I didn't really know very much.

"Anyhow, Geoff's car was parked by the side of the road and he was waving for me to stop and so I did. I didn't recognize him at first and I didn't see he had a gun. He was carrying a gym bag. So he came up to my car and I put my window down.

"'I need your car,' he says. 'It's very important. You'll get it back. Get out.' He goes to pull open the door but it's locked. Then he stuffs the gym bag through the window into the back seat. He has a sort of worn-out desperate look on his face. Then I see the gun. He's holding it in his hand but at least he's not pointing it at me. I don't think he recognizes me but I recognize him. He was my boss fifty years ago and he treated me terribly. I won't go into that but I'll tell you I could never forget him or what he did.

"And I know at the time, he'll wind up in jail for hijacking my car and threatening me with a gun. I'll see to it. I'll give him the damn car and then I'll call the police. I know his name. He's not going to get away with this.

"But I'm still thinking about the tournament I'm going to. I'm in charge of it and I want to be there. My revenge will be that I'll go on with my normal life and this guy will get arrested and go to prison.

"'Let me get my golf clubs,' I say. I'm trying to stay calm. He's very agitated and I'm afraid he's going to shoot me without thinking. I act like his taking my car was a minor inconvenience, no worse than the windshield wipers not working. I use the release inside the car to pop the trunk where my clubs are. Then I'm not sure what happened. He looks back toward the trunk and suddenly it's got his full attention. He raises his gun and starts toward the back of the car. Then I hear a loud bang. It must have been the shotgun but I don't know very well what a shotgun sounds like. All I can think about is I want to get away. The car is still in gear and I step on the gas as hard as I can. Then I know I'm going too fast and I slow down." Elizabeth stopped talking and caught her breath. She'd put off telling this for a long time. No one asked her a question and she went on.

"Then, you know, I think, 'I'm okay. The car's okay. I'm still on my way to the Woodlands. I'm no part of what happened and I want no part in it. I don't want to think about it.' So I decide it didn't happen. It was a dream and now it's over. I'm gone, going about my business. Let somebody else worry about what happened. I went to Bend for groceries after the tournament and got the car washed. I thought there might be traces of blood on it that I couldn't see. I didn't remember about the gym bag until later."

"You are one tough lady," said Bud. The others ignored him.

"Elizabeth," said Leon, "why didn't you tell me? We should have shared this."

"There was nothing we had to do," said Elizabeth.

"Did you see who shot Geoff?" asked Sarah.

"No. I didn't see anyone. I just heard the shot."

"Was that my shotgun?" asked Leon. "And how the heck did it get there?"

"It must have been yours. I had it in the trunk. I was planning to turn it in to the police on my way home from the tournament. I'm sorry, Leon, because I know it meant a lot to you. But I hated having it in the house and you hadn't used it in years. It took all my will power to pick up that gun and put it in the trunk."

"But you took it out of the trunk when you got home and reloaded it?"

"That was the worst, touching those bullets."

"Cartridges."

"Whatever."

Bud spoke up with an awkward question. "How did the gun get back in the trunk?"

"I don't know. Whoever shot Geoff must have put the gun in the trunk right after he fired it. He must have been quick because I took off only a second or two after I heard the shot."

"Would you have wiped the man's fingerprints off the gun?" asked Sarah.

"No. I guess my fingerprints would be on top of his. I cleaned the trunk when I got home but I didn't dare try to wipe down the gun."

"I wiped down the gun when I cleaned it," said Leon. "The only fingerprints on it will be mine from putting it away."

"We'll want to give the shotgun to the Sheriff as evidence," said Sarah. "It will be a while before you get it back."

"I definitely want to get it back," said Leon. "It was my grandfather's."

"It's not a good thing," said Sarah, "that you brought the gun to the crime scene. But I think the law will understand you had no intention of using it."

Leon could see Elizabeth didn't want to talk anymore about the gun. He changed the subject.

"How did the killer happen to be there? And why did he shoot Geoff Pennstead? How did he even know Pennstead would be there?"

"We don't need to know all that," said Sarah. "We're here to make sure Elizabeth is protected from prosecution."

"Because she brought the gun that killed Pennstead?"

"No, not in and of itself."

"Because she left the scene of a crime and didn't report it?" asked Leon.

"That's not a crime in Oregon," said Sarah. "It would be in Ohio or Texas but it isn't here."

"Then why should Elizabeth worry about prosecution?"

"The Sheriff and the DA have a murder. The public wants them to solve it, to arrest someone, and put them on trial. The Sheriff only knows of two people who were there. One is dead and the other brought the murder weapon to the scene. I don't think either Carl Breuninger or the district attorney believes Elizabeth shot Geoffrey Pennstead. But they may be influenced by political pressure. We need to be prepared."

"But let's move on," said Sarah, turning to Elizabeth. "You still had the gym bag," said Sarah. "What did you do with it?"

"I took it home and opened it with gloves on. It had cash in it, a lot. I don't know how much. If I took it to the police, they would ask me where I found it and I didn't want to say. And I certainly didn't want to tell them I was there when Geoff Pennstead was shot. I thought of leaving the money at the door of a charity when they were closed—Habitat for Humanity or Andi's Kitchen or something. But then I thought the money belonged to Geoff Pennstead, at least as far as I could tell. If it belonged to him then it most likely now belonged to his wife. Let her decide what to do with it. I left the bag on her doorstep in the middle of the night. Next thing I know, the money's in manila envelopes in Leon's golf bag and there's a man with a gun who shows up looking for it. Detective Breuninger shoots the man dead in my bedroom and I'm hiding out from some criminal gang."

"Fine," said Sarah. "I think you're safe from prosecution. We should get a criminal attorney involved and then go to Detective Breuninger and the district attorney. Get a pledge of immunity from prosecution and tell them everything that happened."

Sarah took her phone off the white wicker table next to her and called the criminal attorney she knew best in Bend, Tod Morgan, and asked him to represent Elizabeth. Tod was not quick to take the case, he said, because he thought Elizabeth would never be prosecuted and never go to trial. His fee for representing her would never amount to much. And if he represented Elizabeth, he couldn't represent the actual killer, assuming the man was caught. He might miss out on a big fat fee for defending a murderer.

"Suppose he's a bum with no money," said Sarah. "Elizabeth can afford to pay you. Promptly, no horsing around."

Tod agreed to take the case. After talking with Elizabeth himself, he'd set up a meeting with Carl Breuninger and the district attorney's office. He'd insist that the DA grant Elizabeth immunity from prosecution in return for her testimony at the trial of the killer, assuming he was caught and went to trial.

Chapter 39

Cries and Whispers

Had this case gotten simpler? Or had it grown more complicated? After a long interview with Elizabeth Martinez and Sarah Chatham, Carl had many facts he hadn't had before. But Geoff Pennstead's killer, instead of emerging from the murk, was sinking further into it. Carl told his wife Estelle that he was turning over rocks and finding nothing underneath them.

The next rock he turned over was Joe Rheel, the guy calling himself Che who came to Sunriver looking for missing coke, then shot Dave Pasciuti, went after money when he couldn't get the drugs, and wound up dead in the Martinez garage. Carl looked him up in the criminal database. Multiple arrests and convictions in Phoenix and Flagstaff, starting with car theft when he was young, graduating to burglary, possession with intent to sell, and possession of a handgun while on parole. Affiliation with a gang called the Amigos. Currently on parole in Coconino County where Flagstaff was the county seat. Carl called the county sheriff, gave Joe Rheel's name, and was connected to a detective.

"We've been looking for him," said the Coconino detective.

"He's in the morgue in Deschutes County, Oregon," said Carl, "along with a local named Geoffrey Pennstead. We don't think Rheel killed Pennstead but there's a connection between them and I'm trying to understand it better."

"Never heard of Geoffrey Pennstead and I know Rheel's associates pretty well."

"I never heard of Joe Rheel until yesterday. He came up here after a package of coke that was left in a plane. We already had the drugs so he went after the money Geoffrey Pennstead was paid. He was about to kill Pennstead's wife when I cut him off."

"So you don't know what happened down here?"

"Not a peep," said Carl.

"We learned that Joe Rheel's gang, the Amigos—I mean he wasn't the head of it but he belonged to it—the Amigos had gotten a shipment of coke and they were cutting it up in one guy's basement. They were all together when we surprised them. You'd think they'd surrender when we surrounded the house. They'd hire lawyers to persuade a judge they were only having a party and none of them knew where the coke came from. But some fool starts shooting. They're in a cellar with one exit and we've got all the windows covered. Five of them dead and four of them in the hospital. But Joe Rheel isn't there. That's how come we're looking for him."

"He won't testify," said Carl.

The other man snorted a laugh.

"Down here anyway, the guys in the morgue are the least cooperative."

Carl asked if the detective knew where Joe Rheel was on the day Geoffrey Pennstead was shot.

"Let see if I have anything on that." The detective still had his phone to his mouth. Carl could hear him humming softly to himself as he searched for the information. "He had a meeting with his parole officer and he made it. Rheel is supposedly working in a body shop but the report says he was dressed like he was going to a party. Ironed shirt, creased pants, and dress shoes. Not a spot of dirt on him."

"If that's the case then he wasn't in Oregon killing my victim. One possibility eliminated. How about his buddies? Are these guys with some sort of cartel?"

"The cartel is who gave us the tip. They don't like competition. So tell me about this Geoffrey Pennstead."

"A guy with a plane who needed money. We know he flew to Flagstaff and we think he flew into Mexico and back. He may have brought in the drugs you found."

"We'll probably need your help when and if we have a trial for the guys who survived."

"I'll tell my boss I might be needed in Flagstaff."

"You'll feel right at home. I've been to Bend once and they've got their similarities—high desert, mountains, lots of ponderosas. Used to be timber and cattle and now it's tourism."

The next rock Carl turned over was to look at the tips that had come in from the public. The department encouraged email but some tips came in by phone and went to voicemail. The voicemails were translated into text by a computer so no one had to listen to them unless they looked relevant or there might be something the computer got wrong in the text. A deputy had sorted out the ones that referred to Sunriver or sounded even conceivably relevant to what happened on the day of the murder.

Going through tips was always frustrating. Most of them, though well-intentioned, were completely irrelevant to the crime at hand. The worst were the ones that sounded related but actually weren't and would take precious time to investigate. Nonetheless, Carl began.

A man reported a small campsite off one of the Sunriver golf courses with a ring of stones for a fire. It was hidden by trees and the ashes were cold.

A small inflatable boat with a leak in it had been abandoned on the bank of the Deschutes opposite the airport.

A bike rental store in the Sunriver Mall reported a woman who promised to bring a bike back but would not fill out the paperwork.

A Sunriver resident reported a group of teenage boys who walked through her backyard two days in a row. She wanted them arrested for trespassing.

A man reported an unknown car parked overnight on his dead-end street. Parking along the roads was illegal in Sunriver, day or night. He didn't get the license number and the street was a long way from East Cascade Road.

A man reported a boy in the woods with binoculars while the man's teenage daughter was getting dressed.

A man who had a stranger drive him and his car to Corvallis reported that the stranger had a serious black eye and might have been in a fight.

Two people reported a boy going door-to-door trying to sell a used bicycle.

The week of the murder several homeowners complained of package thefts from their front doors. None of the people had doorbell cameras.

A man complained that someone had stolen a For Sale sign from in front of his house. He didn't know that For Sale signs were illegal in Sunriver.

Two boys separately reported a man driving a golf cart on a bicycle path. The boys knew that was illegal. The man was fat with gray hair and wore a yellow and black checked shirt.

Two days after the murder, a cleaning service had found a magazine with bullets in it under a bed. They hadn't found a gun.

A set of keys had been found outside of the church on Cottonwood, within walking distance of the Pennstead crime scene.

A month before the murder, a shotgun had been stolen from a house on Harney Road in Sunriver.

Who to call first? What to follow-up first? The illegal campsite, the peeping Tom, the golf cart, the abandoned boat, and the package thefts did not sound promising. The stolen shotgun was irrelevant. Carl was sure the murder weapon was Leon's.

One coincidence stuck out that Carl would have to track down. Maybe it would actually lead to something. When he called the tipster, he got voicemail and asked the man to call him back. If he didn't call right away, Carl would call him again in the evening and then the next day. After that he would use an online database to learn the caller's true name and address.

Chapter 40

Can I Get A Witness?

"Were the tips any help?" asked Gordon when Carl came to his office to give him an update.

"Not inspiring so far. People want to be helpful but no one's come forward who saw the shooting or anyone near the scene. We didn't tell the media about the money Pennstead was carrying and none of the tips mention anything about the money. But I've got one coincidence I'm tracking down. A parole officer in Seattle, Alma Oshiro, says the brother of a guy who has a house near the shooting has a black eye from an injury at work. And I've got a tip from a man who rode over to Corvallis with a young man who had a banged-up eye on the afternoon of the murder. If the tipster doesn't answer my next call, I'll track him down some other way."

"Keep at it," said Gordon.

Carl went back to his cubicle and reached the tipster, Hal Shalen, on his next call.

"Sorry I didn't return your call right away," said Shalen. "I was in a meeting. The reason I needed someone to drive my car was that I can't drive myself. I'm narcoleptic, I can be wide awake one moment and fall asleep the next. I could run off the road or into another car. I take Uber or Lyft around town but I want to take my own car when I go out of town. So I posted a notice at the bus station and this fellow called me."

"Did you get his name?"

"He said it was Taylor Smith. I think he made that up. But I did get a good look at his face. He didn't want to take off his sunglasses but I needed to check his pupils to make sure he wasn't high on something. Sober as a judge but his right eye was really banged up, black and blue."

"Any explanation for that?"

"He said it was an accident at work."

Carl took a breath. "What did he look like?"

"About thirty. Medium height. Blond hair but not bright blond. Kind of a narrow face. T-shirt with a collar. Green backpack. A small pack, like for a day hike. He wasn't sunburnt but he'd been out in the sun, like hiking or biking or playing golf."

"Eye color?"

"Light brown or maybe hazel."

Shalen's description matched the picture of Dylan Crabtree that Alma in the Seattle probation office had sent him.

"Did he say where he was coming from or where he was going?"

"He was visiting friends in Bend," said Shalen, "and he was going to see some other friends in Corvallis. That was a little strange because he wanted to be dropped off at the bus station, not at a house."

"How did you and your car get where you were going without this man driving you?"

"Oh, I drove to the hotel. Short distance, low speed. I only nod off a few times a year. It's pretty safe. I'm going to get a self-driving car once they get the kinks out of them."

"Anything else you can tell me about the man?"

"We didn't talk much. I listened to a book on my phone. He seemed like an okay guy."

"Did he act nervous?"

"Not at all. Drove carefully. Stayed close to the speed limit."

"If I send you a picture, do you think you can recognize him?"

"Maybe. Between the sunglasses and my not paying attention, I only looked him in the face that one time."

"Okay, thanks. If you think of anything more that might help, give me a call."

"Will do."

Ben Crabtree's brother Dylan, with his black eye and matching Shalen's description, definitely deserved further investigation.

Carl's eagerness led him into a mistake that he later regretted. His logic was sound at the time. Dylan, if it was Dylan, was in the area the day of the shooting, presumably at his brother's house, and he left soon after Geoff Pennstead lay dead on the road. If Dylan wasn't the shooter, he probably knew something about it. If Carl could prove that Dylan was at his brother's house in Sunriver on the day of the shooting, he'd have enough evidence to arrest him. At the very least, Dylan would wind up back in prison for violating parole by leaving the State of Washington. Carl quickly got a search warrant for Ben Crabtree's house and his car. It was a generous warrant, allowing Carl to search for fingerprints or DNA on anything Dylan might have used or touched. It would take a team of deputies a full day to scour the place. But along the way, Ben might be scared enough to admit his brother had visited him.

The team arrived at Ben's house at 6:30 in the morning. Ben read the warrant carefully.

"Search away," he said. "You won't find anything but go ahead. Is it okay if I get dressed and make breakfast?"

"Go ahead," said Carl. "When you are settled, you and I should sit down and have a chat."

Carl thought the car might be the best bet for fingerprints and DNA. Dylan would have wiped down the house before he left after the shooting. But Ben had been fishing and had the car with him. Dylan could not have wiped the car down. Carl sent two deputies to the car while others began methodically lifting fingerprints from one end of the house to the other.

Carl and Ben sat outside in the enclosed patio off the back of the house.

"We have two witnesses who saw your brother in the area on the day of the shooting. We're sure to find more witnesses and other evidence he was here," said Carl. He was exaggerating on all counts to bring as much pressure on Ben as he could. "When we do find that evidence, he'll be charged, at a minimum, with violating parole by leaving the State of Washington. You can be charged with harboring a fugitive. You can do yourself a big favor by telling us, before we find specific evidence about your brother's visit, when he got here, everything he did while he was here, and when he left."

"You're imagining all of this," said Ben, "and I want you to get out of my house." Carl recognized this as the worst possible answer. Ben hadn't admitted Dylan had been there, the best possible answer. But he hadn't denied it either. He couldn't be charged with lying to law enforcement. "And given the way this is going," Ben went on, "I'm not going to answer any more of your questions. Our talk is over. I'm going for a walk."

Carl sat still in his chair, trying to think of a way to get Ben to talk. Ben got up, walked through the house, and went out the front door. He walked down the road to where he was no longer visible from the house.

Dylan was getting a brand-new tire down off a rack when he got a call from Ben.

"The Sheriff is searching the house," said Ben, "looking for signs you were here. Of course they haven't found anything. They haven't found any because you weren't here."

Dylan didn't correct him.

"It's another beautiful day in Sunriver," said Ben. "How are things in Seattle?"

"Light rain, cloudy sky. It may clear up by the time I'm done with work."

"Well, good. Enjoy."

A deputy came out to the patio to tell Carl about the car.

"It's been detailed recently. We're getting fingerprints on the driver's side but none on the passenger side or in the back seat. Hardly any fingerprints inside or outside of the trunk and they look like they're the same as those on the steering wheel and the driver's door handle. Do you want us to do the engine compartment?"

"Save it 'til last," said Carl. "We'll do it if we have time." Carl stayed in his chair commiserating with himself and trying to think. The search was getting nowhere and now he'd tipped off Ben that he was interested in Dylan. That was Carl's mistake. Ben probably left the house precisely so he could call his brother.

The patio was small. But it was a cheerful place, the sunlight descending down the western wall as the sun rose over the house. A person could be happy here, drinking their morning coffee and imagining the trees went on for miles, no roads or houses to interrupt them. Carl stood on a chair and looked over the patio wall. He wasn't as tall as either Dylan or Ben. But through the pine trees, he could see East Cascade Road where Geoff Pennstead had pulled his car off the road. He could see the place where he had put the tarp over Geoff's body.

"You should see this," came the voice of a deputy behind him. The deputy led him to the smaller of two bedrooms. A rug was rolled up to one side and a hatch door lay on the floor beside a doorway into the space below. The crawlspace below dropped three feet to a bare lava rock. In the rock was a dark steel door, about the size of a cabinet door.

"Dust both sides of the hatches, the floor around the hole, and any flat spot you can find on the rock. And see where this damn thing goes. Take two of you in case somebody gets stuck." He stood beside the trapdoor while the deputy dusted for fingerprints.

"Whoever was here last was wearing rubber gloves with ridges on them," reported the deputy, "like dishwashing gloves. Do you want me to keep dusting?"

"Yes," said Carl. "We need to be thorough. But only dust a few places on the rock as you go along. If you still find glove prints then forget dusting and follow the tunnel."

After more minutes and multiple fingerprint samples the deputy crawled into the tunnel with his flashlight. Another deputy, a woman, followed him. She was smaller and had an easier time of it. The sounds coming back from the tunnel grew fainter and the fleeting shafts of light from the moving flashlights disappeared entirely. Carl listened carefully for word of what they had found. He was surprised when the deputies appeared, not in the mouth of the tunnel but in the doorway of the bedroom.

"It comes up in the laundry room of the house across the road," said the deputy. "Another trapdoor under another rug. We dusted the trapdoor, the floor, and the back door."

"You shouldn't have done that," said Carl, unhappy but not angry. "The search warrant doesn't cover that house." The deputies stoically accepted Carl's reprimand. "Probably doesn't matter. I doubt he took his gloves off for us. Run the fingerprint lifters from that house through the shredder when you get back to the office and don't put it in your report, or tell anyone that you got them."

"The good news is," said Carl, "we know how Dylan Crabtree could leave the house without anyone seeing him."

Carl went back to the patio to find Ben reading a book.

"Find anything?" asked Ben with a hint of mockery in his voice.

"We'll let you know," said Carl. He didn't mean today. He meant eventually, like when Dylan Crabtree went on trial. When he got to his car, Carl called Alma at the probation office in Seattle.

"I need to come up and talk to Dylan. When is he next coming in to see you?"

"Let me see," said Alma. "Four o'clock tomorrow. He has an appointment to see me and he's always shown up in the past. Are you going to arrest him?"

"I don't have a warrant yet. I just want to talk with him."

"You're going to come all the way to Seattle and you don't know if he'll answer a single question?"

"Have to," said Carl. "I have to know where he stands if I'm going to move this investigation forward. Silence implies guilt—maybe not in court but to me it does. If he doesn't give me information, I'll have to investigate him further. But he might tell me something useful. Or even deny something and that would be useful. If he lies to me and I can prove it, then I've got leverage to get more out of him. Anyhow, he's the best avenue I've got whether he cooperates or not."

Chapter 41

Lifesaving

"There's something you need to know," were the words Leon heard when he answered the phone. He was about to shred his painting of the scene on East Cascade Road. He hesitated, thinking Carl Breuninger might want the painting for some reason. Leon could not imagine what use Carl would have for it.

"I saved Elizabeth's life," said Dara. "Whatever happens to me, I want you to know that."

He knew he should hang up. He had promised Elizabeth he would. But he hesitated.

"I was there when Geoff was killed. I never told anyone."

Leon waited.

"There are people out to kill me. I want to tell you everything that happened that day. I may not get another chance."

No reply.

"I'm sorry I told that Che man the money was at your house. And I am very, very sorry your friend Maria died because of him. I was desperate. I didn't know what else to do. He'd already shot Dave and I thought he would shoot me. I was hoping he would take the money and go away."

Apologies had always worked well for Dara. They were in her range. She sounded a little mixed up, not quite as smart or as worldly-wise as she actually was. Emotionally wrought but trying her best to be responsible, to do the right thing.

"I'm sorry I put the money in your golf bag. It was for a reason. It was the only thing I could think of. I can explain that too."

Elizabeth would be furious to know Dara called, even more so to know that Leon talked to her. But whatever Dara had to tell him, Leon thought, affected Elizabeth. Leon should know the answers.

"I can't tell you over the phone," said Dara. "Breuninger has me staying at the Riverhouse in Bend for my protection. I'm not supposed to tell anyone I'm here. I could meet you outside the back door at the north end of the building and we could walk over to Sawyer Park. I'll tell you every detail and you can ask me anything you want. You need to know this."

"Maybe," said Leon. "Is it safe for you to leave the hotel?" If Dara was going to be shot, he didn't want to be shot along with her.

"Nobody knows I'm here except Carl Breuninger and now you. Even the hotel doesn't know my real name. If anybody shoots me, it's going to be later. They're gangsters. They'll get arrested or die sooner or later. Or they'll move on to other things. Anyway, I am not going to worry about that now."

"How about I meet you at Sawyer Park in half an hour?" If somebody was waiting to shoot Dara, she'd never make it to Sawyer Park.

"Okay," said Dara. "I'll walk there. Thank you."

Leon slid the painting back in its rack; put his keys, his phone, and his wallet in his pants pockets; and left. It was a warm sunny day and he wouldn't need a jacket. By the time he reached Lava Butte, he admitted to himself he was going partly out of curiosity. He wanted to hear Dara's story. He knew what Elizabeth had told Sarah about Geoff's death. But Elizabeth did not know who the shooter was or what the shooter was thinking. Did Dara shoot her own husband? Did she see who did?

Passing the High Desert Museum, Leon conceded that part of his motivation was a lingering concern for Dara. She had turned to him for sympathy and advice. Perhaps she did not deserve it. He had done enough already. But his instincts pushed him on.

Dara was waiting for him in the Sawyer parking lot. They said nothing as they descended to the footbridge over the Deschutes and started on the trail that ran midway up a steep bluff above the river. Leon walked on the downhill side of the trail. If anyone missed a step and fell down to the river, it was going to be him. Habitual gallantry.

The rushing water muffled their voices. No one would overhear what they said unless they were well within sight on the same trail.

Dara began. "You have to promise me you won't repeat any of this to Carl Breuninger or anyone else."

"I'll have to tell Elizabeth."

"Okay. But no one else. And she can't tell anyone else."

"Okay." Leon was not a lawyer but he knew his promise was worthless. Elizabeth hadn't promised anything and she could repeat what Leon told her to anyone she wanted.

"I was in the car with Geoff that morning," Dara began. "I never told Carl Breuninger or anyone else that. We were on the way to the bank to catch up on loan payments on property down in La Pine. He had cash from a business trip he'd been on.

"Then the car breaks down. Geoff tells me he's going to flag down another car and get a ride to Bend. He tells me to stay in the car and call Triple A to tow it. Then he gets out with the bag that held the money. Along comes a blue Camry and it stops for him.

"I keep looking back and he's talking to the woman who's driving the other car. I didn't know it was Elizabeth. I'd never met her or seen her before. All of a sudden, he has a gun he's waving around. I didn't know he even owned a gun. This is crazy. We're law-abiding people. We don't point guns at people and threaten to shoot them. And if he does shoot her, there's going to be hell to pay.

"So I jump out of the car and walk back to get Geoff under control. I've never seen him like this. I don't want the woman to see me because I figure Geoff is going to be in trouble over this no matter what happens and I don't want to be a...a..."

"An accomplice," said Leon.

"Accomplice. Whatever. So I walk around the back of the lady's car. I was hoping to calm him down or something. Then the trunk pops open and I jump like it's going to bite me. There are golf clubs and, this is nuts, next to them is a shotgun. What was that shotgun doing there, Leon? How did it get there? Do you know?"

Leon knew Elizabeth had put the gun in the trunk to take it to the police. But he wasn't going to tell Dara that. "I have no idea," he said, as though he was as puzzled as she was.

Dara rolled on excitedly. "I think Geoff is acting crazy and I've got to stop him before he shoots the poor lady. He might shoot her by accident or he might even be crazy enough to shoot her on purpose. It means the world to him to take that money to the bank. He's already hijacking her car. If I tell him to stop aiming that gun at her and he doesn't, I'll show him the shotgun. At least that ought to get his attention. I have no intention of actually shooting him.

"I point the shotgun at him to warn him off but he ignores it. He's still pointing that pistol at Elizabeth. I've never fired a shotgun before and I don't know how sensitive the trigger can be. Next thing you know the gun goes off, the barrel flies up and I almost drop it. Geoff disappears until I look at the ground where it looks like a dummy is dressed in Geoff's clothes and there's a wet jumble of red where its head should be."

They had reached the point on the trail where it intersected a road and they turned around to walk back.

Two people lying to each other, thought Leon. *And yet we go on.* He lied when he didn't tell Dara he knew she was lying. Dara was lying about her husband pointing a pistol at Elizabeth. Elizabeth said he never did that. He just waved it around in the air. And Dara was lying about Geoff standing next to Elizabeth's window when he was shot. Elizabeth said he had walked to the back of the car.

"So I can't believe what happened," said Dara, "and I want no part of that shotgun. I push it away from me and throw it back in the trunk of the car. Then the car takes off with the trunk lid flapping up and down.

"I don't think the lady ever saw me and there's nobody else around. So I take off into the woods. I want to get home. I run on bike paths and a utility right-of-way that I never knew was there before. I get lost. I barely, barely make it before Detective Breuninger gets to my door. Even though I did the right thing, I don't want to tell him I was there when Geoff died. It would mean no end of trouble. But I want to tell you because it affects you. And after all you have done for me, I wanted you to know that I did something important for you. I saved Elizabeth."

Leon walked on in silence, inwardly fuming at the outrageous lie Dara had just told him. He realized he appeared to Dara to be thinking the opposite—how close Elizabeth had come to being shot and how lucky he and Elizabeth were that Dara had prevented it.

"And I need to tell you about the money that made such a hullaballoo" said Dara. "It simply showed up on my doorstep. I don't know from where. I honestly don't. I very badly needed that money and I had to keep it safe. I needed that cash just to live. I knew you wouldn't take it, might not even answer my telephone call. But if I could sneak it to you some way, I thought you would keep it for me if you found it. Or at least you would call me and I could explain why I needed you to keep it.

"I knew about your golf game every Wednesday at Woodlands. And how people take their clubs off the golf cart when they're done playing and put them on the rack near the golf shop. Then they bring their car around to pick up the clubs. I put the cash in three folded-over manila envelopes, wrote notes on them asking you to keep them, and put them in that long pocket in your golf bag while it was on the rack. You obviously didn't find it right away.

"Then if Detective Breuninger or somebody else came looking, I could say I didn't know anything about the money. They could tear the house apart and they wouldn't find it. I didn't allow for some desperado who showed up and started shooting people. I was scared to death. I should have taken a bullet. I wish I had. I'm so sorry."

Leon didn't say he wished Dara had taken that bullet. But he thought it. Maria would still be alive and Gabriel would still have a wife. Leon's garage would not be a crime scene and Elizabeth would not have trouble sleeping.

Dara went on. "So I saved Elizabeth's life and now I'm in trouble. On top of these people who think I have drugs or money that belongs to them, Breuninger suspects me of killing Geoff and of killing him on purpose. I know he's building a case. I just know it. Then I have the debts that Geoff left behind that I can't figure out. Leon, what should I do?"

Leon thought he'd already done enough for Dara. "You have a lawyer, right? Also, this gang doesn't know where you are, right? And unraveling business matters takes time. You have to be patient." Leon was getting impatient himself.

"Maybe that's the hardest part," said Dara. "I'm not patient. And I'm bored silly watching television."

"Try working on your singing. Quietly, of course, in your room. Or maybe on your balcony. It'll keep your mind off other things."

"That might be an idea. At least it won't be so depressing going back to my room. Thanks, Leon. It was good to get out in the natural world. And so good to talk with you. I want so much for you to understand. I don't expect your thanks for saving Elizabeth. I almost did it by accident. All I ask is don't tell Breuninger what I told you."

"That's the deal. And I do thank you." Leon was lying. Lying with his words and with the sincere expression on his face. He almost never lied. He hated lying more than he hated being lied to. But the lies he told Dara did not bother him at all. He called Carl Breuninger as soon as he left the parking lot.

Chapter 42

A New Perspective

Carl Breuninger took his badge but not his gun on the flight to Seattle to interview Dylan Crabtree. He wore a blue shirt and a sport coat rather than his uniform. He was uneasy, strapped into his seat, and worried that Crabtree might tell him nothing, absolutely nothing. The department was paying for what could well turn out to be a boondoggle. He tried to relax and watch the Cascades go by—Black Butte, Washington, Jefferson, Saint Helens, and finally Rainier.

People lied. That bothered him. Not just low-life criminals. Respectable people. People he was inclined to trust. The kind of people he was supposed to protect. When Leon said Dara told him she shot her husband, had she lied? Had Leon truthfully passed along what she told him? Or had Leon, seemingly trustworthy Leon, made the whole thing up? In any case Dara would deny she ever said it. Even Leon's account of what she said would be hearsay and never make it to court.

Would Leon have reason to fabricate Dara's story? He would if the person who actually shot Geoff Pennstead was Elizabeth. She said she'd popped the trunk of her car but stayed in the car herself. Suppose she got out of the car to get her golf clubs? She picked up the shotgun instead of the clubs and shot Pennstead. She threw the gun back in the trunk and high-tailed it out of there. Went on to her golf game. She might just be cool and composed enough to do that, even sink ten-foot putts. She said she hated guns so much she didn't want to touch them. But that could be another lie. These people. Perhaps they imagined they could kill someone and just go on with their lives.

Carl got to Alma's office at three, ahead of the notorious Seattle rush hour traffic. Alma was five-foot-three and about fifty years old. She appeared to be Hawaiian but she had no accent that Carl could pick up on. Another woman was sitting in a chair beside Alma's desk facing her. Alma said something to the woman then stood up to shake Carl's hand and lead him by the elbow about ten steps away to a space in the aisle between other desks. She spoke in a low voice, almost a whisper.

"I called Dylan to make sure he'd be here at four and he confirmed the appointment," said Alma. "I didn't tell him you'd be here. I have a few standard questions for him before you get started. They won't take long. By the way, he's been to church the past two Sundays. I checked with his pastor. He's making an effort for the straight and narrow. At least the appearance of it. I've got this other appointment right now and another one before Dylan. Can you hang out in the breakroom until then?"

Carl said he would come back at four.

Instead of staring at the walls in the break room, Carl left the building. He walked ten minutes down to the ferry terminal. Bainbridge Island formed a low green line eight miles away across the water. No lake anywhere in Central Oregon was that wide. But the Cascade Lakes, surrounded by towering mountains, were each unique and, Carl thought, more beautiful. He wondered whether Leon Martinez would like painting this expanse of water with the ferries and ships coming and going across it.

Alma was doing paperwork when Carl returned. He sat in the chair by her desk without interrupting her. He wore a sport coat, not a uniform, but he'd pinned his badge onto his lapel. He recognized Dylan when he arrived. The black swelling around his eye was almost gone.

"This is Detective Breuninger from Deschutes County, Oregon," said Alma. "He thinks you might be able to help him with a case he's working on. I got us a conference room."

Dylan kept his balance and his poise, the only change being a quizzical look on his face.

Alma led the way to a room with six chairs and a gray metal table. It had an indoor window to the office space but no windows to the outside. Alma asked Dylan if he was still at the same address and whether he was still employed at Les Schwab. He said yes with a smile on both counts and showed her his latest pay stub. He sounded cheerful, working hard to maintain a good relationship with Alma.

"How's your attitude?" Alma asked him.

"Good," he said. "I've met a woman at night school and I might get to know her better. We're taking it slow. We get along but I know she's worried about my record. Job's good. Saving a little money."

"Good, good," said Alma. "Keep up the good work. I'm going to leave you two to have your own conversation." Alma firmly closed the door on her way out.

"Alma assures me there are no microphones in this room," said Carl. "This conversation will be off the record, though we may have a later conversation on the record. Are we clear on that?"

"I need to get back to work," said Dylan. "Why do I even need to talk to you?"

"We have a photo of you looking over the patio wall of your brother's house in Sunriver. We have proof that you drove a man and his car from Bend to Corvallis. We will definitely find more proof that you were in Oregon and you violated your parole. If we give our proof to Alma, you'll probably go back to prison. But we don't have to give her that evidence. We think while you were at your brother's house, you witnessed a crime."

Carl had an open mind. It was entirely possible that Dylan had been the shooter. But Carl didn't say that.

"I'd like to know everything you saw or heard or know about that crime. You tell me what you know and the evidence you were in Oregon stays in Oregon."

"You're going to pin this crime on me, aren't you?" said Dylan.

"I'm not trying to 'pin' this crime on anybody and certainly not you. I have no evidence that you knew the victim or had any contact with him. He was carrying a large sum of money which we have recovered. You don't have the money and we have no reason to believe you knew that either the victim or the money would be there at that time or place." If Dylan had shot Geoff Pennstead, he would clam up or insist upon a lawyer. But if he'd seen who did shoot Pennstead, he might possibly open up.

"Are you going to give me a Miranda warning?" asked Dylan.

"No, I'm not. Because if I don't give a Miranda warning, you'll know I can't testify to anything you tell me. You're a witness and I'm trying to get to the facts." Carl did not mention that lying to the police was a crime, whether Dylan was Mirandized or not. If Carl could catch him in a lie or two then the district attorney's office would have added leverage over him. But Carl wasn't looking for leverage or lies. He was looking for the truth.

Carl waited while Dylan looked down at the table and thought about his response. He was sure the policewoman had never pointed her camera in his direction while he was looking over the wall.

"There's no photograph," said Dylan. "You made that up."

Carl took out his cell phone and found the photo Leon Martinez had sent him. He showed it to Dylan.

"It was taken from across the road by a man who was painting what he saw. The photo was so he could remember the light. That's your brother's house back in the trees. When we blow up the photo, you'll see that's you looking over the wall." That last part was a lie. The crime lab had worked that photo every way they could think of. The face in the photograph was too far away to be recognizable.

Bob Fielding from the crime lab had told Carl, "It could be Pablo Escobar for all we can tell."

Dylan looked down at the table and weighed his decision. They'd never convict him of killing that man. But they could easily prove he'd violated parole. He'd be back in that miserable prison and it would take years to restart his life. The woman he was dating would be long gone.

"If I testified at the killer's trial, it will be on the public record that I was in Oregon. Washington could revoke my parole."

"If you don't tell me what you know, I can show Alma the proof you left Washington. That's prison again for sure. On the other hand, if you tell me what you saw, I'll know where to look for more evidence and I'll try to make sure you never testify. Besides, there may not be enough evidence to have a trial, with or without your testimony. And if the case winds up in a plea bargain, which it probably will, you'll never have to show up and I never need to tell Alma a thing. It's a risk worth taking."

Dylan thought some more. "Okay," he said. "You promise this is not being recorded or videotaped?"

"Promise."

"Very well. It was like I was on vacation, even like being a kid again, being with Ben in that house. We talked. We watched TV. We played Monopoly. I slept in my old bed. When Ben left in the morning, I took a cup of coffee out on the patio."

Now that Dylan had decided to talk, he wanted to relive the visit, to share the happier parts of it. "I could see the blue sky and the light on trees up above. I could hear nuthatches and ravens calling and cawing away. I pulled a chair over to the outside wall and looked over the top. I thought it would be safe. The house is back in the trees from the road and there's no bicycle path between the road and the house. The road had hardly any traffic and nobody driving by would turn their head or look in my direction long enough to see me.

"But this Mercedes comes along from the left, on its way toward Cottonwood, and it starts to slow down. It's an older model, gray or silvery. It gets slower and slower until it pulls off the road and stops. A man gets out of the driver's door and walks to the back of his car. He's got a bag, like an airplane carry-on, in his hand. I don't see the gun at this point. He must have been holding it in the same hand as the bag because his other hand, his right hand, is empty and he starts waving at another car coming along in the same direction. It's a blue Toyota sedan. I can't see who's driving it but I think it's a woman. The car stops in the road, doesn't pull off to the side, and the man with the bag walks back to the driver's side of the Toyota. I guess the driver rolled down the window. Anyhow, he shoves the bag into the car, practically throws it in.

"At the same time, a woman gets out of the passenger side of the Mercedes. Dark hair, medium height, and she starts walking back past the cars on the side away from the road. She's half bent over like she doesn't want anybody to see her. As soon as she gets to the back of the blue Toyota, the trunk pops open. I think I'm remembering this right. It didn't make a lot of sense at the time."

"Go on," said Carl. Dylan was getting into his tale, even excited to be telling it. Carl had seen this happen before. The witness had been keeping his story bottled up inside of him but he'd been thinking over and over about what happened. Dylan was spewing out everything he knew, no holds barred, but Carl could not be sure it was true. Crabtree had been polishing the story for so long, over and over. Subtly, without even remembering he'd done it, he would make the story more likely, more believable, or more dramatic. Details would stand out or recede in importance, according to Dylan's tastes. The story would take on a life of its own, more important to Dylan, really, than the actual facts. Carl listened carefully.

"The woman, I mean the dark-haired woman, looks in the trunk and pulls something out. It takes me a second to realize more or less what it is. She was facing away from me. I think it was a shotgun but it could have been a rifle. A long gun. She presses it tight against her chest like she's going to fire it. Then the man walks around the car toward her and I see he's got a pistol. It's squarish, I think, like an automatic. I don't think it was a revolver. Next thing you know she shoots him, blood and flesh and hair exploding all over the place. I'm no expert but I think it must have been a shotgun. Sounded like a shotgun but, once again, I'm no expert. It was more of an explosion or two quick explosions than it was a sudden crack.

"Anyhow, she throws the gun back in the trunk of the car and starts running right toward me. Well, I don't want her to see me. I don't want anyone to see me. I want no part of the whole thing. I get down in the patio and I think, 'Why can't I sit down like I was before, sip my coffee and look up into the trees? Pretend I didn't see anything. Pretend I don't know anything.' I try to relax but it doesn't work. A minute goes by before I realize that this isn't a TV show I can forget about. The police are going to be all over this. Sometime pretty soon they're going to come knocking on the door of this house to see if anyone is here and asking whether they know anything about the shooting. And I'm not supposed to be here. I can stay quiet and not answer the door but they'll be back. I could leave but there's a family in the driveway across the street, obviously renters, and they're taking forever to stop playing with the dog, load up their car, and get the hell out of here.

"I remember a lava tube I can follow to sneak out but now the house is full of evidence that I've been here. So I scramble like a madman cleaning up, all the time listening for the doorbell. I can't move too fast because I don't want anyone to hear me. The police have to be convinced the house is empty and has been empty since before the shooting. I put my sheets in the laundry. I clean the bathroom and the kitchen. I clean or wipe down every surface I can think of that I might have touched.

"The lava tube comes up in the back of the house where the family is leaving and I can get into the forest from there. The family finally looks like they are ready to go. The father locks the front door and walks to the car. The rest are already in it.

"Before I go, though, I want to see where the police are and if they are coming this way yet. I don't see them out in front of the house. The view from the one window at the back of the house is blocked by the patio wall. I pop above the wall and here come two people in uniform, a man and a woman, walking up through the woods toward Ben's house. They don't notice me looking over the wall but they scare me to death. I get down in the tunnel and pull the trapdoor shut with a throw rug over it." Dylan stopped and thought a minute.

"That's it," said Dylan. "That's all I know. I got out through the other house and never saw another soul until I got to Bend."

"I may have more questions later," said Carl.

"But we have a deal," said Dylan. "You won't tell Washington I left the state and you will do everything possible to see that I don't have to testify?"

"I promise," said Carl. "We have a deal." He half regretted letting a parole violator off the hook. But Dylan had identified the murderer. It might not be enough to convict her, or even arrest her. But at last Carl knew exactly who she was.

Chapter 43

Arrested Development

Carl had overlooked something the first time he met Dara, something that was right in front of his eyes. He'd been thinking about how to tell her that her husband was dead, thinking about how to cope with her emotions, thinking about the questions he wanted to ask her as soon as she calmed down enough to answer them.

Dara had been breathing hard when she answered the door. Her face glowed with perspiration. Her t-shirt and shorts were ready for the washing machine. She'd been on her Peleton, she said, all bright and cheery, and hadn't heard him when he first rang the doorbell.

But Dara had been on East Cascade Road an hour earlier, Carl now knew, taking her husband's head off with a shotgun. That was three miles away in a direct line, more if she stuck to the woods and bike trails and didn't walk straight across the golf course and right past the lodge. She must have walked the whole way.

People must have seen her walking. But who were they and how could Carl find them? Renters mostly, now gone back to wherever they came from. And who would remember after all this time? Women went out walking every day.

"I bet she wished she had a bike," said Estelle when Carl told his wife what he was thinking.

"Good thought," said Carl. He remembered the tip about the woman who tried to hijack a bike from Deschutes River Bike Rentals.

The person who phoned in the tip was Jay Belaunzaran at the bike shop. Carl called the next morning to make sure Jay would be there and then drove down to Sunriver to interview him.

Jay was in his early twenties, long and lean as though he rode bicycles for hours every day of the week. The shop and the asphalt in front of the shop were jammed with bikes but empty of customers. Jay gave Carl a bigger smile than Sheriff's detectives usually saw.

"We're all waiting to get laid off," said Jay. "Business is way down for the whole mall. Tourism's way down. Rentals are cancelled or people simply aren't showing up. The forest is scorched earth and everything smells like smoke. Nobody wants to ride bikes."

"How about the golf courses?" asked Carl.

"Well, they're playable. The resort ran irrigation on them all through the fire so the tees and greens are fine and the fairways aren't too bad. But the native grasses in the roughs burned to the ground and some of the tree bark looks like charcoal. It's not pretty but the courses are open."

"Tell me about this woman who tried to steal a bicycle the day of the shooting on East Cascade."

"She rolled out a bike and hopped on it. I yelled, 'Wait a minute,' and she stopped. Then she tried to charm her way into it, said she lived in Sunriver and she just needed the bike for a few hours. She'd bring it back that afternoon and pay the rental. She said her car wouldn't start and she needed to get home to meet a repairman. She was all friendly with me, you know, as though we had an instant bond between us, her and me against the world. But the policy is no credit card, no deposit, no bike. We have all kinds of customers every day. They all play by the rules. I could tell she was trying to hide how upset she was about it. But she didn't have cash or a credit card so I wasn't supposed to rent to her. She didn't even have a driver's license with her."

"Did you get her name?"

"If she told me, I forgot. Do you think she's connected to the murder? She looked like such a normal person, aside from being uptight."

"What did she look like?"

"Dark hair, not too long. Not down to her shoulders. Fairly trim but with some curves. Maybe in her forties. Kind of a round face. Nice looking."

"Eye color?"

"I don't remember, though I remember she worked them."

"What do you mean she worked them?"

"I don't know. She gave me sort of a sly look one time, like a woman in the movies."

"How tall was she?"

"I'd say she came up to about here on me." Jay held his hand level with his heart. It was about five-foot-six, Dara's height.

"Would you recognize her if you saw her again?"

"Definitely."

"So what did she do after you wouldn't give her a bike?"

"She took off walking, fast, like she was in a hurry."

"Is there another bike rental shop in the mall?"

"One more in the mall and another one on the other side of Beaver Drive. But they aren't in the direction she was going. And they have the same policies about identification and deposits that we do."

"So thanks. Tell me where I can reach you."

"Probably not here," said Jay. "I'll give you my cell, my email, and my home address. I don't know the law, you know, but I wouldn't think you could arrest her for trying to steal a bike. She didn't get very far."

"I'm not interested in the bike," said Carl.

"I didn't think so."

"Good luck with the layoff."

"Oh, I'll find something else. In this economy, it won't be hard."

Carl went back to headquarters in Bend to draft a warrant for the arrest of Dara Pennstead. She was still in the hotel in Bend for her safety and he wouldn't have to drive out to Sunriver again to make the arrest.

The warrant would be for manslaughter, not murder. Dara might have thought about killing Geoff in advance but she could not have planned what happened. How could she know that a car with a loaded shotgun in the trunk would stop behind Geoff's Mercedes and that the driver would open the trunk to get her golf clubs? The opportunity to kill Geoff presented itself and Dara took it.

What gave Carl the "probable cause" he needed to arrest Dara? He would use Jay's description of her visit to the bike shop. Carl himself could vouch for her tuckered-out appearance at her house an hour after the shooting. He would subpoena Dara's history on the Peloton and was sure it would show she hadn't been on it for more than a minute or two, if on it at all, when Carl arrived at her house. She must have walked all the way from the crime scene to her house to get there before he did. Surely he could find someone who had noticed her.

Then there was Dave's testimony about the plot he hatched to stop Geoff's car and take some or all of the money in the gym bag. Dave had never said that Dara knew about his plan. Dave had never said that he expected Dara to be in Geoff's car or that he'd seen her at the site of the murder.

Carl would not mention Dylan Crabtree in the warrant or what Dylan saw from his brother's patio. He would keep his promise. For now anyway.

The warrant would not mention that Carl had recovered the shotgun Dara had used. It wasn't needed for the arrest. It would be important at the trial. Jocelyn Nelson, when she prosecuted the case, would have to explain how Elizabeth Martinez brought the shotgun to the scene and how it got back into Leon's closet.

The judge who signed the warrant would be more interested in time, place, and facts than in theories of motivation. The jury would consider motivation but that was months if not a year or more away. The motivation, as Carl briefly stated it, was money. Dara had seen Geoff's fortunes rise and fall and she wanted to keep some money of her own. Sure, Geoff was in trouble paying off a loan but Dara had seen that happen before. She would make the bet that more assets were out there somewhere and, no matter what debts Geoff had to pay off, there would be something left for her.

Late in the day, Carl emailed his draft of the warrant to Jocelyn Nelson in the District Attorney's office and to his boss, Gordon Knapp, the Sheriff. He'd give them an hour to look at it if they wanted to before he took it over to the courthouse for a judge to sign. After an hour Gordon had emailed back, "Go for it." Carl hadn't heard from Jocelyn. The judge he found to sign the warrant, staying late in his chambers, read the warrant over carefully and signed it.

Carl took Rachel Newton, the deputy who had met Dara before, to make the arrest at Dara's hotel. After no answer in her room, they headed to the front desk to ask if the clerk could tell them where Dara was. The hotel was supposed to keep an eye on her, of sorts, and let the Sheriff's Department know right away if anyone was skulking around or asked what room she was in. Or if housekeeping found the bed still unslept in from the day before.

There was a trio playing in the hotel bar off to the side when they headed for the lone receptionist at the front desk. A pianist, a drummer, and a man holding a saxophone were crammed into a corner. All men. In front of them, close behind a microphone on a stand, was a woman singing "All the Things You Are."

"Let's have a listen," said Carl. Rachel looked at him dubiously, surprised at his sudden interest in music, but she went along with him.

The singer smiled at Carl without missing a beat. Carl smiled back and gave her a small wave.

"Here's Dara," Carl said to Rachel. People in the bar were watching Dara and didn't notice Carl and Rachel. "Let's sit down." They sat on a banquet at the back of the room. Dara finished the song and turned to talk to the band.

"Now?" asked Rachel.

"Let her sing a while," said Carl. "She's going away for a long, long time."

Carl had comforted Dara after Geoff was killed, though he had misinterpreted why she needed comfort. He had protected her and ultimately saved her life. Criminal as she might be, she'd had a rocky life. It was in his power to give her a few last minutes of happiness and why shouldn't he? Even if her songs were sad, she must be happy singing them.

A waiter came to the table and asked if they wanted anything to drink.

"Ginger beer," said Carl, "and bring the bottle." He'd enjoy the music more with a liquid in his hand but he couldn't let anyone claim he was drinking alcohol while working.

"Lemonade," said Rachel.

Dara and the band had settled on "The Last Time I Saw Paris" and followed it with the more upbeat "Falling in Love with Love" and "This Can't Be Love". The tunes were eighty-year-old songs that Carl barely recognized and Rachel didn't know at all. Carl enjoyed them and enjoyed watching Dara sing them. No wonder Geoffrey Pennstead had fallen in love with her. Every word in every song came from her heart, or seemed to. She meant every one of them.

The band stopped at nine o'clock. Dara thanked the audience and enthusiastically introduced the members of the band, though she had to ask each musician's name before repeating it into the microphone. The band was called the River House Wranglers and they would be back next week.

Carl and Rachel walked slowly up to Dara while she was talking with the band and the players were packing up their instruments.

"Hello, Carl," she said brightly, still in the glow of her performance. "Can I finally go home?"

"Afraid not, Dara. I have a warrant here to arrest you for the manslaughter of Geoffrey Pennstead."

"That's ridiculous, Carl," she said lightly. "How did things get so messed up?" Then, with a touch of anger in her voice, "How did you let them get so messed up?"

"If you'll come along quietly, we'll hold off the handcuffs until we get to the parking lot."

Dara glanced around the room for a way to escape. Or for someone who could come to her rescue. No help. No relief. What happened next was up to Carl. Dara wished the lady deputy wasn't here.

Dara might wile her way out of this. At least she could try. But even that remote hope went away as long as Deputy Newton was there.

"Can I get some things from my room?"

"You won't need them," said Carl. "Time to go."

"I hope you enjoyed the set," said Dara coldly as they walked out together. Anyone in the bar might imagine two old friends of Dara's, who happened to be in uniform, had come by to hear her sing.

"Very much enjoyed it," said Carl. "You're a wonderful singer."

Even Rachel managed a smile for Dara's benefit. The hammer would fall soon enough.

Chapter 44

The War Between the States

"The case isn't strong enough for trial," Jocelyn told Carl. He felt his anger rising and tamped it down as well as he could. The two of them sat in a windowless conference room in the district attorney's office. The offices, in the gray Deschutes County Courthouse, had been refreshed over time but retained the thick concrete walls and claustrophobic feel of the original 1940s building. Jocelyn continued. "When Leon Martinez told you Dara said she was at the crime scene that was hearsay. He can't testify to it in court. No one saw Dara at the scene of the crime. You've got the bicycle shop guy who says she tried to rent a bike sometime later. He's not sure of the time. He's sure it was Dara but a defense attorney can cast doubt on any witness identification. You have David Pasciuti who never saw Dara at the crime scene because he backed away when he saw the blue Toyota Elizabeth Martinez was in. Mrs. Martinez says Geoff Pennstead tried to take her car but she was focused on Geoff and never saw Dara. She says Geoff looked at something or someone behind her car and walked toward the back but Mrs. Martinez couldn't see who or what it was because the trunk lid blocked her view. When she heard the shot and saw Pennstead fall, she stepped on the gas and left the scene.

"We have your testimony that Dara Pennstead was perspiring and winded when you got to her house. And we can show she hadn't been on the Peleton as she told you she was. But you still haven't found anyone who saw her walking between the crime scene and her house."

"She lied to me and she misled me in my investigation," said Carl.

"She may have lied to you about being on the Peleton but that doesn't prove she was anywhere near Geoff Pennstead when he was shot. She didn't tell you about her husband getting paid to smuggle drugs but we can't prove she knew anything about it. She didn't tell you about the money Elizabeth Martinez dropped off at her door but we can't absolutely prove she knew it was evidence in a murder case.

"Bottom line, Carl, I'll never convince a jury, beyond any kind of reasonable doubt, that Dara Pennstead shot and killed her husband—either with prior intent or on the spur of the moment."

Carl turned over Jocelyn's arguments in his mind. She was right, given the evidence he'd brought her.

"I think you had probable cause to arrest her," said Jocelyn. "But even that's a little iffy if she wants to sue the Sheriff's Department. I expect though, that she'll want to be done with the whole thing and she won't even think about suing."

"What if I could produce a witness who saw the whole thing?" asked Carl. "He saw Dara get out of Geoff's car, walk to the back of the Martinez car, get the shotgun out of the trunk, shoot her husband, and run off into the woods?"

"For God's sake, Carl, if you had such a witness, why didn't you say so?"

"For one thing, I promised we wouldn't subpoena him…"

"You shouldn't have done that."

"It was the only way I could get his story. He's on parole in Washington State. If he admits coming to Oregon, he goes back to prison."

"We could still subpoena him," said Jocelyn.

"I'm not the lawyer here. But if he testified he was in Oregon, he'd be testifying against himself. The fifth amendment lets him off the hook."

"Did he go back to Washington?" asked Jocelyn.

"The same day he saw the shooting. Has a job and a stable life. His probation officer says he's on the road to go straight."

"I can call Washington and see if they'll give him a pass," said Jocelyn, pausing to look at the ceiling. "I wish I had something to offer them in return, though, and I don't."

"I don't know about the parole board," said Carl, "but his probation officer, Alma Oshiro, acts reasonable and she's rooting for him."

"I'll start with her."

Dara Pennstead borrowed the money to post bail using her house as security. Even though she was behind on the mortgage, she still had equity in the house. She was more angry about posting bail than she was about spending the one night in jail after her arrest. After that she chose to stay in the hotel, supposedly for her protection, but actually because the county was still paying her hotel bill.

Craig Hathaway, the same defense attorney who took Tommy Westlake as a client, took on Dara and made the bet that Dara would inherit enough money to pay him. Five days after Dara posted bail, Craig made an appointment with Jocelyn. Jocelyn asked Carl to be there. They met late in the day in the district attorney's office.

"I've looked at all the forensics," said Craig, "and the witness statements from Elizabeth Martinez, David Pasciuti, and the first on the scene who called 911. I've talked with my client. You can't win this case."

"We have a witness who isn't on the record yet who saw everything," said Jocelyn. "He saw Dara at the scene get out of her car, pick up the shotgun, and shoot her husband."

"How close was he to the shooting? What angle did he see it from? How well could he tell what happened?"

"We're not ready to present his testimony yet or to answer those questions," said Jocelyn. "Really, Craig, I think it may be too early for us to be having this discussion."

"Tell you what I think," said Craig. "I think you've got Geoff Pennstead with a gun in his hand. He is upset about his debts and he's a seventy-seven-year-old man who has gotten little or no sleep for two days while flying to a place he's never been, breaking the law, and doing a deal with hardened criminals. In other words, he's not functioning with a full deck. He's already threatened Elizabeth Martinez with the gun he still has. Our first line of defense will be you can't prove Dara was at the murder scene. Our second line will be that if she was there, she acted in self-defense. And to protect the life of Elizabeth Martinez. She's not guilty of anything. She's a hero."

"She was there," said Carl. "She had motive, means, and opportunity to murder her husband and she took it. Why would she pick up the shotgun if she didn't mean to use it?"

"One or two on the jury may see it that way," said Craig. "But some will see self-defense and none of them will ever believe she came there intending to kill her husband. She didn't know his car would stall. She didn't know the car he hailed down would happen to have a loaded shotgun in the trunk or that the trunk would be open. Call it self-defense. Call it lack of evidence. Call it what you will. But I think you need to save the county a lot of time and money and give my client her freedom."

"She saw her opportunity and she took it," said Carl. "That's manslaughter if not murder."

"We'll get back to you," said Jocelyn.

"I'll be waiting," said Craig. He left Jocelyn and Carl to themselves.

"That defense will be hard to beat," said Jocelyn. "I'm glad we found Pennstead's killer but I don't see how we can convict her."

"Dara had no reason to think her husband would shoot her," said Carl. "Why would she feel threatened? And if it was self-defense, why did she flee the scene? She wanted to kill him and get away scot-free.

"And," Carl went on, "forensics says Geoff's thumb caught more of the shotgun pellets than his other fingers did. That's consistent with his pointing the pistol at the ground, not at Dara."

"His hand was a bloody mess," said Jocelyn. "A lab tech might conclude the gun was pointing at the ground but will the jury be convinced?"

"How about I bring in my witness from Seattle?" Carl offered.

"That won't solve our problem," said Jocelyn. "Whoever he is he cannot possibly convince a jury that he saw from a distance, through the trees, whether Dara pointed her gun at Geoff first or the other way around."

Two weeks later, the district attorney's office dropped all charges against Dara Pennstead. No murder, no manslaughter, not even assault.

Dara was not charged with smuggling or drug possession because Carl and Jocelyn could not show that she knew where Geoff had taken the plane or why. Dara clearly didn't know the smugglers had accidently left two kilos of coke in the plane. Even Geoff didn't know that.

Dara got none of the cash and that made her more angry than ever. The dollars were the proceeds of a crime, namely drug smuggling, and the State of Oregon took them.

Two months after Dave Pasciuti was shot, Carl got a call from him.

"A man called me from Arizona," said Dave. "I want you to have the number he called from. It's probably a burner phone but if anything happens to me, you might like to have it. The man said people were unhappy about what happened to Che. The 'people' he said would be content if they were paid for the two kilos that Geoff Pennstead took with him and they figured I could help get it.

"The guy admitted, when I asked him, that he knew Geoff Pennstead was dead and that the county had both the coke and the money Geoff had been paid to smuggle it. I told him that I was not part of the plan to smuggle the coke and that I never had either the coke or the cash in my possession. And that, as far as I knew, Geoff's wife never knew about the smuggling and never knew there was coke in the plane until the sheriff's detective found it.

"I told him I thought someone in Arizona had slipped up and missed that last two kilos of coke and that was not Geoff's fault, Dara's fault, or the fault of anyone else in Oregon. And, I told him, the Sheriff was all over this case and if the 'people' sent anyone like Che again the law would descend on him and everyone else he knew. Then he hung up."

Carl asked Dave if the man said anything that would help identify him. Dave said the man sounded "kind of young" and he had a twang in his voice, like a cowboy.

"How did he know to call you?" asked Carl.

Dave paused. "I'm not going to go there. I have no idea. I'm getting as far from those kind of guys as I can. I've got a new job with a tech firm. I'm only bartending on weekends. I shaved my beard and cut my hair."

"Sounds like a plan," said Carl. "How's your recovery from the gunshots going?"

"On schedule. I get physical therapy twice a week. I can't run or walk very far but I can swim and I'm getting better at it."

"Thanks for the tip," said Carl.

He and Dave both hoped they'd never talk to each other again.

Carl traced the phone number Dave had given him. It belonged to a cell phone with minutes already in it that had been purchased off the rack for cash in a CVS Pharmacy in Flagstaff.

Carl did not give the State of Washington any evidence that Dylan Crabtree had visited Oregon while he was on probation. Dylan got a raise and proposed to his girlfriend.

Chapter 45

Ashland

Dara moved to Ashland, Oregon and volunteered with the theater. She sang sometimes with local bands. When Geoff's estate was finally settled, she would buy a small house and get by on a reasonable income. No more trips to Paris or even Los Angeles. She had her eye on a wealthy and widowed rancher from Medford but his children wanted no part of her and he stopped calling.

She became known around Ashland as the woman who had shot her husband. She told different stories to different people at different times. In one version, Geoff used to tie her up, insult her until she wept, and then beat her where he was sure it would not show. One night he started waving a pistol around but he was drunk and put the pistol down on the kitchen counter. Dara picked it up and pointed it at him when he came after her with a carving knife. She didn't remember pulling the trigger but the gun went off and Geoff was dead.

In another version, it wasn't Dara who had shot Geoff. The two of them were driving at night on Highway 97 and they flashed their lights at an oncoming car that had its high beams on. The other car turned around and ran them off the road. The three men in the other car surrounded Geoff and Dara's car. When Geoff pulled a pistol from the glove compartment, they shot him. They told Dara that if she reported them to the police they would come back and kill her. She called 911 but could not describe the men or their car.

One of Dara's stories had it that Geoff died the day of the big Sunriver fire. Most of Dara's listeners had heard about the fire and that added to the credibility of the story. Geoff went outside with a hose to spray water on the house. A burning branch, carried by the wind, fell on him, knocked him down, and set his clothes on fire. He started screaming. Dara came out of the house, picked up the hose, and turned it on him. The clothes had burned through by then and the skin on Geoff's upper arm fell off when the water hit it. His face and his hands were blistered black and red. Dara put the fire out but Geoff kept screaming. He begged her to kill him. She ran to the house, got his gun, and shot him once in the heart and once in the eye. She turned the water on herself and watched her house burn down. The coroner said Geoff would not have survived his burns and, morally right or morally wrong, Dara had saved him from unimaginable pain.

In a tale closer to the truth but still far from it, a stranded motorist stopped Geoff and Dara on a road in Sunriver and tried to take their car. When Geoff got out, the man raised a shotgun he'd hidden behind his leg and shot Geoff. Dara already had her door open and she took off into the woods as fast as she could run. She was afraid the man would follow her so she stayed away from the roads and bike paths until she got home and called 911.

Dara's new acquaintances were so taken with her stories, they passed them on to others. Gaps were filled in. Details were dropped. Embellishments were made. Her closer acquaintances brought contradictions to her and asked her which version was true.

"I don't know how some of these stories got started," she said. "I've decided the best thing to do is to ignore them. I don't want to think about what happened. I want to put all of that behind me. My husband, the house, the fire, Sunriver, the shooting—all of that was in another life."

Chapter 46

Resolutions and Reconciliations

Elizabeth had the garage repainted soft white and light blue. Leon put his shotgun in a new cabinet with a lock on it in the back of the closet. Together they replaced the living room couch and gave the old one, thoroughly cleaned, to Habitat for Humanity in Bend.

Leon went back to painting abstract acrylics and oils in his studio. It was a retreat from the wider world and he expected it would be a temporary one. He felt more comfortable at home and he could silently assure Elizabeth that he was safely in her orbit. He liked to hear the sound of her talking on the phone. He couldn't hear the words and he didn't need to.

He received a call on a September afternoon from Lester Westlake.

"Leon," said Lester, "I'm back in Sunriver. How would you like to play a round of golf?"

Leon hadn't spoken to Lester since he'd called him to express his sympathy for Tommy's death. Lester had been distracted and the call was short. That was fine with Leon. He had done his duty. "I'm not playing much golf these days," said Leon.

"Could we get together for a cup of coffee? I'd love to see you."

"I don't leave the house much," said Leon. "I don't think I could do that."

"Leon, the thing is my life has taken a turn for the worse since Tommy died. I feel awful that he and I weren't communicating better when he was still here. I know I didn't work hard enough on raising him. To call a spade a spade, his mother didn't either. But that's beside the point. Now she won't even talk to me. I'm spending too much time watching television and my boss is telling me I need to get back on track. I really need to see you, Leon. I think you are the one person who can help me do that."

Leon spoke sternly but not angrily. "I'm not your teacher anymore, Lester. I've got my own life to lead. I can't help you."

"I appreciate your trying to help Tommy. I'm sorry it didn't work out. I don't hold you responsible."

"One hour with me, or with anybody, was not going to fix a lifetime of neglect."

"You're right. You're right," said Lester. "But please, please, you've helped me before and I need your help desperately now. I've lost my marriage. I've lost my son. I'm losing my wits. I may lose my job."

"And thanks to Tommy, I've had my home invaded," said Leon. "A good friend was killed and her husband, another lifelong friend, has lost his wife. My wife and I were threatened and nearly lost our own lives."

"I know about that," said Lester, "and I'm very sorry that happened. Very sorry. I know that must have been terrible. But, you know it's totally separate. It had nothing to do with Tommy or me."

Leon thought Lester was blind with selfishness. "If Tommy hadn't set that fire," said Leon, "the four of us would have been hiking that day. My friend would not have died and none of us would have been threatened."

"From what I learned from the news, that guy would have broken into your house and taken the money."

"Money that wasn't mine and I didn't even know I had. Let him take it. Lester, you give no thought to other people. I can't fix that and it's not up to me anyway. It's up to you. Can we agree you won't call me again."

"Leon, please."

"This is what you can do for me, Lester. Can we agree you won't call me again? Or email me? Or text me? Or try to get in touch with me any other way? Can we agree on that?"

"Oh. All right. We can agree."

"Good. Goodbye." Leon hung up, blood boiling but satisfied. That was, hopefully, the end of that.

Late that night, when Elizabeth and Leon were by themselves in the house, reading in bed before going to sleep, Elizabeth put her book down and turned to her husband.

"I'm glad Geoff Pennstead is dead," said Elizabeth. "May God forgive me for that thought but it's the truth and I need to tell you. I've wished him dead most of the years of my life. I've woken up at night hating him. And hating myself sometimes too. I didn't have to do what he asked. But I was ambitious. I realized I was debasing myself but I thought I would get over it. I didn't know it would keep me awake and tug my thoughts in rotten directions for the rest of my life."

"Until now?" said Leon.

"Maybe. He's finally gotten what he deserved and I was part of it. At least I was there to see it."

"But you told Breuninger you didn't see it."

"I didn't see who shot him but in my side-view mirror I saw him at the back of my car. I saw the look of surprise on his face. I saw his whole head explode. I saw him fall backward as though he'd been standing in the surf and a big wave knocked him over. After he'd stood outside my car with a gun and threatened me all over again. He must have seen the hatred on my face. I'm not sure he recognized me but I'm sure he saw my look. And then he was obliterated. Forever and ever and ever. I wanted to be done. Done with the whole thing. I knew I didn't want to answer questions about it. So I stepped on the gas and left."

"That sounds like a scene that could haunt you more than the old one."

"Not a bit. Mission accomplished. I didn't feel guilty, not in the least."

"Why didn't you tell Carl what you saw from the beginning?"

"I didn't know who had shot Geoff Pennstead but whoever it was deserved to get away with it. At least that's how I felt until Dara was coming to you for help and I realized she might be the killer. If Geoff Pennstead stopped haunting me, that horrible woman threatened to take his place. I never wanted to see her or hear about her again. But of all things, she gets your sympathy. She hides the money, the money that everybody is looking for, in your golf bag. Then this Che or Joe or whatever comes to our house and nearly kills us. I shouldn't be happy people are dead, and I'm certainly very sorry about Maria, but I'm glad Geoff Pennstead is dead. I'm glad Joe Rheel is dead too. Can we get on with our lives?"

Acknowledgements

I am extremely grateful to the people who helped put this book on a solid footing of reality and generously shared ideas to make the book more exciting. Thanks to my pilot friend, John Rogers, for his advice on airplanes, flight tracking, and Sunriver Airport operations. Many thanks to the Sunriver Police Department, especially Sergeant John Beck who spent hours informing me on police and sheriff's department operations. Also Chief Stephen Lopez, and Captain Tory Kornblum. Alex McClaren of Sunriver Fire and Rescue provided critical information on fire scenarios and responses. I am also grateful to my longtime friend Ellen Leich Moon who painted the watercolor on the book's back cover and advised me on my descriptions of watercolor and plein air painting. If I have misrepresented any of the real-world facts supporting this book the fault is entirely my own.

My brother, Jared Haynes, who taught writing at UC Davis, contributed immensely to making this book a better story and making the characters more credible and interesting. I am very much indebted to Jessica Powers for her perceptive and insightful advice on the story and her thorough copy editing. Also to Cindy Davis for her early development editing and marketing advice. As always, my greatest thanks are to my wife, Joan Haynes, for her encouragement and her wise comments on drafts and ideas throughout the writing of this book.

Fact and Fiction

Sunriver is a very real place and the descriptions of Sunriver, its airport, the Deschutes River, and the Deschutes National Forest across the river closely match reality. Some of the streets and the houses on the streets are fictitious.

Upriver Ranch is fictional but incorporates elements of two communities south of Sunriver, Crosswater and Vandevert Ranch.

This book's murder investigation is led by Carl Breuninger, Deschutes County Sheriff's Detective, who cooperates with the Sunriver Police Department and draws on the resources of the county medical examiner and a contractor for crime scene investigation. In reality the county would form a major crimes task force, to investigate the murder. The county does not contract with crime scene investigators but trains its deputies to document crime scenes.

No fire has ever threatened Sunriver on the scale of the "Conklin Road Fire" described in the book. Forest fires are largely unpredictable, as are the plans for fighting them. The fictional fire in this book is informed by conversations with Sunriver Fire and Rescue and by the book, *Firefighter's Handbook on Wildland Firefighting* by William C. Teie.

The Cascade Lake Races that Dan swims in are sponsored every year by Central Oregon Masters Aquatics and Bend Metro Park & Recreation District. The author has been on the kayak safety patrol for these races.

About the Author

Ted Haynes is the author of both history and fiction set in Central Oregon. He and his wife first visited Bend in 1975 and built a log house on the Little Deschutes River in 2007. In addition to writing, Ted is a fisherman and competitive master swimmer. He has studied fiction writing with Hillary Jordan, Lynn Stegner, Nancy Packer, and Martha Conway. He is a member of Mystery Writers of America and a founding board member of the Waterston Prize for Desert Writing, now incorporated into the High Desert Museum. For more about Ted and his books please see www.tedhaynes.com.

Books by Ted Haynes

The Northwest Murder Mystery Series
Suspects
The Mirror Pond Murders
The Mt. Bachelor Murders
Pole Pedal Murder
The Sunriver Murders

On the Road from Burns – Short Stories from Central Oregon

The Dot.Com Terrorist

Vandevert – The Hundred Year History of a Central Oregon Ranch
(non-fiction, co-authored with Grace Vandevert McNellis)

Milton Keynes UK
Ingram Content Group UK Ltd.
UKHW012131110624
443988UK00001B/82